THE LAND OF DEATH
AND DEVIL'S CLUB

By the Author

Come Find Me in the Midnight Sun

The Land of Death and Devil's Club

THE LAND OF DEATH AND DEVIL'S CLUB

by

Bailey Bridgewater

2024

ISBN 13: 978-1-63679-659-8

This Trade Paperback Original Is Published By
Bold Strokes Books, Inc.
P.O. Box 249
Valley Falls, NY 12185

First Edition: June 2024

CREDITS
EDITOR: ANISSA MCINTYRE
PRODUCTION DESIGN: STACIA SEAMAN
COVER DESIGN BY INKSPIRAL DESIGN

Acknowledgments

Thank you to the staff of Kenai Fjords National Park, who remember park tech from 2009 in surprising detail. Thanks, as always, to Anissa.

For Dad, who always wanted to see Alaska.

Author's Note

This book features Native Alaskan characters. Alaska would not be the captivating land that it is without Native Alaskans, and I felt that leaving people of the Alaskan tribes out of this story would further erase Indigenous identities. I do not, however, delve deeply into the customs or beliefs of Dolly, Ryne, or Jeannie out of respect for Native Alaskans, who should maintain the right to tell their own stories when and as they see fit. I hope that readers who want to learn more about Native Alaskan history and culture will seek out writing by Indigenous authors.

CHAPTER ONE

July 2009

I grin when I walk into the Bake, though I begged Mikey—Chief Michael Harper, and my former partner—not to make me do this. He's gone all out. The chalkboard near the door announces the entire place has been reserved by the Seward Police Department. All other patrons are politely asked to make reservations for another evening. A couple in front of me wearing nearly identical blue sweaters and khaki pants turns around looking somber. A cruise ship is in town, and this was likely their only chance to try the best restaurant in Seward. I want to apologize personally, but I restrain myself. This is, after all, my party. No apologies this evening.

Of course, it's a sham. There's no way I would let Mikey throw a going away party for me otherwise. I'm only here because I'm not actually going away. I just need the wealthiest, most well-connected drug lord in town—Mr. Drew—to think that I am. That means everyone else in town has to think I'm leaving too. I stop at the podium and scan the room. Mr. Alaku stands in a corner surveying all while he supervises the wait staff. The Seward Police Department is here, including former Chief Willington. Anna and the medical forensics team are present, as well as a couple journalists I recognize from five years ago when we closed not one but three missing persons cases, all within a week of one another. Granted, one of the bodies was misidentified, but we didn't know that at the time. Anna has already spotted me. She's wearing a huge grin, even though she's talking to the police department's intern.

The biggest surprises, and the people I find myself walking to immediately, are Chief Myla Rodriguez and Fritz of Whittier. They found the body of one of those missing people, Kyle Calderon. Fritz, the

Whittier medical examiner, taught us some very important information about poisonous berries in Alaska. My hand is out, ready to shake before I even reach them. Chief Rodriguez removes her napkin from her lap, placing it on the table as she rises and extends her own hand.

"Chief, it's so great to see you. You didn't need to come all this way—"

"None of that. Fritz and I are always delighted to get out to Seward in the summer. We've all been cooped up in the Tower for nine months—you'd be hard pressed to keep us there once the weather is nice. Besides, meeting you and Harper on the Calderon case made us realize that we really need to be better connected to our fellow officers across the state. We've been working on that ever since you left us."

Fritz stands to grasp my hand in his chilly palm.

"And you may not have known this, but Dr. Fenway and I go way back to med school. I never pass up a chance to see her if one arises." He winks dramatically and glances toward her. She laughs and waves her napkin at him in what could be a gesture of either dismissal or surrender. Anna is open about her sexuality, so I'm assuming Fritz's crush is something of a joke between them.

When Rodriguez sits, Mikey indicates a chair between him and Anna, which I take. The waiter approaches and places an old-fashioned in front of me. I raise my brows at Anna, who grins. She knows my love for good whiskeys.

"You really shouldn't have, Mikey."

I speak as if the crowd is truly a surprise, and some of it is. I didn't want to know all the details because I'm not a natural actor. Mikey and I simply agreed, sitting up late in my hotel room like we'd done years ago, that there should be a going away party at the Bake (owned by Mr. Drew), that Willington (a friend of Mr. Drew) should be invited, and that all the staff who worked closely with the Branden Halifax, Kyle Calderon, and Lee Stanton cases five years ago and more recently should be invited, because they deserve to be celebrated too. There's no doubt in my mind Mr. Drew is already aware of the party and that the reason behind it is that I'm leaving Seward and the department wanted to thank me for my help. He may know that I'm now also a special liaison to the FBI. That fact has been kept very quiet—only Mikey and Anna know it here in Seward—but I'm guessing Mr. Drew's police connections run far and wide.

That's why only three people—Mikey, Anna, and a National Park Ranger I haven't met yet—know I'm coming back to Seward tonight

THE LAND OF DEATH AND DEVIL'S CLUB

after I deliver the Tank to the Anchorage station. It's why the only people in Anchorage who know are my chief, Chief Quint, and my FBI handler, Senior Special Agent Mensel, as well as anyone else they've deemed it crucial to tell. The rest of the Anchorage officers—that rowdy group in which I've finally managed to find my place—have been told I'm being sent on special assignment in Seattle. It's where I initially came from, so it'll make sense as long as they don't dig too deep.

From across the room, Valeria Close, who works the Seward PD desk at night and has an amazing memory for town history, calls out.

"Hey! Where's Tails?" The entire room laughs.

"I thought the food would have enough texture without his hair added in." Laughter again. The entire crowd is looking our way; Mikey stands and clinks his butter knife against his wine glass hard enough I worry he'll break it.

"Since we already have your attention, I'd like to just say a few words about why we're here tonight." The wait staff, who had been circulating with water and taking orders, stop and make themselves nearly invisible in some trick I wish I could learn.

"This is Officer Linebach's last evening here in Seward, at least for the foreseeable future, and before she goes back to catching the big bads in Anchorage, we wanted to give her a proper send-off." There are *hear, hears* from the group, some of whom raise glasses already mostly drained of wine. "As you all know, Officer Linebach reunited three families with their missing loved ones and, even though I know it's not the way we ever want those reunions to happen, it is an extraordinary accomplishment. Most families here in Alaska never get to put their loved ones to rest, and on behalf of the police department, medical examiner's office, and the town of Seward, I wanted to say thank you."

I look directly at Mikey as he talks, though sweat seeps into the armpits of my pale gray suit jacket. I should take it off, but not now while everyone is looking at me. I make myself smile. I was hoping Mikey would keep this short and sweet since he knows I hate being the center of attention, but he continues.

"I know there might be some other folks here today who would like to express their thanks to Louisa, but as I'm sure everyone here knows, she's awfully modest." *That's a nice way to say socially anxious.* "So please, if there's anyone else who'd like to say a few words, or a whole string of them, please feel free to do so now." I swat at Mikey instinctively and everyone laughs. I'm already rehearsing the full round of shit I'm going to give him in my head. If he had done this five years ago, I would have killed him. I silently thank my therapist for the sessions we've had on coping in social gatherings. "Oh, okay, okay—no need to get violent, Officer!" Mikey holds his arm as if I've really hurt him and makes a face. "Well, since the lady doth protest so much, feel free to come by our table and interrupt her while she's eating."

The wait staff is promptly there taking my order. Next to me, Anna places her order. I try not to laugh when I hear her request three separate dishes. I wish for a second that it was just me and her, that we could share food like we did here before, but only Mikey knows we're interested in each other. We can't risk Mr. Drew finding out. I may need her professional help, and it won't do for the very man I'm trying to catch to have eyes on her.

The meal passes pleasantly enough. When I've finished my scallops, I make the rounds of the room, checking in with each of the tables, thanking everyone for coming out and expressing my appreciation for everything they did in helping to solve the cases. It's usually the lead officer who gets all the credit when a case closes, but no case is solved in isolation—a lesson I've learned here in Seward. Without Mikey, Anna, my colleague at the DNA lab, and the families of the men themselves, we would have gotten nowhere.

But for this next part, I have to go it alone.

The thought causes butterflies in my stomach, which is unusual. I preferred working alone at the beginning of my career, but now the thought makes me uncomfortable. This is a special assignment of my own design—though I have Chief Quint's support, there's not much he can do to help me from Anchorage. I'll still report back to him as my primary boss, but I'll really just be informing him of what I find. If I get in a bind, Seward PD will have to help me out of it. And while Mensel and the FBI approve of the work I'll be doing, the fact that I'm not a full special agent means they'll only really invest in me if I find something concrete that absolutely merits the full force of their resources. They don't like speculation and uncertainty, so my job is to get them evidence. The thought of not being able to do that makes me sweat.

I find reassurance in Mikey's smiling face as he speaks to another table visitor. He'll still be there, just down the mountain, behind his desk at the station. Anna will be there too—either at the hospital or in her adorable little yellow house. And I'll have Tails.

Still, I'll be isolated at a seasonal outpost that I've never even seen, somewhere in Kenai Fjords National Park. And I have no idea for how long.

My pulse begins to accelerate, and I try to be subtle as I look at the fitness tracker on my wrist, tapping it until it shows my heart rate. *Ninety-seven, ninety-nine.* I take a deep breath in, then exhale slowly through my nose. *Ninety-two.* Better. I smell Anna's amber and jasmine perfume before I see her.

"It can't be time already, can it?" she asks. "We're all talking about going over to the Hotel for a drink. I want to see Marge."

"Oh no, I just…I wasn't looking at my watch. I mean I was looking at my watch, but—" I try to wave at my left wrist to indicate the fitness tracker…which is on my left wrist. Anna laughs, a delicate tinkling sound like windchimes that makes my heart leap. "Okay, let me start over. I was checking my pulse."

Anna raises an eyebrow. "Do I need to take you down to my office?"

I blush. It's a morgue joke, not a sexy joke. Probably.

"Oh! No, it's…I'm fine. My…" I don't want to say *my therapist* in front of a crowd. Some people are still weird about anything related to mental health, especially when it comes to law enforcement. "It helps."

"I get it." Anna knows a little about my struggles with anxiety. She starts to reach out but glances around and wraps both hands around her glass of white wine instead. "Think you'll join us?" She's stunning this evening in an ankle-length blue and white striped linen dress. Anna always looks so effortlessly put together—even when she's working in the morgue as Seward's medical examiner. I adjust the scooped neckline of the knee-length jersey dress I bought for the special occasion. I'm not usually one to wear dresses, but this one felt like I could go for a run in it if need be, and the coral color complements my brown skin and eyes nicely.

"Honestly, I probably shouldn't. Please give my regards. It's a long drive back to Anchorage."

She nods. She knows it'll be at least five hours round trip, and I'm not even sure what getting up the mountain in the semi-dark will look like. I won't know until I meet the mysterious park ranger who will follow me to Anchorage and take me to my new home.

"That's true," she lowers her voice, "but I will miss you an awful lot." She doesn't just mean at the Hotel. If all goes well, I might not see Anna for weeks. Possibly even months. I'll be staking out Mr. Drew's operation, and no one can come and go that he wouldn't already expect to see. I'm likely to be lurking around his airstrips, his property, and wherever it is he's sending his men to run drugs and quite possibly kill one another off. Anna and Mikey coming and going will raise his suspicions unless they're obviously on a call that's not related to him.

"Mind walking me out after I say goodbye to everyone?"

She agrees and turns to chat with Fritz as I go around the room one last time.

CHAPTER TWO

I make it outside before Anna does, and I stroll to the end of the block to look out over the harbor. The sun sparkles across the waters, which shimmer in shades of turquoise and deep purple. The sun will remain there, supervising the movement of the orcas and the sea otters until finally relinquishing its place in the sky around midnight. If I leave now, I should arrive back in Seward after the sun is as safely tucked away as it gets in mid-summer, when it's up from about four a.m. to midnight. I can peruse my new home under cover of that all too momentary darkness. I'll be thankful for these impossibly long days while I'm watching Mr. Drew's operation, but right now I'd love to be standing here with Anna, holding her in the dark and watching the stars.

A sea lion gasps a half-laugh and I jump, he's so close by. He looks at me.

"I know, but a girl can dream, right?" He slaps one of his enormous flippers against the rocks. I huff. "Well, you don't have to be judgmental about it."

My rude friend is right, though. Whatever it is that's rekindled between me and Anna doesn't stand much chance with me out in the middle of the mountains and her here. Combine that with the fact that I'm not exactly the best at relationships, with all their elusive unwritten rules, and the odds seem pretty stacked against me. But that's the way it has to be. And really, it's probably better that I'm going now. If things had already developed the way I hope they will, it would be impossible to leave her, and that would mean never catching Mr. Drew. For myself, for the families whose loved ones I found, and for the entire community, he needs to be behind bars. But putting him there isn't going to be easy. Circumstantial evidence isn't going to cut it—not when he can buy the best lawyer in the state. Hell, he could fly someone in from wherever he wanted.

I remind myself to not let my thoughts spiral, and focus on the sea lion instead. I'm still staring at it when Anna approaches.

"Ma'am, this guy bothering you?" She imitates a cop. As if he understands, the sea lion slides into the harbor with a slap of water against blubber.

"Yeah. He was giving me a reality check that I didn't entirely appreciate."

"Pretty sure that's why they're here." She leans her elbows against the rail that stands between us and the rocky slope leading into very, very cold water. "This scenery's a little too picturesque. You could convince yourself you've died and gone to heaven if some asshole sea lion wasn't there making rude noises."

I laugh as I glance behind us, then lean into her briefly. Her skin is cool against mine despite the warm day.

We're quiet as we stare at the water. She's right. I'm not religious, but if I was going to picture the heaven my mother believed in, Jannah, it probably would look like this.

"I wish you could come with me."

"Me too." It's a safe and easy thing to say because we both know it's impossible. It's a beautiful fantasy, like all of Seward in summer, sea lions included. But winter always comes.

"Maybe I can con Mikey into letting me bring you some home-cooked dinners every once in a while."

"Oh, please no," I say quickly, and she hip checks me. "I still haven't recovered from the lamb korma."

"Ugh, do you have to remind me?"

"Absolutely. It's the most wonderful culinary failure I've ever experienced."

"Why don't you go ahead and hurry up that mountain?" She contradicts her mean words by brushing her hand swiftly down my spine. Despite my jacket and jersey dress, I quiver. Though Anna and I have enjoyed some amazing kisses, both circumstances and my own foolishness have kept us from enjoying much of anything more, and the sexual tension is killing me. I'm so attracted to her, but once again, I find myself having to leave her.

There are footsteps behind us, so we both tuck in our arms. It's just tourists taking pictures. Anna and I move over slightly so as to not block their view.

"It won't be for long. You'll get him in no time."

"I *want* to hope so, but that could also mean going back to Anchorage. There will be a trial, and all that paperwork, and then who knows what the next assignment will be."

"Don't worry about all that. You've wanted this for so long, and you've worked so hard. You deserve to finish this case." I hear my therapist in my head telling me to repeat after her. *You deserve happiness.* But it seems I can't have both happiness and Mr. Drew. At least not yet. *Trooper* Louisa pushes my therapist out of my headspace. The greater good. It's for the greater good that Mr. Drew has to be gone. A relationship with Anna benefits only me.

"When this is finished, do you think we—"

"Oh yeah. Once this is over, you're not escaping again before we've figured out what we're like together. Properly together."

I smile. "I'm going to hold you to that."

"Don't you go running off with any Bigfoot hunters in the meantime."

"Great. Way to add Bigfoot to the list of things to be worried about."

"Hot tip. Around here, he's known as Nantinaq. Or Aula'aq."

"Good to know."

We both sigh. It's time for me to go. She's the first to turn away from the water, taking my elbow. I follow her to the Tank. As we get there, several partygoers spill out of the Bake and head down the sidewalk that leads to the bar. I watch the crowd, wondering if I should dare a quick kiss goodbye. I could kick myself for having wasted the last five years not even speaking to Anna. Several people cast their glances toward us, and I sigh again, reminding myself of my role here. I don't get to give Anna a kiss goodbye, and I feel the disappointment in my chest. Instead, she gives me a half-smile as I get into the cantankerous vehicle. Before I close the door, she grabs my hand and squeezes.

"Dolly will take care of you."

CHAPTER THREE

A white Land Rover pulls out behind me as I exit the Bake's parking lot. It parks across the lot from me when I stop at my hotel to change and get Tails. When I leave again moments later, it follows. I've never met the person who will meet me at the Anchorage police station. Once I've settled into the drive, I glance over at Tails, the dog Mikey and I found while searching for Lee Stanton five years ago. The boxer mix is sitting up straight in the passenger seat, his mouth open in a grin, tongue hanging, staring out the windshield. I smile. Despite the fact his first act as friend was to lead me to a decapitated, decomposing body, Tails is a happy, sociable dog. The happy part is contagious at least. As cars pass, he tracks them until they disappear.

"Sorry, bud, we'll be on the road for a while. You don't have to stay on duty, you know. You can take a nap." He looks at me, cocking his head to the side as if he doesn't understand the instructions. His ears flop, and I reach over to give them a scratch. "It's gonna be just you and me for a little while."

When I'd initially suggested bringing Tails to my new place in the park, both of my bosses had been skeptical. Eventually Quint was persuaded and then he convinced Mensel and the FBI. Quint knows how excellent a tracking dog Tails is, and that's likely to come in handy. Since I have to stay out of sight, any time I follow someone it will have to be from a distance, and Tails's nose could be invaluable. Besides, he's also been trained to take down suspects. He's used that skill a couple times when criminals fled the scene with a good head start. Most importantly, Tails helps me manage my stress and the bouts of depression that, thank goodness, come on less frequently now that I've got a good management plan and a few containers of medication—enough to last me at least three months. Still, there's nothing that helps me calm down in the evening like curling up with my warm dog, stroking his auburn fur and watching TV together. He especially likes the nature documentaries.

I've already got my bags packed. It's just a matter of transferring them to the Land Rover. I try to picture Dolly. Most likely a woman, and a National Park Service ranger at Kenai Fjords, which means she has to be tough. Even though it's popular with tourists, most of the massive park is extremely remote and very rugged. The majority of its trails are closed for most of the year because of the heavy amounts of ice and snowfall that cover the terrain. The glaciers are in constant movement, and the wildlife, including a large number of grizzlies, often shut down particular routes. The entrance is just a few miles from Seward, and its proximity to town can mislead tourists into thinking a visit will be, well, a walk in the park. But it takes serious preparation to spend a significant amount of time there.

Other than Dolly's job, though, I know nothing about her. I assume the National Park Service rangers work closely with Mikey and the Seward department, given that most people who come to visit Seward also spend time in the park, and vice versa. She and Anna must know each other through Anna's role as the closest medical examiner. The national parks in Alaska find their fair share of remains. I've been called to Denali several times now, and even to Gates of the Arctic once.

The station looks deserted when I arrive, though the officers assigned to night duty are nearby. I don't go inside. I park the Tank in the staff lot, where it lives when it's not rumbling like a Victorian locomotive up the side of a mountain. After I jump out, I knock my fist on the vehicle's hood three times like I always do.

"Well done, Tank." It's a kind of superstitious thing around here. Any time one of us takes the Tank, we talk to it like it's our baby. The general consensus is that this is what keeps the ancient monstrosity going. If you don't remember to thank it, it might leave you stranded in the middle of nowhere next time.

I pull my bags from the back just as the Land Rover swings alongside me. Tails stands up in his seat, wagging the nub where his tail should be, tongue hanging out of his mouth in anticipation of meeting someone. He assumes everyone is a friend until I indicate otherwise.

I stop to watch a woman in jeans, light sweater, and a fedora climb out of the vehicle. She's not wearing the ranger outfit I expected. As she walks toward me, I note confident, long strides. My officer brain compiles a description. She's average height, five foot five maybe. About one hundred fifty pounds. Possibly Native Alaskan. Chin length hair, wavy, black with significant gray. Narrow eyebrows, mostly drawn on her wide, square face. Significant laugh and scowl lines. Around sixty if I have to guess. Age is where I tend to be off. Dark brown eyes, birthmark on the lower left cheek. Scar above the right eye. Animal attack? I'd need Anna for that one.

"You're Dolly?"

She stands there staring at me like she's also putting together a description. I wonder what hers says. *"Shorter side of average, one hundred forty pounds, athletic build, brown skin, South Asian heritage, dark brown braid almost down to the waist."* That's how I'd describe me, at least.

"I am."

I wait for more information.

It is apparently not forthcoming.

"I'm Officer Louisa Linebach." I extend my hand. She looks at it, then approaches and shakes it, scowling at me.

"I know."

"I've got a dog traveling with me. I hope Chief Harper made you aware."

"I'm aware." She reveals nothing of her feelings about this. We both stand there. I wait for her to add something.

Anything.

"Mind getting a move on? Long drive to the cabin." She's apparently waiting for me to hurry the hell up.

I snap into action, transferring bags to the back of the Land Rover. She doesn't offer to help and instead stands with her arms crossed, looking at my bags as if she's scrutinizing them.

"How long you planning to be up there?"

"I wish I knew. Did Harper tell you why I'm going?"

"Nope. Don't want to know, either. Forget I asked."

I want to ask why she agreed to let me stay, but I bite my tongue.

"Okay. That's it for the bags. Any particular place you want the dog?"

"Behind you. Don't need a dog trying to climb on me when I'm driving."

After he visits his favorite grassy patch, I open his door and Tails jumps into the back seat of the Rover on the passenger side, sitting like a gentleman. As soon as he realizes he can't easily see out the windshield, he curls into a ball and lays his head down.

"Good boy." He no longer needs my positive reinforcement, but it's automatic at this point.

I should be relieved that Dolly isn't a talker. I hate small talk. But I get the impression this woman does not like me, and my muscles tense as I automatically prepare to defend myself. I fight the urge to interrogate her and get to the bottom of her attitude. This silence is anything but peaceful.

She doesn't even turn on the radio.

CHAPTER FOUR

As anticipated, we are in Seward again after the sun has set, though the mid-July sky is more charcoal gray than black. I duck in my seat out of excess caution. There's no need to worry about anyone spotting Tails, either. He's been snoring lightly for the past half hour.

"You can sit up now," Dolly says as we turn off Exit Glacier Road and enter the park. Within minutes, we've pulled alongside a simple cabin with lights on inside. It's way too close to the park entrance. During the day, this place will be packed. I furrow my brows, considering how to tell Dolly that this isn't going to work. Before I can open my mouth, she's out of the vehicle and headed toward a neat line of trucks, ATVs, and snow machines. She picks a heavy-duty SUV and opens the passenger door.

"You comin', or what?"

I jump out and start pulling my bags from the back of the Land Rover. Tails's face appears in the window. Dolly opens the back door of the SUV. This isn't my cabin—awkward conversation avoided. Once we're all packed into the new vehicle, Dolly steers us down a muddy, rock-speckled road marked *Authorized Vehicles Only*. The SUV bounces on the uneven ground. I reach back to stop Tails from sliding onto the floorboard.

"Cabin's at the northeastern boundary of the park. You head east almost at all, you're gonna run into Resurrection River. Other side of that, Resurrection River Trail. Do not attempt to cross that river. It's high and fast this time of year. You come back down the way we're coming and cross over the road. Soon as you cross the trail, you're out of park boundaries. Harper left me some maps to give you. They're in the cabin. He's got a couple things marked on there that I'm guessing will make sense to you."

"I'm going to need to cover a lot of ground. What are my transportation options?"

"You'll have free use of the park service vehicles." She sounds annoyed. "There's a decent pickup, a Jeep, and a good ATV with a silencer." *Jackpot.* A lot of the officers in Anchorage who hunt use silencers on their snow machines and ATVs so they don't scare animals. I'm guessing the park uses them to not disturb wildlife. It'll certainly come in handy for not being obvious while poking around Mr. Drew's. I tune back into Dolly saying, "...bike, and obviously skis and snowshoes." She pauses for a long time. "You spent a lot of time in Kenai Fjords?"

"Almost none, I'm afraid."

She sighs, then starts into some information that sounds rehearsed. I'm guessing she's delivered this speech to tourists many times. "Be cautious of any small river crossings. If you have to cross, do it early in the day. You wait until later in the day and something that looks like a stream can become impassable. Carry GPS with you at all times. Carry a paper map too. I don't have to tell you about wildlife, do I?"

"No." I've been in Alaska long enough now to know about food storage and how to handle the various types of bear and moose. Which is to say, I know enough to avoid them, so I don't have to deal with them. I may sound like a dumbass singing 90s grunge music while I run, but it's effective in scaring them off ninety-nine percent of the time. It probably scares away other runners too.

"Any time you're in the park, you'll have a satellite phone, PLB, and high frequency radio. They're already at the cabin. The satellite works fine most places, unless you're under a rocky overhang or in a cave. Emergencies only. Calls are expensive."

"Thanks. I already have my own." I mentally run through my emergency inventory in the bag behind me. "Well, except the personal location beacon."

She looks at me out of the corner of her eye and squints, her face bouncing up and down in my field of vision as we ascend a steep slope.

"Let me see your radio."

I twist around and pull my backpack into my lap, digging through it until I produce the black hand-held device. Dolly shakes her head when I hold it up.

"Show me the battery."

I open the casing and pull out the rechargeable.

"Nope." I start to object but she cuts me off. "No rechargeables. Double AAs."

I blink at her. I want to argue, but her face is set so sternly there's no point. *Trust her. Don't get cocky just because you've been here for five years. It's her park. She knows emergency protocol.* I stuff my apparently useless radio back into my pack and we fall back into silence. Dolly makes a sharp turn onto a path I never would have spotted had she not started down it.

"So how long have you been a ranger?"

"Fifteen years."

"Always at Kenai?"

"Yeah."

I am determined to get this woman talking. She must be a wealth of information, and if she's been in this area that long, she knows something about Mr. Drew and his Seward operations. After all, Kenai Fjords is close to his stomping grounds. That's why I'm here.

"What got you interested in the park service?"

She keeps her eyes on the road. "We're almost there."

I flare my nostrils and my cheeks warm. Usually, I'm the one annoyed by others talking. Being on the receiving end of that irritation is not pleasant. I exhale heavily and look out the window. Nothing but trees.

CHAPTER FIVE

A minute later we approach a cabin that can only be described as rustic. The logs from which it's built are weather-worn and nearly black in places. The roof is pitched at such a steep angle that the whole thing has the silhouette of a tent with a round metal chimney sticking up through it. A narrow porch is under the overhang of the roof, and a large window sits immediately in the cabin's center. An old maroon mountain bike is on the porch leaning against the railing. As Dolly swings the SUV around the side, I can see a few other small windows, but they can't let in much light; the place is densely surrounded by pines that attempt to engulf it entirely. The pines come nearly to the back wall. The seclusion must be why Mikey—or NPS—picked it. Even flying over, you'd need to know what you were looking for to realize it's here.

Which makes me wonder why it is here.

"What is this place?"

"Ranger cabin. Usually emergency use only. It's also on the boundary. We like to keep an eye out."

I wonder what they're *watching for*. It could be illegal hunters. It could be drug activity. Then again, Mr. Drew has to be smart enough to avoid federal land and stick to his home ice. Of course, if he thinks no one is watching all this mostly unoccupied land…

"How many rangers patrol the park?"

"Two full times, but one's on furlough. Four seasonals. They're all staying at Exit Glacier, so you get into a bind, that's where you go. They'll patrol down to Aialik Bay with the Naiad occasionally, stay overnight in the cabin there a couple days and come back. Most of the park's unpatrolled. Once the season ends, it's down to one volunteer at Exit and one full-time. Once in a while, we take the plane out if the weather cooperates."

So, Mr. Drew could have the run of the place and be nearly guaranteed no one would see a thing.

"Naiad?"

"Our boat. Rigid hull inflatable."

"Ah." In Anchorage we call them RHIBs, but I make a note to myself that for now, it's Naiad.

She unlocks the door, and it swings into a small, cool space. The log walls look almost the same inside as outside, and my eyes travel to a lofted sleeping space requiring use of a ladder. Tails will have to make do with the leather loveseat. I glance at him, and he begins walking the perimeter of the cabin, carefully sniffing anything he deems interesting. When he's finished, he returns to me and sits. Now it's my turn to check the place out. I immediately open the kitchen cabinets. They're well stocked with non-perishables, which makes sense given that a person could easily get trapped here for weeks. The kitchen accounts for a disproportionate amount of the cabin with its full-sized stove and fridge, plus a long chest freezer and pantry. A variety of mismatched skillets hang against the wall. I guess I'll get to practice my cooking skills. No pizza delivery here.

I turn back to Dolly.

"This'll do."

"I'm so glad." Again, I experience the unpleasantness of being on the receiving end of snark I typically dish. She shifts her satchel on her back. "I'll be around every few days. You have an *emergency*, there's the phone." She indicates the satellite phone laid out on the two-person dining table.

"Thank you." My skin crawls. I'm not satisfied letting her leave when I have no idea why she's so pissed at me. I won't sleep right until I know what's going on. She's already turned for the door.

"Dolly, hang on."

She turns back with a sigh.

"I'm sorry. Did I do something? Is there a reason you're being so short with me? I mean, I'm used to people trying to avoid me after a couple conversations, but I didn't even get a fair chance to stick my foot in it this time."

She looks at me, eyes slightly narrowed as if she's examining the details of my face.

"I just wonder why you agreed to this if you're so unhappy."

"Because Anna asked."

Anna?

"I thought you were working with Chief Harper." I sit in one of the dining chairs, hoping she will too. She doesn't.

"I am helping you because Anna asked, and the Park Service approved. This is a favor to her personally—not to the *Seward* Police." Her stony facial expression has cracked. The lines around her mouth quiver.

I consider what to say to that and decide less is more.

"History, huh?"

We're locked in a stare standoff for a minute before she exhales, then flings her bag onto the sofa and sits next to it.

"You could say that." Her voice is even. Tails curls at my feet.

"What happened?" I lean forward, hands on my knees. She glances at Tails, who gets up immediately and goes to her. She places a hand on his head, and he sits, enjoying a light ear scratch.

"I live in Nanwalek with my family. Always have. We're Alutiiq. My ancestors traveled all over the park and the peninsula. Nanwalek has always been safe for us. Everyone looks out for each other, so I never worried. My children were grown but my niece was living with me—Jeannie. She had just turned eighteen years old. I was raising her and my grandchild Ryne, who was young. We were all happy. One day, I drove Ryne to Anchor Point to buy things for school. When I came back, Jeannie was gone. I waited. She didn't come home that evening. I knew something was wrong. I called the police. They told me to keep waiting. I called her friends. No Jeannie. The next morning, she was still gone. I called the police again. The wind is bad, they said. We cannot get someone out there right now. *By boat*, I said. *You can get here by boat.* Yes, but they can't spare anyone right now. They'll send someone as soon as they can. *Four days later…*" She pounds her fist against her thigh. "Four days later they show up. One officer. He acts like he doesn't want to be there. He asks me five questions. *When did I last see her? Who are her friends? Had we fought?* We had not. *Was she depressed?* She was not. *Did she have a boyfriend?* She did not."

I am getting upset as Dolly's anger rises. These were the same questions the police always asked when a kid in the foster system went missing. It's a way of coming up with a nice clean explanation that makes the kid responsible for their own disappearance. Must be a runaway.

"This officer told me he'd investigate. He just talked to the same friends I'd talked to. He came back to me that same evening…" She struggles for control and stops to take a breath. "*That same evening*. He barely even looked! He came back and he told me he'd talk to his chief, and he asked me if she could have run away." Dolly stops, looks away from me, and wipes the edge of her eyes.

When Dolly has relaxed into the sofa and her eyes are dry, I ask if they ever followed up.

"The same officer came back three days later. Said they were classifying her as a runaway. They put her picture on a website somewhere and told people to call a tip line if they saw her. That's it."

"How long ago was this?"

"It will be ten years next week."

I sigh. *Chief Willington.* There's nothing I can say that has any meaning.

"I'm sorry. The way that was handled was not right. I know you know that. That's a horrible thing to go through, and it sounds like the police department made it even worse."

She doesn't respond, but her face softens a little. "Well, you weren't the officer, were you? But since you needed to know why I don't enjoy working with the police, there you go."

I stand because she has. "I respect that. And I respect you helping even though you've had this shitty experience. Hopefully the work I'm doing will help everyone around here."

She shakes her head. "I don't want to know."

"Okay." I follow her to the door and present my hand, ready to drop it if she doesn't want it. She shakes it briefly. "I'd say the FBI is at your disposal but, well, I'm still working to try and get them at *my* disposal." She steps back. Maybe I shouldn't have mentioned that I work with the FBI, but that compulsive need to prove that it wasn't me who did wrong rears its head.

I make a mental note to talk through that with the therapist when I see her again.

Dolly inclines her head.

"Noted."

I watch until the SUV disappears into the trees, then I conduct a full inventory of the cabin.

❖

Despite the late hour, I cannot fall asleep. The loft is stuffy, and my face is closer to the ceiling than I'm used to. It's dead silent. No birds chirp. No crickets. There are no drag races down mostly deserted city streets. No muffled fragments of conversation heard through apartment walls. Between the complete blackness and the silence, I'm claustrophobic. To make matters worse, Tails isn't in bed, which I hadn't realized would feel so weird. When I flip myself around and hang my head over the edge of the loft, I can see that he's snoozing on the sofa, his face pointed toward the front door. How dare he sleep so well without me. I get back at him by clambering down the ladder as loudly as possible. He lifts his head and jumps off the couch, ready for action.

"Oh, get back to sleep, you traitor." I turn the television on. The picture quality is awful, and I don't even bother flipping through what I'm guessing is a sad selection of channels. I set the volume just loud enough to mimic people talking on the other side of the wall, then I climb back into bed, watching the light change on the ceiling as the scenes of the show progress.

CHAPTER SIX

The ruckus of the birds wakes me. When I stumble down the final rung of the ladder, Tails already looks alert. Then he's up, butt wagging.

"No chance, buddy. Just because the sun's up doesn't mean it's breakfast." I check the clock on the wall, then confirm it's correct with my phone. It's barely past five a.m. The winter dark may be psychologically distressing, but the light does far worse things to my sleep schedule. If I was in Anchorage, I'd use this awkward time where my brain says it's time to move, yet nothing is open, to run. Here, I plan to use the early hour to full advantage. I remember the six-cup coffee maker in the cabinet and pull out it with a can of grocery store brand grounds. I dress while it brews. I'll shower when I get back.

For now, I want to know exactly where Mr. Drew's airstrip is in relation to the cabin.

I sit down at the table with my coffee and pull Mikey's maps toward me. One is a massive National Geographic topographic map of the whole park. Another shows the park's eastern boundary, near Seward; to the north, Primrose. On it, Mikey has drawn a tiny castle and two instances of what would look like part of a road to most people. The castle is Mr. Drew's house, and the *roads* must be airstrips. The one close to the house is the one everyone knows about. The other is the secret strip where Branden's footprints disappeared years ago. Whatever illegal activities Mr. Drew is engaging in, they're moving through there.

The map makes it look like the secret airstrip is an easy ride from the bridge near the Visitor Center, but I know better. There are few easy rides in Alaska. I grab the satellite phone, Dolly's personal beacon, and radio with the required batteries, and stash them in my backpack along with the maps. I confirm my GPS is working. In Anchorage, my smartphone is usually enough, but out here I don't trust cell batteries or towers. Chief Quint recently said that having so many GPS tools is making people incapable of navigating on their own. He may be right. We've had to recover quite a few hikers who got lost when their phones died. They either hadn't brought maps or didn't know how to read them properly.

The ATV is a Polaris four-seater with plenty of space for me, my dog, and my gear. I click my tongue at it in appreciation and tap the roll bar like it's the Tank. As we leave the cabin, I get a feel for how loud the vehicle is with the natural background noises. It's not totally silent, of course, but not bad at all. Between the birds and the insects, it shouldn't be too obvious unless I'm pulling right up to the front door. I follow the rough path Dolly and I took last night, then turn off toward the Resurrection River. She's right—it's totally impassable. I find my way to the bridge, then head immediately north after crossing. I pass over the Resurrection trail, which is nicely deserted this time of morning, and continue on using the map. It seems like I should be getting close to the airstrip, but the landscape gives away nothing. It's so densely forested and rocky that I can't tell if I'm anywhere near my destination.

It's a completely different world here in the middle of summer than it was that winter when Mikey and I followed a dead man's footsteps and marveled at their termination in the middle of the strip. My working theory, and I've had a lot of time to think about it, is that there was a plane waiting for him and that Branden had driven out there to pilot that plane for Mr. Drew one final time based on orders he was given while picking up his check. Was he flying drugs? The dead body of Calderon? Was he going to pick something up? Those are the answers I want to find.

The sun is making a sprint up the powder blue sky, already well above the horizon. The air smells fresh and herbal, and at least for the moment, it's cool as the wind whips across my face. Soon I'm slowing the ATV to a crawl, trying to find a path that's not covered in dense shrubbery. Along animal trails grow clumps of wildflowers in pinks and purple, some yellow scattered throughout. The Devil's club is covered in its enticing white flowers. That at least I recognize—primarily because the plant's defense system is just about as good as Mr. Drew's. The entire thing is covered in sharp thorns that will happily become infected if they find their way under your skin. I should get better at Alaska plants. So far, I only know the ones that have injured me and those that are highly poisonous. I never knew the names of plants in Washington, but for some reason it seems like a thing to know when you plan on growing old somewhere.

Checking Mikey's map against GPS, I should be in the general area of the airstrip. I don't want to accidentally drive right onto it, so I park the Polaris next to a particularly memorable wall of gray rock with a few scraggly trees barely hanging on to the top. Tails and I continue on foot. Good thing—beyond the rock wall, nothing even comes close to passing for a makeshift trail. My ability to navigate in forests has gotten a lot better since I started working with the FBI. They got me out of Anchorage and into more remote areas a lot, and I didn't want to look like a dumbass getting lost, so I started paying attention to my colleague Bogg's stories about hunting deep in the woods and asked questions. He even took me to his cabin outside the city once; not to kill anything, but just to talk about pathfinding and survival stuff. He seemed to enjoy it, and I learned a fair amount. I'll have to be sure to thank him again when I get back to Anchorage.

I pat my leg so Tails stays by my side and doesn't run ahead. I'm glad he knows both voice commands and hand signals. Mr. Drew knows I found a dog while investigating the cases five years ago, and I'm not taking any chances having Tails spotted. It's not long before I glimpse the narrow and flat clearing in the trees. The runway. I stop and make some notations on the map that will make it easier to find in the future.

Runways are everywhere here, but most people put down gravel so they're more visible. Not Mr. Drew. Not on his hidden runway, at least. This one's grown over. It's just long enough for a small plane to take off and land, and even then, the pilot would have to know what they were doing in order to avoid clipping the tops of trees. I'm at the western end of the strip, which means Mr. Drew's house is northeast, probably a ten- to fifteen-minute ride away on the Polaris. He can't see the strip from his house, dense as the trees are between them, which is good for me. And good for him too, I guess. He can easily pretend he doesn't know what goes on here. Still, I suspect he keeps eyes on it somehow. I scan the trees for anything that could be a camera. I approach, but the hairs on the back of my neck warn me not to step through the tree line and out into the open. Tails makes to run out into the clearing, tongue hanging out of his mouth like it does when he smells something interesting, but he sits when I tell him to stay.

This was all I came out here to do—find the airstrip in relation to the cabin. Of course, I'm never satisfied doing simply what I came to do. I walk, still hidden in the trees, around the perimeter of the strip. Tails trots alongside, sniffing the ground. Nothing unusual. Nothing to indicate any signs of recent activity. At least not at first glance. When I use my binoculars, I see the grass is flattened in two long strips. Something has taken off or landed recently, and that means Mr. Drew hasn't given up using this spot.

I take some pictures, though they don't show much, and head back to the Polaris. I want to see if the bush plane I once spotted next to Mr. Drew's house is still there.

CHAPTER SEVEN

The plane is gone, at least for the moment, but I spot something even more interesting just outside the gates of Mr. Drew's place—the tallest commercial kitchen refrigerator of a man I've ever set eyes on. I've never seen him before, and I'd certainly remember. He is about six foot six with hair so light and short that it's almost transparent. There's a distinct cleft in his chin and a sharp black sliver of tattoo creeping from below the right sleeve of his fitted T-shirt. Even through binoculars, his face is not friendly. A guard. Has to be. I keep my distance, making sure I'm well concealed behind a tree as I watch. I order Tails to sit and stay where he is.

The real-life Incredible Hulk isn't doing a whole lot, and he seems to take his job pretty casually. He has his back leaned against the wall as he talks on a cell phone. Occasionally he walks around like he's trying to get a better signal. I try to glimpse through the windows. All the shades are drawn, and I can't tell if there's a light on. Mr. Drew's office is on the top floor, per my intel. He's likely in there. If what Mikey says is true, he rarely comes out anymore. I aim to confirm that.

In the meantime, I sketch the guard in my notebook. It's rudimentary—usually I have the department's contracted artist on hand to create sketches from witness descriptions—but it'll be enough for Mikey whenever I can forward it to him.

I'll come by here again later today.

My search of the woods behind the house yields a very discreet path that leads out the back of Mr. Drew's wooded property and toward the secret airstrip. It's overgrown and there's nothing to indicate a small, grounded plane could navigate it. Unless, that is, you know what you're looking for. I saw that maroon and white plane next to Mr. Drew's house five years ago, and now I know how it got here. The route to his other airstrip is much more obvious. That airstrip is also only a quarter mile from his house. Any coming and going from it could in theory be visible to folks downhill. He must use that strip for legitimate business and the secret strip when he doesn't want anyone to know what he's up to, though I'm sure it's a lot more complicated than that. Mr. Drew doesn't exactly check in with control towers and register his flight plans when his minions are flying drugs or dropping bodies on top of mountains. He probably has loads of rules for how the plane is used and by whom. I need to figure them out. And I need to figure out where that plane goes. Mensel hinted a couple months ago that the FBI was working on small tracking devices that could be used to monitor the movement of cars. Maybe I'll check with him to see if I can test one out on a plane.

Back at Mr. Drew's place, little has changed. The blond man is still there. Just as I'm about to give up on him, he walks quickly toward the gate. I train my binoculars at the driveway, and indeed there is a car crunching over the gravel. I can hear it now from where I am. The blond man types something into the keypad and the gate opens, letting the car through. The driver emerges and greets the guard. I shift to get a better look. Eliyah. Mikey and I met Eliyah when we were investigating Branden's disappearance. Eliyah's wearing a full beard now, but otherwise he looks the same. I scowl. I like Eliyah. I was hoping he'd stop whatever he was into with Mr. Drew after Branden's death, but that doesn't seem to have happened. As I watch, the blond man says something to him, then disappears into the doorway for just a few seconds before re-emerging with several large manilla envelopes. From what I can tell, they're blank—no addresses or labels. The two men exchange a few sentences before Eliyah gets back in the car and leaves. The guard stays standing outside the gate for about half an hour before he goes into the house. Twenty minutes later, he exits the house, gets into a black Bronco, and leaves the same way Eliyah approached— the only way to the road.

I move through the trees as quickly as I can, trying to keep the departing Bronco in sight. Thankfully, it's moving slow. Before it's lost in the pines, I see the Bronco turn onto the road. He's not heading for Seward. He's headed toward Kolit's Hole.

CHAPTER EIGHT

After a dinner of canned beans, well after the park Visitor Center has closed, I pull into its large lot and retrieve my cell. No need running up a bill on the NPS satellite. I have decent reception, so I can walk and talk while Tails watches for wildlife.

I call Mikey. I can hear him clearly enough to make out the scrape of cookware as he talks.

"Hey, sorry, am I interrupting dinner?"

"You mean are you interrupting me preparing to eat in front of the TV and then fall asleep in my chair? It'll be all right just this once, I think. Can you hear me all right? Did you get the maps I left you? Were you able to find the airstrips from there?"

"Yeah. The cabin's great. I found the airstrips. Got a couple things for you to check."

"Shoot!"

"First, I wanted to talk about Dolly."

"Oh?" He sounds cautious. "Something wrong?"

"No, it's just…Well, yeah, I mean…I guess something kind of is wrong. Was. She certainly wasn't happy about bringing me here, though I think we're okay now. It's just…why didn't you tell me?"

"You mean that she's…maybe not my biggest fan?"

"Yeah. She said *Anna* asked her to help me out."

There's a pause and what sounds like scrape of a spatula on the bottom of a pan. "Oh. Yeah that. That's true. It was Anna who asked her. She and Anna are good friends."

"Well, some warning about how she feels toward police would have been nice."

"Oh. I didn't want to bias you or anything."

"Bias me? It's not like I'm not used to dealing with people who are skeptical of cops, Mikey."

"Well, true. It's just…I don't know. I wasn't sure how she'd be with you."

I walk toward the signs for Exit Glacier, bypassing the chain meant to block off the trailhead since the park is closed for the evening.

"Do you know *why* she's skeptical of the police?"

There's a long pause with no utensil noises. "Her niece. Yeah, I know about that."

"You could have told me. I was confused as hell about why she seemed to hate me without even having met me."

"Yeah. It's…well, it's kind of embarrassing, I guess. Even though I wasn't chief, I mean. It was still Willington. It's just…the way the Seward department handled it was not exactly pretty. I didn't want to pull you into that since it's not relevant to Mr. Drew."

"Are we *sure* it's not relevant?"

Now I hear a sizzle and I picture bacon. My stomach growls despite having just eaten. I probably burned a lot more calories today than I ate.

"I don't…I mean…I don't think it's relevant, do you? Dolly's niece is, you know—female."

"Yeah. One of lots of Native Alaskan females who have gone missing. Why wasn't it investigated?"

"Honestly, I'm not totally sure. At first, I thought maybe Nanwalek had a tribal police presence. I didn't find out till later that they didn't. You know tribal police work separately."

"But once you found out they didn't, why didn't you look into Dolly's niece?"

"I just…" There's a creak, and I picture him settling into his chair, phone to his ear and a plate of food in his hand. "It had been a long time. You know there were some politics under Willington. I looked at the file, but there wasn't anything helpful in there. Filed under *Runaway*. I wasn't sure there was a whole lot I could do, and I heard Dolly wasn't always easy to work with."

"You heard that from officers who totally ignored her." I shake my head. Women who are firm in what they want are very quickly labeled *difficult*, while similar men get the *ambitious* moniker.

"Well, yeah…maybe. That's true."

"Well, when this is done, I think it's worth looking at again. It should be *you* who does that, don't you think?"

He laughs, but it doesn't sound natural. "Are you threatening to bring the FBI to town?"

"I mean, technically the FBI is already in town, right?" There's an edge to the conversation. We both laugh awkwardly.

I hear him chewing. "I'll look into it again, Lou…It would help if Dolly would talk to me."

"Might help if you try talking to Dolly."

"All right. Touché. You know I'm not a big fan of confrontation, that's all."

"You're a police chief. And once upon a time, you wouldn't let *me* get away with not meeting people where they are and doing what's right."

"You know, I didn't exactly miss all these Louisa Linebach reality checks."

"Aw, sure you did!"

"Okay, maybe a little." There's more chewing and a loud swallow. "So, what was it you found?"

I wait for him to grab a pen, then I describe the guard, but he doesn't ring a bell for Mikey. He could be staying in Kolit's. I ask Mikey if he can check it out.

"Sure thing. I promised I'd stop in to see Mrs. Butler anyway."

We both have a genuine laugh over that. Mrs. Butler knows all the conspiracies about the Kenai Peninsula—aliens, military, Sasquatch, all the Bermuda Triangle of the North stuff. You name it, she's got a theory. She took a liking to Mikey when we were here investigating years ago, and it seems as soon as he came back to Seward to stay, she invited him over for some of her infamous spiked tea. He's been expected to look in on her about once a month since, or so he told me. He clearly finds her entertaining, and she seems to like the company. If that guard is staying anywhere near Kolit's, she will know. She might try to convince Mikey he's a werewolf, but still.

After I end my call with Mikey, I contact Senior Special Agent Mensel to ask about the tracker. My boss hints he might have something soon and assures me he'll call back in a couple days.

I debate whether to call Anna. I haven't been here long enough.

I sigh. I ration things that make me happy for no reason. I remind myself that her phone's not tapped, and that no one is listening to me out here on the Exit Glacier trail. There's no risk in calling Anna while I have reception, and if I'm going to be here for a while, it will be important to hear friendly voices.

I'm glad I called. She sounds like she's been crying.

"Anna? What's wrong? Are you all right?"

"I'm okay. I mean, I'm safe." She doesn't brighten her voice or conceal the fact that something is the matter. "It was a really bad workday is all."

She talks about the toddler she autopsied, and I shut my eyes, part of my brain resisting the picture of what she describes, but another part wanting to understand her experience.

"His mother left him at home alone to go shoot meth, and she ended up away for nearly three full days. The neighbor finally called the police because the dog she kept out on a chain was barking nonstop. The Primrose officer found the baby already gone."

"Oh, Anna. That's horrible." I stumble, never knowing what to say to comfort a person. My instinct is to try to fix the situation. Every ounce of my being wants to help Anna feel better, but it's not possible. There's nothing I can do.

"The mother is in jail. She seems to have no comprehension of what she did. The officer said she was confused. She admitted she left the house and went to do drugs, but she also kept asking for the little boy. He died of dehydration all shut up in his attic room. Even after they told her repeatedly that he was dead, even after she saw his body, she kept asking where he was."

"Shock?"

"Probably part that and part drugs. She'll go through one painful withdrawal in prison. And when she realizes what she's done, well…"

"Is she on suicide watch?"

"She is."

I want to rail against the mother, but I can't. Anna doesn't either. What punishment could be worse than realizing you've killed your own child? She'll sit in prison with nothing to do but think about what she's done.

"I keep thinking about how that baby must have felt, alone up there, crying and crying and no one coming. Then I think about what his life would have been like if she *had* come home, and he'd survived. He would have been taken away eventually."

"Child Services."

"Right. And then what? Foster homes? Residential facilities?"

"Both, probably. An adoption if he was lucky. But with a drug-addicted mother…" My time in Child Services taught me that only the most special of parents will adopt when it's suspected a child was born to an active user. Most people want infants taken straight from the hospital with medical records showing nothing in the mother's system at the time of birth. No chance for drugs to have affected the baby.

"There's no point even thinking about it, but I can't stop myself."

Well, that's something I certainly understand.

I sit with her in total silence. She's not crying anymore. I wonder if she cried herself out. Still, I can't stop picturing Anna leaning over that tiny body, scalpel in hand. I shiver.

"Can we talk about your day for a while?"

I have to clear my throat before I can speak. "Sure, if you like."

"I'd like!"

I smile. I can't tell her much about what I saw at Mr. Drew's house, so I talk a little about riding through the woods and how pretty it is around the cabin. Then I shift focus to Dolly and my conversation with Mikey. At mention of her friend, her voice becomes a bit brighter.

"I'm surprised Mikey didn't tell you about Dolly's experiences!"

"Me too. It would have been good to know."

"I'm sorry. It didn't even occur to me that he wouldn't have said anything, or I'd have told you myself."

"Not your fault in the least. I'm just glad I know now."

"She's a wonderful woman, but she really did have a horrible time. She's told me that whole story. It wasn't just Seward that did her wrong. Homer had its own emergency, so they couldn't spare an officer. She went to Seward because they had a bigger force and a good reputation, then they ignored her, like she told you."

"She didn't go to Anchorage?"

"I don't think so. But for people who live remote, Anchorage seems like a whole other world. A lot of people are put off by the idea of folks from Anchorage investigating."

"I can see that." I've run up against the rural bias against the urban Anchorage department before. It's not just that the officers are more diverse—some rural Alaskans assume people who live in a city can't understand their lifestyles or their problems. At times that can be true. Of course, the reverse is also true.

"I've asked Mikey to reopen Dolly's niece's case when this one is wrapped."

"He'll probably want to pull Homer in, close as they are."

"Good call." I've reached the end of the Exit Glacier, and I stop. Tails runs to me and sits by my side. The glacier is quiet right now, but they're not always so. When they calve, the reverberation can echo like a gunshot over water. "It's amazing to me how little the departments work together here."

"It's a problem. But it's hard, you know, logistically. We might only be twenty miles away from another department, but if it takes an hour and half to drive there because of mountains and water, well…"

"Yeah. I get it. It's just that I wonder how many cases go unsolved because of the lack of communication."

"A lot. I can pretty much guarantee that."

"Exactly."

We both sigh. It's an obvious problem, but there's no obvious answer.

"Well, I offered Dolly my help too once Mr. Drew is done. Who knows? Maybe we can turn something up."

"If anyone can find Jeannie, it's you." I smile at Anna's optimism. "Where are you, anyway? Does the cabin have reception?"

I laugh. "No. I'm staring up at Exit Glacier."

"Ooh. As close as it is, you know, I rarely go out there. It must be nice with nobody else around."

I turn my head to take in the trees and the ice and the expanse of pinkish-gray sky. "It really is."

She asks about the cabin, and I describe it. She promises she'll find a reason to come visit. I'd love that, and I tell her so.

"I'm really glad you called. I feel better than I did, so thank you."

I assure her I'll call again soon. After we disconnect, I stand there looking at the glacier, thinking about the sheer size of it and how it affects everything around it. Yet when I walk with Tails back to the car, I notice the signs marked with years, indicating how much the glacier has receded over time—a reminder that time comes for all of us, no matter how powerful we might think we are.

My thoughts return to Mr. Drew.

CHAPTER NINE

For the next two weeks, I watch. That's it. It is not a comfortable pastime for me. I like to act, and spying on Mr. Drew's property from a distance is deeply unsatisfying. I'm not even gathering all that much new information. So far, I've confirmed Mikey's assertion that Mr. Drew rarely leaves his house. I've noted a second guard, a man almost as muscular as the blond who's a few years his senior with a short beard and a distinct birthmark on his left cheek. That man stands perfectly straight and spends most of his time staring straight ahead. His posture reminds me of a military man.

The maroon and white plane has come and gone a couple times from the secret airstrip, each time with the same pilot—a man who would match the same physical description of Lee Stanton, Kyle Calderon, or Branden Halifax. When he returns the plane to the airstrip, the guard sees him back to his vehicle, then drives the plane back along the makeshift path that leads to the back of Mr. Drew's house. It is parked in plain sight, and I'm absolutely sure there are cameras on it at all times. After it's in for the evening, the guard spends a lot of time inside the plane. He comes out with a trash bag and a spray bottle, so he's giving it a thorough cleaning. Mikey confirms that there's no mandatory tracking of flights around the Peninsula. Pilots are supposed to register their routes, but many choose not to. When I call her quickly from the satellite phone, Dolly informs me that the park doesn't monitor small planes in their airspace unless they're flying particularly low.

I take pictures of both guards, though they're from far away and not of ideal quality. The FBI finds absolutely nothing on the blond guard. I was right about the other one, though. When they match his picture to a name, they tell me he was a Marine. Unfortunately, there's nothing on him for the years following his honorable discharge, and his record before that is as clean as a straight shot on an empty net. I have to wonder how much he knows about his employer, which makes me question the younger guard's level of involvement too.

In the evenings, lying there staring at knots in the pine of the pitched ceiling, it's easy to feel restless—especially when I'm trying to sleep and there's still daylight. I remind myself that this is a long game, and that if this doesn't end up being the route to catching Mr. Drew, that's okay. I'm still gathering important information. I tell myself that because it's what my therapist would tell me, not because I am convinced of it. Two weeks and nearly nothing new feels like a massive waste of time.

One bright spot is that Mensel informs me that he's got his hands on a prototype for the new tracking device, and he's been itching to put it to good use. I'm the lucky recipient of both the device and a lecture on not letting it fall into the wrong hands. Mensel describes the tech as a small magnet so strong it can rip out the underside of a car upon removal, so I have to place it exactly where I want. That's not going to be easy, given that I want that tracker on the maroon and white plane, and there's no chance I'll be able to attach it while the plane is at the house. I've confirmed Mr. Drew has cameras all over the property. The blond bodyguard took one down from a tree to work on it—perhaps it was malfunctioning. He then very helpfully went around the entire property and checked all the cameras. I now have a lovely little hand-drawn map with each one's location, though I don't know what directions they face and exactly how much ground they cover. Sure, I could risk it, knowing that he can't monitor the cameras all the time, but if there's any sort of motion sensor, it might alert him. My best bet, as far as I can tell, is to attach the tracker while the plane is at one of the airstrips waiting on a pilot. I'm guessing a wheel well will be my best bet for keeping it hidden during cleaning.

I am in the cabin when the door opens, and Dolly enters. She doesn't knock—she just pushes the door open with her shoulder. When she sees me, she jumps like she wasn't expecting me to be home. She's got armfuls of brown paper bags. I rush to take some from her.

"Is it Christmas already? I must have lost track of time."

She fishes around in one of the bags and hands me a midsized padded envelope labeled *From Chief Harper*. I grab a knife and slice the top open, then peer into the envelope. It's a tiny device that can only be the tracker. I poke at it.

"Don't wanna know," Dolly reminds me. "The Park Service

agreed to house you to assist your investigation, but that's the extent of NPS involvement." I half expect her to whip out a liability waiver.

"I remember. And I certainly do appreciate it. I know the parks have their own operations. Thank you for liaising with Chief Harper and bringing this. It will be very helpful." *Or it might be at least.* I turn the device over with my fingers while it's still in the envelope, thinking about when I'll be able to attach it without getting caught.

"Your face looks like there's a dirty diaper in there." And here I thought I was getting better at controlling my facial expressions. I try to force my eyebrows into a neutral stance, which feels unnatural.

"Oh. Yeah. Just a…logistical problem. Not sure how to get it where it needs to go."

Dolly looks at me and exhales sharply.

"What? I didn't tell you what it is!"

She shakes her head and empties the bags. It's a random assortment of goods that she unloads—a couple puzzles, some scotch tape, some toiletries and tools, some antibacterial cream and other first aid potions. She goes to the first aid kit in the kitchen and rifles through it, throwing out various creams and ointments and replacing them. Expired, I guess.

"You found three men a few years back," she states. *So, she's been asking about me.*

I nod. "Branden Halifax, Kyle Calderon, and Lee Stanton."

"They were involved in drugs?"

"You want to know?"

She shrugs. "I have my hunches. As a private citizen." After a second, she adds, "And it's always nice to know you're right."

I laugh. "I definitely understand that. We know a couple of them were definitely in the drug trade. They all died because of it."

"You think they were murdered."

I want to nod, but I don't.

"Can you talk about it?"

"I shouldn't, no."

"*Will* you talk about it?"

I put on a fresh pot of coffee. "You said you have a hunch. How about if you tell me."

She makes a low, contemplative sound in the back of her throat, then nods once. After a few moments, she begins. "They're all connected to the men who go missing around the peninsula all the time. The men all look alike. You've realized that?" I nod. "Why would these disappearing men who are running drugs look alike?" I tilt my head and raise an eyebrow. "They're being identified by someone who orchestrates this drug trade." She stops, waiting.

"Sounds reasonable to me. And why pick men who look alike?"

"Added level of anonymity. One goes missing, few go missing— harder to find them if the description is just young man, average height, white, brown hair, brown eyes, possible beard. Then if they do find one, hard to positively ID. More so if they've been in the elements." The corners of my mouth lift slightly. She's good.

I pour the coffee into two cracked ceramic mugs, offer Dolly one. She accepts it with both hands, adds nothing to it. We sit in a silence that's far more comfortable than the last time she was here.

"Who do you think is orchestrating this, Dolly? If this is a major operation, it needs someone in a powerful position leading it."

She narrows her eyes at me. "You already have an idea." I nod but say nothing. "My idea is that it's that old police chief, Willington, and a couple of the other old Seward officers." It takes all my effort to keep my eyebrows down and say nothing. She stares at me, then shakes her head. I'm sure she knows I can't say more. She jumps up to top off her coffee.

"So, a decades-old drug operation that involves dozens of identical men is what you're trying to crack. By yourself."

I laugh. "Not quite."

"Anna is helping you."

"And the FBI. And Chief Harper."

She sighs. "Well, if Anna is helping, there must be something to it."

I smile at the mention of Anna's name. These past two weeks have been a misery when I think of how close and yet far away she is from me. *How was I away from her for five years?* I was a dumbass to waste all that time. "You think highly of her."

"I do."

"How do you know each other?"

"Ah. She didn't tell you?" I shake my head. "Anna used to train with my uncle, who was part of the Qutekcak community near here. He's a great hunter. Was. But not just that. He knew animal behaviors, the way they interact, way they attack even. Anna wanted to learn about injuries they inflict."

"Ah yes. She did mention that. Said it was very helpful to her work."

"I used to visit with him when I was in the park for the summer.

He introduced us. I was skeptical at first, but she is a genuine person. She wants to help."

"You're right about that."

"You met her when you were on those cases in Seward." I nod. If she knows Anna well, she knows she's a lesbian, and I'm sure she can tell just by the way my face changes when I talk about her how I feel about Dr. Anna Fenway.

Dolly drains her cup and goes to the sink to wash it. When she's finished, she pats Tails on the head and stuffs the empty bags under the sink. "I should go. Educational program today."

"You teach programs?" She nods just once. "What's the topic?"

"Today? Wildlife. Kids' favorite."

I smile. I'm a little jealous. I miss interacting with kids since I no longer work for Social Services. "That must be a blast."

"Best part of my job."

"Well, enjoy."

Tails walks Dolly to the door. As soon as she's left, I turn to the tracking device.

CHAPTER TEN

The maroon and white plane doesn't move for days, and I'm impatient waiting. I bide my time watching the guards. Then one morning I arrive at Mr. Drew's and immediately spot that the plane is missing. I get to the secret airstrip as fast as I can – the plane is unattended, which makes the hairs on my neck stand up. The guard wasn't outside the mansion, and he doesn't seem to be here. Maybe he's inside talking to Mr. Drew. I don't have time to look for him; I'm guessing a pilot is on the away, which means no matter where he is now, the guard will be back to watch his takeoff. He'll head back to Mr. Drew's as soon as the plane is in the air, but that will mean I've missed my chance. I have little time. I unzip my backpack and retrieve my raincoat stuffed in the bottom. It has a massive hood I pull down over my eyes. I sternly command Tails to stay while I sling the pack back onto my shoulders. Then, tracker in hand, I sprint for the plane.

I slide underneath the white belly of the plane so I'm not as visible. The tracker will be too obvious here, so I reach for the back wheel. The tracker will fit inside the black metal casing, and no one should have reason to look in there unless they need to replace that wheel sometime soon. There is no time to second-guess myself. I try to keep most of my body under the plane while I reach inside the wheel casing. I can't see in there, but I can feel the pull of the magnet as the tracking device attaches.

I roll out from underneath and run for the trees. The wind threatens to whip my hood back, but I keep it secured with both hands.

Just as I get to the edge of the airstrip, a massive weight crashes into my back and sends me spilling forward into the underbrush. I'm pinned, hot breath on the back of my neck. The weight is as heavy as a bear, but bears don't speak English, and this beast does.

"Stay down."

Then there's the thud of another impact and a cry as the body on top of me rolls slightly, pinning my left arm. My right arm is partially free, and I struggle to draw my gun. My pack is pinned against me, so no chance of calling for help.

"Fuck. Get off…" The guard's weight shifts more as he fights with Tails. The man is making noises of pain himself now, and finally he rolls mostly off me. I'm up by the sheer force of adrenaline alone, but he's up too—and Tails is hanging from his arm. It's the gun arm. *Good boy.* I slide my own hand into my waistband and pull my weapon, aiming it squarely at his head and as far from Tails as possible.

"Drop your weapon." His gun falls to the ground before I finish speaking. As soon as I go to kick it away, the man kicks out with his own long leg, sweeping my legs from under me. Even as I hit the ground hard with my tailbone, I chide myself for not anticipating that move. It's not every day I end up in hand-to-hand combat. Tails is swinging in the air above me. His grip is relentless. The man dives for his gun, but I'm already up, and my boot comes down hard on his left hand just as it reaches the ground. I shift all my weight onto my lug soles until I hear something give and the man screams. I come around his left side and kick him hard in the ribs. Tails has detached himself but is trying to get to the man's neck. He lashes out with his bloody right arm and hits my dog in the face, which earns him a swift kick to his own face.

"All right. Fucking hell. Enough." He raises both hands.

"Stay the hell down."

"Fine, but call your dog off."

"Tails. Down." Tails immediately returns to my side, where he sits, not taking his eyes off the young guard. The man starts to stand. "What did I just say?"

"Look, I need to just…" As he pulls himself into a crouch, he reaches for his ribs as if inspecting whether they're broken. It's another con, but I'm ready for this one as he pulls a massive hunting knife and lunges toward me. I fire at his chest, but he's in the midst of turning and the bullet hits between his heart and his shoulder. It doesn't stop him. This must be what shooting at a moose is like. Before I can make any decisions, I'm back on the ground, and he's trying to wrestle my gun from my hand. He slashes at my arm with the knife. There's a sting but I don't register much else. *Yet.* I manage to get a grip on his right wrist. He screams. Tails must have done serious damage. Thank goodness, because with our size differential, I'd stand zero chance if he wasn't injured. I bring a knee up into his crotch and his eyes go wide. Hey, I can fight dirty too. I repeat the motion and he falls off me, still managing to keep a grip on his knife. I lift into a kneel, breathing hard, and level the gun at his head.

He gasps. "Who are you?"

"I'm not telling you that."

"You're on private property. I have every right to shoot you."

"And yet." His gun is several yards away from us at the base of a tree. I want to grab it, but I don't dare take my aim off him.

"You were messing with the plane."

"Was I?"

"Don't play dumb. I saw you come out from under it."

Shit. If I let him go, he's going to find the tracking device. I have to distract him.

"You're Mr. Drew's guard."

"That's none of your business." He examines his mutilated arm, blood entirely soaking his sleeve. He doesn't seem particularly bothered by the sight.

"You oversee the men who run drugs for him."

"I don't know what you're talking about." His tone is too casual. He knows exactly what I'm talking about. He places one hand carefully on the ground and raises himself up, still gripping the knife. He takes a step toward me.

"I will shoot you again."

"You need to leave."

The man makes a sudden lunge toward me and I fire again, square into his stomach. He doubles over but still comes at me, albeit stumbling. I can't take my chances on hand-to-hand with him again. My luck can't hold out for another round.

Without taking my eyes off him, I command Tails.

"Attack."

Tails is in the air immediately, his body coming level with the man's chest. Tails goes straight for the throat, and when the man throws up his hands to shield his face, the knife handle, covered in blood, slips from his grip. He falls backward as Tails's ninety-five pounds of muscle slams into him, then he's squeezing Tails, almost as if he's trying to hug him. Blood spurts from a wound I can't identify. The man screams and then goes eerily silent. Tails growls low. I step close. My dog's teeth are in the guard's neck so far that I can't even see them. His face is covered in blood. I don't want to look, it's so brutal and so vicious, but I also can't look away.

I call Tails off. He keeps his eyes on the man as he backs away a few feet and sits.

"You fuckin' bitch and your stupid..." His voice sounds wet and gurgles. He holds his hand to his neck, but blood pours through his fingers. The front of his shirt is drenched. He tries to raise his head but lets it fall back down.

"I can call for help, but you need to answer some questions first. That's the deal."

"I'm not making any fuckin'—"

"You don't have long with those wounds." I look in his eyes. My mind is racing with questions I need to ask this man. I also need to call for help. I slide my phone from my pocket, sincerely hoping it's not damaged.

"Did you kill Kyle Calderon and Branden Halifax?"

He makes a choking half-laugh sound. "You don't know anything."

"Why don't you enlighten me. That wound isn't healing by itself, and I can call for help."

"Real fucking concerned citizen, aren't you."

"Come on. Mr. Drew isn't worth dying for." The phone's screen is cracked, but otherwise it looks intact. I barely look at it as I press the numbers and the call button.

He holds his head still and puts pressure on his neck with his busted hand as he stares at the sky. He must be starting to feel weak from the blood loss now. I don't hear ringing. No signal. I need the satellite phone in my pack.

"He'd kill me if I told you anything anyway."

"Answer the question."

"I didn't fuckin' kill anyone. Now call."

"But you know who did."

"Yeah. Ca—"

"Who killed Kyle Calderon?"

"Gandhi." His hand starts to shake as he holds his neck.

"Look, if you give me an answer, I can call for help and I can make sure you're protected from Mr. Drew." He snorts, but there's little force behind it. He'll lose consciousness soon. "If you live long enough for it to matter."

"Fine. Call now. I'll tell you." This man is going to die.

"All right. I have to get my satellite phone, though there's a good chance you smashed it when you tackled me. Stay down or you get the dog again." I lower my gun arm and slip the backpack to the front of my body, eyes still on him. He doesn't move. I feel pieces of plastic, something busted at the bottom of the bag. The satellite phone is buried among whatever is broken. The case is shattered, but I'm still able to call Anna. I tell her someone's hurt, not me, and it's a serious neck wound.

"Come alone."

❖

"Help is on the way. Now tell me."

The man is so still and so quiet that for a second I think he's already dead. I step closer.

"He has them kill each other. When it needs to be done. No dirty hands."

"Mr. Drew orders it."

"Yeah." His voice is starting to sound very far away.

"So, he ordered Lee Stanton to kill Branden." He chokes out an affirmation. "Did he have Lee Stanton killed?"

"Not that…I don't…" He's fading fast. Anna will be faster in her Jeep than an ambulance on these rough roads, but not fast enough.

"Hey!" I yell at him. "Hey, stay with me. She's almost here." He's closed his eyes. I draw my gun again, but I reach with the other hand and slap him. "Tell me how to catch him."

His eyes open enough for me to see whites, and he opens his mouth, but there's only a death rattle.

CHAPTER ELEVEN

I drag the dead man further into the forest. It's horrible, painful and necessary work. I have no idea when to expect the pilot. Sometimes the plane sits there waiting for just minutes, sometimes it's up to an hour. One thing is for sure, though—people tend to not delay on Mr. Drew's tasks. I sweat through my clothes, bleeding and panting and swearing when I finally let go of the guard's legs, letting them fall in the underbrush. Tails has tried to help a few times, but he's panting hard. I'm sure that fight took it out of him too. I check to make sure no one is nearby, step back into the open, and check that the body isn't obvious. It's not. There's nothing I can do about the blood on the ground, other than hope it's not that obvious against the dark mud and flashes of flowers where the trees let light through. I go back to Tails and collapse against a tree, waiting for a sign of Anna. Shit. She could run into the pilot. I call her.

"Hey, I'm here. Where are you?"

I stand and scan the area. There she is, just emerging onto the end of the airstrip on foot, her medical kit at her side and her backpack strapped on, ready for a wilderness rescue.

"Get back into the tree line." I wave, hoping she'll see me. "There's a pilot coming." She disappears from view. "Head around to your left. I'm about ten yards back from the strip, opposite side of you."

She reaches me in just a few minutes and immediately reaches for her medical kit. I look down at myself even though I know I'm not the one who needs attention. I can see why she thinks I am. The entire front of my jacket is covered in half-dried blood, and a flap of fabric hangs down near my ribs. I take it off and stuff it in my pack.

"It's okay—most of it's not mine." She exhales heavily, then gives me a hug. I get blood on her olive green button-down, but I hug back, leaning my weight into her. The exhaustion hits me now.

"Oh!" She steps back, eyes focused on the body of the guard.

"Yeah. He's who I called you for." She's already checking for a pulse. "I thought maybe he'd make it." She stays crouched, examining his injuries with her eyes, shaking her head. She pulls on a pair of latex gloves from her pockets and prods at his neck.

"Jesus, what did this?" She notices the dog. "Oh. Tails?" Her eyes are big.

"Yeah. The guy had the best of me for a minute. I had to have Tails attack. Twice, actually."

"Given the size of this guy, I wouldn't be too sorry about it. He attacked you?"

"Yeah. He saw me near the plane. He had a gun. Shit, it's still…" I move to retrieve it, but just as I do, I see movement near the plane. I nudge Anna and point. She scrambles around in her pack and pulls out her binoculars, handing them over to me. The pilot's not someone I recognize, though he matches the same description of the men who usually do Mr. Drew's deliveries. He walks slowly, scanning about as he goes. He turns constantly to look behind him. Surely, he expects the guard, who always oversees take-offs. The man pushes brown hair out of his eyes, keeps looking as he gets to the plane. Anna and I crouch low as his eyes glance into the tree line, but his gaze doesn't linger. Before he steps into the cockpit, he looks back toward where he came from, hesitating as if he's unsure whether to proceed. I silently will him to get in the plane and take off. He stands still for a few seconds, then hurries into the plane. Just a couple minutes later, it's in the air. Anna and I both exhale audibly.

I look at her. "I'm so glad you're here."

"We better get this guy out of here."

"Yeah. And we're going to do that…how?"

"I've got a stretcher in the Jeep. Hang tight." She takes a few steps, then turns back. "Odds of Mr. Drew coming out here or sending someone else?"

"Good. Usually, the guard heads back to the house as soon as the pilot takes off. Drew'll notice when he doesn't return."

"Shit. Okay."

While she heads back to the vehicle, I go through the man's pockets. There's a wallet but no ID and no photos or credit cards with a name. There's just a bunch of cash. I take the knife and a few bullets and recover the gun.

When Anna returns, we roll the body onto the stretcher and strap him down. It takes forever to get the man to her Jeep even though she's moved it as close as possible. He weighs a ton. We can't risk the much easier route along the airstrip. Instead, we maneuver the dead weight around trees, scratching ourselves and the body on underbrush. At one point the Devil's club gets him. At least he won't have to worry about the needles in his skin. Tails goes ahead of us, picking out a way through the trees, but it only does so much good. It's entirely overgrown. Good for keeping out of sight, bad for this particular operation.

Anna opens the back of the Jeep and flips the second row of seats down, and we finally give one powerful joint-effort lift and heft the body in, folding the legs at an undignified angle. It's not pretty, but it's the best we can do. The interior is already a bloody mess, but Anna doesn't seem concerned about that or the million tiny cuts in her shirt's fabric and on her skin. With the exertion, I realize the knife cut on my arm is bleeding heavily. Anna cleans it and binds it tightly.

"I'm taking this guy to the morgue. Tell me where I can meet you after."

I just want to collapse into bed and sleep for a decade, but I know I need to be checked over first. My body is starting to hurt, and that's sure to get worse before it gets better. I tell her how to find the cabin, then Tails and I head back to our vehicle.

As we drive away, I hear another vehicle in the distance, but I don't stop, and I don't look back to see who it is. I don't have to.

I can only hope he hasn't seen me or Anna.

CHAPTER TWELVE

I'm not sure a hot shower has ever felt as good as the one I take as soon as I get back to the cabin. I wish it could last forever, but the water heater is small, and it starts to go cold about ten minutes in. I dump half a bottle of shampoo onto my scalp and scrub at it as hard as I can. My hair could probably make at least three excellent wigs—though right now you wouldn't want it to. The water turns cold as I wash it out, but at least it's something close to clean.

I have no idea how long Anna will be, so once I've dressed, piled my tangled hair into a bun, and bandaged my more obvious wounds, I take Tails outside with a dishrag and the trash can, stripped of its bag and full of water. For some reason, rubbing dried clots of blood off him is more disturbing than it was washing them off myself. Maybe it's because he doesn't seem particularly bothered by what's just happened. His large honey-colored eyes look serious, but they always do.

After, I lie down on the sofa and close my eyes. It's hard to get comfortable—my back feels like it's been run over by a semi. I can feel some of the welts and small cuts with my fingers. Tails doesn't try to crowd on the couch with me like he usually does, but he curls up on the rug right next to me. I let my arm dangle, and he rubs his wet nose into my hand. He's sore. I can tell by the way he keeps shifting his body.

"You did a good job today, buddy."

Tails would never hurt me. But I can't shake the image of his teeth buried in that man's throat. The sheer brutal viciousness of it is shocking even though it's what he is trained to do.

I am unsure how long I sleep. I wake to the door opening. When I pry my eyes open, it's Dolly, not Anna. I force myself to sit up and Dolly takes a long glance at me.

"Well, that doesn't look good."

"Thanks."

She grabs my wrists and examines each of my arms in turn, then my head. She even lifts my shirt to look at my back.

"Take this off."

"My shirt?"

"Yes. Your back needs ointment." She doesn't go to the first aid kit in the kitchen, though. She reaches into her fanny pack and pulls out a small glass jar.

I gingerly pull my arms through my shirt sleeves. Something cool goes on my skin, but I can't tell what it is from the smell because there is none.

"What are you putting on there?"

"Devil's club."

"You mean the stuff that's always trying to kill me?"

"The same. I'll leave it with you. Keep putting it on. Helps with inflammation and pain."

"Thanks. I'm guessing the pain is going to really hit tomorrow."

"I shouldn't ask what happened."

We're both silent. I wait for her to ask what happened.

"Does that mean you actually *don't* want to know?"

"No."

"So, you *do* want to know."

"Maybe."

I laugh, but it sounds weak. "I got into a fight with a—"

The door flies open and Anna rushes in. She stops suddenly, then looks between Dolly and me. I'm still not wearing a shirt. She hugs me as gingerly as possible, then turns and hugs Dolly.

"I'm so glad you're here," she says to her. Anna places both of her hands lightly on my shoulders and turns me gently to look at my back. "Oh, good. You already treated it."

She turns me back toward her. "That should start working in about twenty minutes, Louisa."

"I can't wait."

"So, first of all"—she keeps her hands on my shoulders—"are you okay?"

"Yes. I mean, I think so. Nothing's broken."

"Want me to redo your arm bandage?"

"Maybe in a little bit. I'm all right. More kind of shocked and tired than anything, I guess." I look at Tails. "Mind looking him over?"

"Well, I'm no vet, but I'll check for anything broken." She tells Tails to lay, and he lets her check him over, turning when needed. He lets out a whimper at one point, but Anna assures me he's just bruised, like I am.

Dolly looks at me. "Should I leave, or are you going to fill me in?"

"Which do you prefer?"

She sighs, looks at Anna for a few seconds, then at Tails. She removes her fanny pack, leaving it next to the Devil's club salve, then sits.

"I'm supposed to be checking in on you every few days at my boss's request, so I guess if I'm going to do that, I might as well know what's going on."

And here I thought she was just coming by to keep the cabin supplied.

Anna sits next to me on the sofa.

"Don't spare the details either," Anna says. "After checking the body, I'm intrigued as to how exactly all that happened. Especially given that you don't look like you took too much damage."

"Really? Because I feel like I did. But yeah, I had some serious help." I lean down for Tails, who places his chin on my knees and lets me scratch his head while I talk. I recount the fight, blow for blow, at least all I can remember. I mention that I was at the plane, but not what I was doing. I picture the tracker stuck to the plane, airborne. I did my job. Even if someone discovers it, the FBI can see where it lands, and that may or may not answer a lot of questions.

We all lean back in our chairs. I should put on a pot of coffee. I can't move.

"Anna, would you mind doing me a favor?"

She jumps from her seat. "Name it."

Within a couple minutes, the room is filled with the aroma of a nutty dark roast, and we sip in companionable silence. Tails's legs twitch in his sleep. There's a feeling of comfort in the cabin with Anna and Dolly to which I'm not accustomed. I want to be able to tell them everything because I know they could both help. I may not know Dolly well, but my gut says I can trust her. Besides, Anna seems to.

"Dolly, can I trust you with something that you absolutely shouldn't know? Actually, you too, Anna." I know what I'm about to do is an absolute breach of my work with the FBI, but these women could help me. I think of that saying, *better to ask forgiveness than permission.* Both nod earnestly. Dolly makes a sign with her hand that isn't familiar to me, but I assume it's akin to *cross my heart and hope to die.*

"I'm trying to get evidence on Mr. Drew. When the guard caught me, I was placing a tracker on the plane." Neither of them looks particularly surprised. "The pilot took off with it in place, so for right now, no one knows it's there. Though I guess…"

I remember after a few seconds that they can't actually hear my thoughts.

"I guess in theory if there is some sort of camera around there, Mr. Drew could have reviewed the footage when his guard didn't come back, and he could have seen me put something on the plane. I'm not sure we'll know one way or the other, though the FBI will be able to tell me if the device stops working. Or if they just stop using the plane. Thankfully, this tracker is a beast to get off."

"You didn't need a warrant to do that?" Dolly asks.

"Place a tracker? Surprisingly, no."

She nods solemnly.

"Either way, Mr. Drew is going to know something's up because his guard disappeared." I haven't asked Anna what she did with the body. I turn to her. "What happens to him now, by the way?"

"He's safely tucked away in a drawer. I'll let Mikey know, but he'll use discretion. If next of kin come looking for him, of course I'll have to make his presence known. If Mr. Drew comes knocking…well, he's not family. And besides, I suspect he'll never turn up."

"Is there any way you could be traced back here?" *Good question, Dolly.* She doesn't want to risk bringing danger to her fellow rangers, and understandably so. NPS likely wouldn't have agreed to house me if they'd known how dangerous this would become.

I shake my head slowly. "I wasn't followed on my way back, and that's the only way I can think he would know where I'm staying."

"So, Mr. Drew knows his guard has been killed. That's for certain. That means he knows someone is watching his operations. He can likely assume who. And *that* means he'll stop using that airstrip. He'll move the operation elsewhere, or he'll pause."

"When you say it that way, it doesn't sound like the end of the world."

Anna chuckles. "Look at you, being so positive."

I smile. "I've been working on it."

"Well, it's a great look on you!"

Dolly watches us steadily. It's hard to tell what she's thinking from her expression.

"Louisa, do you think you're still safe here?"

I turn to her and nod. "Like I said, no one followed me. Mr. Drew may well start looking around. He's paranoid—we know that. What are the odds of him poking around park grounds?"

Dolly puffs out her cheeks, releases a stream of air.

"Given how big the park is, he'd have his work cut out, though we are right on the border. But he surely knows how few rangers there are, and it *is* summer—it would be easy to mill around in the tourist crowds without us even noticing."

Suddenly I'm starving. My knees creak as I rise. Anna is immediately at my side. I rummage the cabinets and find a box of spaghetti noodles while she pulls out a jar of sauce and a can of mushrooms, ordering me to sit down.

"I'm fine, I—"

"Doctor's orders. You could stand to learn a lesson about listening."

"Yes, ma'am." I slink to the sofa.

"There's venison. I'll make meatballs." Dolly commandeers a spot at the counter and grabs an onion and some garlic.

While they cook, I consider the situation.

"Dolly, you know this park and the area around it better than anyone. What do you think? Should I stay here?"

"Inclined to say no, but not sure where else you'd go that you could keep watching."

"Though like we said," Anna chimes in, "Mr. Drew is likely to stop using that airstrip. Who knows where he'll move his operations."

"Hang on. I'm going to make a phone call."

They both watch me as I half-fall, half-walk out the front door to seek out better reception. Tails follows. On my way out, I hear Anna saying, "I could have sworn I just told her not to…" I smile.

The FBI returns my call within a few minutes. When I come back in, walking like Frankenstein's monster because the soreness in my legs is really hitting now, the place smells like my favorite Italian restaurant. Both women glance up at me, and Anna rushes over to offer an arm. I'm happy to lean against her as she helps me back onto the sofa.

"They tracked the plane. It landed a while ago."

"Where?" Dolly sets my plate down on the arm rest.

"It landed in Seldovia, stayed half an hour, and took off again. It's currently grounded in Port Graham."

Dolly inhales sharply. Anna's eyes widen.

"What am I missing?" I ask.

"Port Graham is right near my home," Dolly says, her phone already in hand.

CHAPTER THIRTEEN

I've lost track of how much coffee we've gone through. I keep glancing out the window thinking it's midday, but when I check the wall clock, the evening is getting well on. Anna and Dolly don't seem to mind. Dolly has the atlas open between us on the table, and she's been staring at the same page for a while now. Her finger is on a location at the very tip of the peninsula, all the way on the other side of the park.

She seems a bit calmer than when I first told her the plane's location. She made some hurried phone calls to members of her community, all of whom are now on a mission to subtly spot the plane. She already knows it didn't land on the Nanwalek airstrip, which would be odd if it wasn't affiliated with Mr. Drew. Now we contemplate the route, trying to figure out what the pilot is doing.

Seldovia and Port Graham are tiny and can only be reached by plane or boat. Perhaps Mr. Drew has told his pilot to find a good place to hide the plane since the guard went missing. That could explain why it's so remote. It'll be Mr. Drew's bad luck if the pilot chose to hide the plane in Dolly's hometown, where she knows every single resident.

Dolly's work phone rings once, then the signal drops, so she heads outside. When she returns, she's smiling.

"Got 'em, copper."

"Where?"

"The plane's in a clearing outside Port Graham, but the pilot's not in it."

"Where's he?"

"They finally found him down at the marina."

"Doing what?"

Dolly shrugs. "Seems to just be talking to some guys down there.

My cousin's going to try to get himself into the conversation and report back.

"Did anyone recognize the pilot?"

"This is the first time my cousin's seen him, and he tends to know everyone."

"Your family works fast."

"Well, it's a tiny community. Outsiders draw a lot of notice. Besides, it's a Tuesday evening. Nothing else will be going on in town."

"No one saw him distributing anything? Taking money?"

"Not yet, but they're on it. We'll know everything he does with all those eyes." Dolly places her hand over her mouth, but a yawn escapes anyway.

"I'm sorry, Dolly. You've been here for ages and I'm sure you just meant to only be a few minutes. There's no need to hang around."

"I probably should check back in at Exit. The overnighter will start to wonder where I am soon." She stands and gathers her things. "If I hear anything tonight, I'll call the satellite." She nods at me, gives Anna a quick hug and a peck on the cheek, and is gone.

Anna also looks sleepy. I'm sure that however she managed to wrestle that guard out of her SUV and into the morgue, it was no easy task. Hopefully she had discreet assistance. Still, she doesn't move to go but pulls her feet up onto the sofa.

"Ah, alone at last."

I laugh. "You mean you were waiting for your friend to leave?"

She smiles. "I love Dolly, but I was looking forward to a little time with you. If you're not just hoping to crash right away."

"I probably should, but I know that once I fall asleep and wake up again, I'm going to be an entire world of sore." I do what I've been wanting to do since she arrived and rest my head on her shoulder. "I'm glad you stayed. I really like Dolly, but I'm still getting comfortable with her."

"Yup, that's Dolly. I thought she didn't like me for months when I first met her. She can seem kind of untouchable, but it's just a front, you know. She's careful about who she trusts because she puts so much of herself into her relationships."

"I think she and I may have some things in common."

"Glad you realized it." She laughs her tinkling wind chime laugh.

I sigh deeply, her perfume faint now but still detectable, with a touch of soil and pine mixed in from our earlier adventure.

"Do you want to talk about it?"

I don't raise my head, but instead bury my nose in her shoulder, intentionally muffling my words. "Yes. No. I think part of me is trying to block it out and not think about what happened."

"That's understandable. It's kind of a huge deal, even if it was justified."

That's the real *question. Was it justified?*

"Maybe. But he didn't just shoot me on sight. Maybe he would have let me go if I hadn't fought back."

"But he had no right to attack you in the first place."

"I feel bad that I don't know his name. Is that weird?"

"No. And I'll try my best to find it."

"Thank you."

Anna runs her hand over my hair. "I've been lucky to never have to take someone's life, but I've worked with a lot of people who have, and it seems really complicated. You're bonded with them in an intimate way, and it doesn't necessarily matter that he was attacking you or that he was a bad person."

"I think if I *knew* that he was a bad person, I would feel better about it, honestly. He was working for Mr. Drew, but I mean, so was Branden, and Kyle, and Lee, and Eliyah. I don't think they are—or were—bad people...I think they just got pulled into something they shouldn't have been involved in. They made a bad *choice*, for sure. But not bad people. Maybe he was the same."

She exhales into my hair. "Maybe. I'm not sure we'll ever know. But one thing's for sure, you made the right decision. He could have killed you just by tackling you. He certainly did some damage. I'm just glad it wasn't worse." She lifts her head, then turns so that I have to remove my head from her shoulder, which results in a bit of dizziness which fades in several seconds. She places her fingers lightly on my chin, turning my face toward her. "It's a shitty, horrible thing that happened, and I'm sorry you had to deal with that alone. And that you'll continue having to deal with it."

I smile as best I can muster, which I'm sure just looks sad and exhausted. "I wasn't alone, though. I had Tails with me."

"That's true," she says before giving a click of her tongue that gets him up and wagging his nub. "Geez, it's hard to imagine this dog doing what he did to that guy. He's such a big sweetie." She starts talking directly to Tails. "But he's a good boy, protecting Louisa like that. You knew just what to do, didn't you?" She turns back to me. "He's well trained. That gun arm wasn't going to be aiming much anytime soon even if he had survived. He would have needed reconstructive surgery."

"What actually killed him?" I'm not sure I really want to know.

"The shot to the stomach."

There's not much else to say, but my mind grasps for every detail, as if by knowing all the specifics I can somehow gain some control over what happened. "Tell me."

She puts her hands on my shoulders and looks into my eyes. I gaze back at hers, so close I can see the little flecks of gold and mahogany in her eyes that would, from a distance, simply read as green. "You're sure?"

"Yes."

She doesn't spare me any details, and I appreciate that. She tells me exactly how the bullet entered the liver, and how profuse the blood loss was because of the liver's function in circulation. She walks me through what the guard must have been feeling, how unfocused he would have become. I'm impressed that he was even able to answer my questions based on what she's telling me. He really was tough. I have an odd sort of admiration for him.

"He knew he was going to die." I look down at my hands, trying not to think about how that would feel, to know you only had maybe minutes left.

"Yes. I think that's probably why he talked. It would have been a serious effort. He would have felt like he could barely even breathe."

"So why? Why talk? Especially to the person killing him." A wave of shame washes over me. I cover my face.

I knew, of course. Getting into police work, I knew there was a good chance I would eventually kill someone. There had been moments I thought it was going to happen, but both times I had hesitated just long enough that a colleague had shot first, and both times the other people who were there had reassured them it was necessary—that they were protecting the pack.

I appreciate Anna, but she wasn't there. And if it hadn't been justified, would she or *could* she even tell me? What difference would it make?

She smooths back some hair that's come loose around my face and just looks at me.

"I've been there for people's last rites a few times, and I've been with people who died without any sort of religious figure there too," she says. I think automatically of my mother wanting the imam at her side as she died, even though I'd never known her to be devout in her religion. "Whether there's someone there to formally hear confessions or not, people want to talk at the end." Anna carefully rubs her thumb beneath my eye, collecting some of the tears gathered there. "You were there, and he needed to unload what he knew. It's a shame that was the only way for that to happen."

"If he could have held on longer...I could have learned more." I wince, realizing how insensitive I sound. "That's *awful*. Shit."

"Don't beat yourself up for having complicated feelings about all this. That man had secrets that could save a lot of lives, I'm sure. But you'll find them. He helped you in his way. You know your theory was correct now."

"But what he said holds no weight in court. There's no way to even prove he said it."

"No, but you know for sure that you were right, so you don't have to waste any of that lovely brain space"—she lightly taps my temple—"doubting yourself or trying to pursue alternative explanations. You know what you have to prove. Now you just gather evidence."

"Thanks, Anna." My vision swims. The walls of the room slowly advance forward, then retreat when I turn my head. "Speaking of my brain, though, I'm wondering if I have a concussion."

Anna has me follow her finger with just my eyes, then do a couple of balancing tests.

I don't pass with flying colors.

"Your recall is obviously good, and you don't seem disoriented, but you do have some physical symptoms, so I want you to take it easy for the next week. You know concussions can be dangerous."

I nod carefully.

"Don't read or look at a screen for more than a few minutes at a time." She goes over to the television stand and opens a drawer. She pulls out a bunch of cases, flips each open and checks inside. "You've got a good stock of books on tape here. Well, CD actually." She reaches into the back of the drawer and finds a Walkman. I laugh.

"Wow. I haven't seen one of those in a while."

"Count on remote Alaska for all your old-school technology needs! This should entertain you while you're recuperating. Maybe some books on tape, a little music, and sitting outside and enjoying these beautiful surroundings will be just what the doctor ordered."

I won't touch those books on tape, but I won't tell Anna that.

"What does the doctor think about some light hiking with a guard dog?" I'd rather be moving around in pain than sitting in pain.

"The key word there is *light*. Walk, but don't push yourself. I'll come back in a few days to check on you."

My heart wants to smile but the corners of my mouth want to let gravity take hold and drag them to the floor with the rest of my body. Anna is clearly worried about me. She leans forward and places a kiss on my forehead.

"I hate leaving you alone up here."

"I know, but Mr. Drew is going to be looking for anything out of the ordinary. He could be watching your place as we speak. We have to act as normal as possible."

"I know. At least he shouldn't have reason to be watching Dolly. If there's anything you'd like, you just let me know and I'll coordinate with her to get it to you, okay? Food, entertainment, whatever."

"I will. And Anna," I touch her arm, "can I ask you to do something weird for me?"

"Absolutely anything."

I blink a few times. "Can you tell the guard I said I'm sorry?"

It sounds like a crazy request to me. I hold my breath for Anna's reaction. She smiles.

"That is not weird. People speak with the dead all the time. I'll pass the message along for you."

She leans over and, so delicately that it feels like a moth's wings fluttering against my skin, she kisses the side of my mouth.

CHAPTER FOURTEEN

As soon as I'm alone, the guard haunts me. I rest on the couch, afraid to navigate the ladder to the loft. I leave the lights on even though my head is pounding. When I close my eyes, hoping for a peaceful night's rest and recovery, he's there. When I get up after only a few hours to make some instant oatmeal, I feel eyes on me, spin around, and nearly fall. I swear he even watches me in the bathroom. My hand shakes when I make a cup of tea. I tell myself it's just a side effect of the pain—my whole body aches from that fight—but I know what this is. I've been haunted by dead men before. The next time I get out of my makeshift bed to make a cup of tea, I toast him with it.

Thankfully, I don't have to spend too much time alone with my ethereal companion. It's not even nine a.m. when a series of heavy, rapid-fire knocks bombard the cabin door. I draw my gun before opening the door.

Dolly looks so pissed I consider shutting the door again. But there's also a youth standing beside her hanging his head. Dolly's anger isn't directed at me.

"We're coming in," Dolly announces.

The kid follows her in, head still down. Tails immediately conducts a thorough investigation of all his smells.

"Louisa, this is my grandchild Ryne. Ryne, this is Louisa."

I extend my hand. "Nice to meet you."

The kid looks up and flips a curtain of chestnut-brown hair away from his eyes. He's wearing eyeliner and a hint of gold eyeshadow just at the outer corners of his large, thickly lashed lids. His complexion is much like Dolly's, as is the slightly square face shape. Based on the sheepish facial expression, I feel bad for this kid, and I don't even know what's happened yet. As soon as our handshake is finished, Ryne drops to a crouch to hug Tails, who happily accepts—a fact that I note. Tails is a great judge of character.

"We won't stay long. We just can't be in Nanwalek, and I didn't know where else to go."

I wave toward the table, but Ryne's face is buried in the dog's fur. Dolly goes to the coffee maker instead of sitting.

"Want to tell me what's going on?" I look at Ryne. Ryne's face sinks even further into Tails. Dolly raises her voice and also looks at Ryne.

"I found out what your pilot was doing in Nanwalek. He was there trying to recruit young foo—" She's fuming, and she stops herself, takes a breath. When she starts again, she seems a little calmer.

"He was trying to recruit naïve young people to participate in the little endeavor you're investigating, and my grandchild here was silly enough to get pulled in."

Maybe it's just the concussion, but it takes me some time to process this. I speak carefully, unsure of how much Dolly told Ryne about what he's gotten himself into.

"The pilot was trying to get Ryne to…join the team?"

"Apparently. Ryne can give you more information since they had what I understand was *quite* the in-depth conversation with the pilot." Her nostrils flare as she speaks, and I wonder how hard she's having to work to contain the fact that she's livid. I suspect it's not so much at Ryne as it is at the pilot she feels is threatening her family—and at Mr. Drew.

"Ryne, would you mind telling me about it?"

"Ryne *will* tell you because they have no choice in the matter."

I just nod and make Ryne a cup of tea. My Child Services brain notes the pronoun Dolly has used twice now to refer to her grandchild. Ryne turns away from Dolly but accepts the sugar container.

Ryne's voice is soft and low. "Where do you want me to start?"

"Tell me about the pilot first. Is this someone you've seen before? How did you meet?"

The curtain of dark hair shakes back and forth. "We'd never met, but I knew about him. Or I guess if I'm more accurate, I knew about pilots *like* him." They speak slowly, as if carefully selecting and polishing each word before uttering it.

"What do you mean?"

"Some of my friends who go out on the boats told me that they had encountered pilots who all look similar while they were out in different parts of the community. They said it seemed as if the men were waiting for them. As if they knew them. One of my friends felt like they were destined to meet these men somehow." I nod, though I'm not sure if Ryne can see it through the hair. "They told me they'd had conversations with the pilots, and the pilots told them how they can make a lot of money and have these really good educational opportunities that they wouldn't get anywhere else. Some of my friends just ignored them because they think it's a scam, but a couple of them listened and agreed to meet up the next time the plane showed."

"And did they?"

"Yes. They said it was a different pilot the next time, but that he told them the same things—how they can make money and support their families, but how they'd have to prove they were trustworthy, and how that could take a long time. They'd have to keep meeting up and doing small things for the pilots to show they were serious." I blow out a puff of air. *Shit.* Ryne rushes to continue. "But it never happened. It never got to that point. This pilot had just given us envelopes to deliver. And then—"

"Then I found out what the hell was going on and I took that envelope and told the council about it. They tracked down these other children and confiscated the envelopes before they could do anything with them."

"Did you open them, Dolly?"

"Better believe it. Just some fake money, but real addresses. My guess is the boys and Ryne would have delivered them and the recipients would have reported back to Mr. Drew or the pilots to let them know who had come through and kept quiet. If they'd messed it up, nothing lost."

I shake my head. Some nerve. I'll be sure to make some house calls once Mr. Drew is safely tucked away in a cell.

"And you planned to deliver your envelope, Ryne?"

I'm sure if Ryne could will themself to melt through the floorboards, they would.

"Yes. But I didn't know. I just wanted to see what would happen. Whether it was a scam or not."

"Like I didn't teach you better than that." Dolly narrows her eyes at her grandchild. "You're a smart child, Ryne. How could you be so…" She inhales deeply, then exhales and takes a sip of coffee. "Tell Louisa what you told me about how the pilot already knew things about you."

"Oh. Yeah, the second pilot, not the one from a few nights ago, but the one before that…he talked to me and one of my friends alone when he saw us together. He knew my friend plays soccer at school. He knew I got to go to Anchorage for the chemistry competition last year and that I won a silver medal."

"So, he's been gathering information about you. From where, do you think?"

"I thought about that a lot. I don't know."

I lean back in my chair, thinking out loud. "He knew your friend was on the soccer team. He knew about your chemistry competition. Did he know your grades or who you hang out with, other than the friend he saw you with?"

"I don't think so."

"Ryne, was the chemistry competition in the newspaper? Or did someone publish something about your silver medal online?"

Dolly answers. "There *was* an article in the paper. I cut it out and put it on the fridge." The lines around her mouth soften a little as some of the tension leaves her face.

"And I'm guessing the school publishes the soccer team roster online. So, my bet is the pilot was gathering information from afar. He could easily find demographic information about Nanwalek online, and probably stories about town concerns."

Dolly speaks again. "He also knew about our financial situation."

"Sure, but he could just be making assumptions. It's easy to find income information for the village, so he probably just guessed that Ryne might be looking for work, and then they accidentally confirmed it by getting excited about making money."

Dolly looks heartbroken. Enough so that I put a hand on her shoulder. Suddenly, Ryne starts to cry.

"I'm sorry. I didn't…It's not because I think we don't have enough. You work really hard, and you've been raising me all these years, and I always have everything I need. I just talked to him because I wanted to be able to contribute."

"All these years I've worked and gotten promotions, and now I make a good living." She shakes her head, lower lip trembling. "I've always done my best. We aren't poor. The Park Service is fair to me, and I pass everything I make along to the children."

Ryne has their face in their hands now. "I know. I'm sorry. I didn't mean it that way."

I feel for both of them. I can see why Ryne would want to help a grandmother who works so hard to support them. But I also see why

Dolly is offended, though I don't think Ryne meant to make her feel inadequate. Tails nudges his face into Ryne's side. Dolly and I watch them pet the dog for a few minutes in silence. When Ryne is more composed, and when Dolly has cleared her throat a few times, I speak.

"Dolly, maybe Ryne should stay until things calm down a little. You know I have the means to protect them if need be."

Having a teenager hanging around might not be the most convenient thing while I try to investigate Mr. Drew, but then again, I can't exactly do much until I've recovered, and having someone around who knows the local landscape might come in handy. Besides, Ryne has spoken to a pilot as a potential recruit—that's a perspective I will never have.

Dolly's facial expression is a mix of concern and relief. I wonder if she was hoping I'd volunteer to watch Ryne.

"What about Ryne's friends that these men talked to? Are they safe, Dolly?"

"Their families know to keep them under lock and key. I didn't tell them much, but I told them enough."

"Okay. I'll need to let Chief Harper know." I'll need to inform the FBI of the new household addition too, but I don't want to mention that affiliation in front of Ryne. It's hard to say what will make them uncomfortable. "I'm also going to ask him to pull a list of all the young men that have gone missing from your community and the ones around you, even if the police concluded that they left of their own free will."

Dolly does not look comforted by my plan. "It will be incomplete."

I cock my head to the side in silent question.

"After Jeannie, it was clear that the Seward police weren't going to take our missing young people seriously. We stopped calling them in every time someone disappeared. Tribal Council has its own investigations and its own list."

That will make investigating these missing people more complicated, but given what Dolly has told me about her experience, I can't say I'm surprised.

"Do you think the council would be willing to share the information they have?"

She looks at Ryne in silence for a long while. "With me, yes." I don't press her further. Dolly's voice is softer now as she turns to Ryne. "Go get your bag."

I hide my smile. If Ryne is coming with luggage, having him stay here was Dolly's hope all along. In the brief time that they are gone,

Dolly gives me a stern warning about not letting anyone I don't know and trust close to them. I sober even more as she speaks. I can see the panic in her face because I've seen it on the faces of hundreds of parents before. She's terrified of losing another child.

Ryne returns with a small bag, and Dolly hugs them before she leaves. As soon as Dolly is out the door, Ryne puts their head on the table and exhales heavily.

It's such a teenage expression of exasperation that I smile outright.

CHAPTER FIFTEEN

D ammit, you win again." I throw my cards back onto the pile and
Ryne grins, revealing a row of slightly overlapping upper teeth. I
hop up to stir the pot of chili simmering on the stove.

"The more you play, the better you'll get."

"Yeah, well, I won't be heading to Vegas anytime soon, I guess."

"I'm pretty sure they don't play cribbage in Vegas."

"Oh good. Maybe I still stand a chance."

"Probably wouldn't quit my day job."

I give Ryne a playful glare. Our first day was a little awkward.
I love kids, but taking care of Dolly's grandchild seemed a little
intimidating. When I worked with Child Services, I visited the kids in
their homes, and then I went back to my home. I never lived with any
of those kiddos. Turns out, there was no need to worry. Ryne and I get
along great.

In just a few days, we've established a routine of quiet mornings,
lunchtime hikes in the park with Tails, and an evening game while
we cook dinner. Ryne makes a great sous chef, which I appreciate.
Chopping vegetables tries my patience. But there's something I've been
meaning to ask them, and I broach the subject now since all potentially
difficult topics go down better with food. I hand them their bowl of
steaming chili.

"Do you mind if I ask you a question?"

Ryne looks a bit like a deer in the headlights for a moment. "Is it
about my gender?"

I blink and prepare to pivot the conversation. "Well, no, but we
can definitely talk about that if you like."

"Oh no! That's okay. Just most people want to know about that
after they get to know me."

"Ah. I see." I throw a whopping helping of cheddar cheese onto my bowl of chili. The whole cabin smells like onion and peppers.

"So, what did you want to ask?"

"Well, I was able to track the other towns that pilot has been visiting, and I'm just trying to figure out why *these* towns. I've never been to them, though, so I'm probably missing something. You talked to that pilot. I'm wondering if you might see something I don't."

"Maybe. Where else did he visit?"

I grab the map Dolly, Anna, and I were using and lay it out between our bowls. I point out the villages the plane was tracked in.

"Well, they're all really remote. They're all small too." Ryne places their finger on Homer. I wait patiently for them to speak. "Did they stop in Homer?"

"No. About ten miles outside of it."

"That's interesting. It's the biggest town near here. Why would they stop outside it like that?"

"Homer has a police department, right?"

Ryne nods slowly. "The pilot was afraid of getting caught?"

I nod. "That's my bet."

Ryne looks contemplative, eyes staying on the map even as they spoon chili and chew. "Most of these villages can only be accessed by plane or boat. They're really cut off, you know?"

I nod again. I'm impressed by how thoughtful Ryne is.

"If I'm understanding the conversations you told me about with the pilot, it sounds like he'd done maybe a little cursory research on the communities he was visiting, then he came in and sought out young people he thought might be interested in making some fast money. He sold the idea as a way to help the community."

"That sounds right. I don't think he talked to anyone younger than maybe fifteen or sixteen."

I take a few bites of my chili. It could be spicier, but most people don't like things as spicy as I do. Ryne is scarfing it down, so it must not be too bad. Then again, in my experience, teens will decimate any food. I swallow and voice a few of the going theories.

"Dolly thought he was targeting people who were particularly vulnerable. If this guy is under the assumption that all the tribes are struggling, that could explain why he's targeting villages with a lot of tribal members. And the fact that these places are so far removed, so it would be hard for people to compare notes about these random men flying into their towns." I eat my last spoonful, then lean back. I can totally go for seconds, but I want to make sure Ryne is full before I go for it—growing teen and all. "How do you think the pilot identified you and your friends? Was he talking to all the young adults in the village?"

"No. No, I think he'd picked us out specifically. He didn't talk to the kids who have relatives on Tribal Council. And he didn't talk to my teacher's daughter or the principal's son."

"Interesting. So, avoiding kids he thinks are well-connected."

"Maybe. When he was talking to me, he knew about my mom, and that she's gone. He didn't know anything about Grams, like he didn't know I lived with her. I bet if he'd realized, he wouldn't have approached." This confirms another idea I've been considering.

"I wonder if he's pinpointing kids who he thinks might not have a lot of family or support, and he thought you fell into that category."

"He's wrong, of course. Grams is like a mom. She's way more involved than any of my friends' parents, even. I used to go stay with my dad when she had to be here in the park over the summer, and she'd call me twice every single day."

"You don't go stay with your dad anymore?"

"No. I turn eighteen this fall, so Grams said I could make the choice myself this year. I chose to stay in Nanwalek and take care of the house for her. My dad's fine, I guess, but I don't know him well, and he thinks something's wrong with me because I don't feel like just a boy."

"Ah. That's not easy."

"No. His tribe recognizes two-spirits like me—all the tribes do now. Everyone adopted that term right after I was born, but two-spirits have always been around. His tribe even has an elder who's like me. I think it's because I'm my dad's kid that it's not okay. Like I have to be macho like him or something." They jump up and ladle more chili into their bowl.

"I left enough for you to have seconds too," they say as they sit.

That's my cue. I clean out the rest of the pot.

"I wonder why that guy would think I was vulnerable just because my mom isn't around. He must not know the tribal villages at all."

"You don't feel like an outsider there?" I correct myself immediately. "Not that you should. I just wondered because a lot of queer kids do. Hell, a lot of kids your age do, period."

"No way. Some of my friends didn't understand when I told them I thought I was kind of male *and* female, and some of them stopped talking to me for a while, but once we got a little older and they still saw me in school all the time and saw that I was like, the same person, then they were cool again."

I smile. My experience of being queer was so different. I'm glad that Ryne's has been positive.

"I'm kind of embarrassed that I don't know more about two-spirit people, or nonbinary people. I'm a lesbian, but that's the only queer identity I know a lot about."

Ryne shrugs. "I get that. I don't know a lot about what it's like being a lesbian either."

I laugh. "So, being two-spirit means you're male and female?"

"For me, it means I feel like I'm male and female. Some days I'm a little more feminine, like the day I came here. Other days, I have more male energy. But I've been talking to people online, and some two-spirited people don't have a gender. I think it's different from person to person."

"That makes sense. And thanks for telling me about yourself."

"So did you know you were a lesbian when you were my age?"

"I was still kind of figuring that out. I think you're probably a little ahead of where I was maturity-wise."

"It was helpful to have Grams around. She doesn't really like to talk about sex *or* gender, but she always told me, even as a little kid, that she'd love me no matter what. And she always listened and encouraged self-love when *I* wanted to talk. I think she always knew. She let me learn about myself and didn't shame me."

I hear their strength even while the words are softly spoken. I think about my own mother and try not to feel irrationally jealous of Ryne and every other queer kid with a supportive parent—or grandparent, in their case.

They grab the dishes off the table. "So, what's next?" I can barely hear them over the sink, Ryne speaks so quietly.

"I'm kind of in a holding pattern right now because of this stupid concussion, but at least we know the pilots are still active, and thanks to you, we've got some idea of what they're doing."

"Trying to recruit young people."

"Yup. Smart young people. The question is, what for?"

"Yeah, going to all that work to get people to deliver envelopes of fake money or whatever seems kind of not worth the time."

"You're right. It has to be for something bigger." I need more info. I'm restless, and I wish I could get back out there.

I *have* been feeling better...

Tomorrow maybe I can make a little excursion.

CHAPTER SIXTEEN

I give Anna a call the next morning to see if she's heard anything about Mr. Drew. According to Anna, he hasn't made an appearance around town. She hasn't heard anyone say anything about the missing guard. It's like no one in Seward even knew he existed. No one has called the hospital asking about a body, so the guard is, in Anna's words, "still chilling" in the drawer. The plane is active, but it hasn't been back to either airstrip. It's been moving around the west coast of the Kenai Peninsula, still circulating amongst those small villages. I'm worried that Mr. Drew knows the plane is compromised and isn't using it anymore. Hell, he could have sold the thing and someone else could be flying it and I wouldn't necessarily know. I only know where it is.

Ryne asks if I'm okay over coffee. Apparently, I was screaming in my sleep. I know why, too. I was dreaming about the guard again. I just shrug it off. Ryne certainly doesn't need to know about that. Still, they can tell how restless I am.

"If you want to go out, it's totally okay. I can check out one of these books on CD." I'm guessing they could probably use a little alone time too. It's been almost a week of cabin fever. Maybe I could just pop over to the airstrip, then swing by and check out Mr. Drew's. It wouldn't take more than a couple hours. Besides, Tails is probably going stir crazy.

I look at Tails lounging on the rug.

Okay, maybe I'm just projecting my restlessness onto him. Tails looks pretty relaxed. Still, I need to get out of the cabin. Ryne's presence is a welcome distraction, but as I go to sleep—rest—at night, all I can think about is that guard.

I've imagined so many lives for him in my head. He had a past. Maybe he had a family. He had parents and maybe siblings and possibly children. A partner, maybe. He had people, and I've taken him away from them. They don't even know it. Maybe if I can go back to the airstrip, back behind that dumpster where he used to smoke, maybe I can find some clues as to who he was—other than Mr. Drew's guard.

"Are you sure you won't mind if I go out just for a couple hours? Do you feel like you'll be safe here?"

Ryne laughs. "It'll be fine, Louisa. Remember, I've been home by myself for the whole summer while Grams is at Exit. I don't mind my own company."

I wish I was the kind of person who could just relax happily on their own, but it's always been a struggle for me. Still, I respect that Ryne operates differently than I do.

"I'll leave Tails with you. He'll bark if he hears anyone." I wonder if I should leave Ryne a weapon, but I need my gun with me.

"If anyone shows up, Tails is trained as a police dog. If someone tries to grab you, Tails will stop them." I have Ryne give Tails some basic commands—sit, lay, shake—to make sure Tails will listen to them. The first couple times Tails looks at me for confirmation, then he quickly catches on to the fact that Ryne can give him commands too. Once that's established, I tell Ryne how they would give the command for Tails to attack, and I tell them what to expect if that happens.

"Tails has attacked someone?"

"Yeah. Mostly just trainers who were wearing serious padding, but once in a real situation. It was…upsetting to see. But Tails will absolutely defend his person, so you're safe with him. Just be aware that it can be scary when he's defending."

"Well, I don't think we have anything to worry about."

"I'll be back by lunchtime, okay?"

"I'll fix us something to eat for when you get back."

"That would be amazing."

With a wave, I'm off. I feel that same worry I always felt in social work leaving the home of a child whose safety wasn't one hundred percent guaranteed. Then I remind myself that Ryne is nearly an adult. I understand why Dolly brought them here, but they'd probably be perfectly fine back at home too.

There's nothing much to see around Mr. Drew's. Both airstrips are empty. I don't risk going out into the open. Whatever alerted that guard to my presence, I don't want it alerting the other guard, who I confirm is standing outside Mr. Drew's house. His gun is prominently displayed in its holster. He's actively surveying the grounds. The curtains are drawn.

Mr. Drew is surely holed up in there. I return to the cabin disappointed and a little pissed at myself. I'm not sure what to do next. I'm at a dead end. I know where the plane has been going and why, so there's nothing else to learn about that. Mr. Drew isn't showing himself, and there's nothing new to learn from his more disciplined guard. What else can I learn from watching the house? But if I'm not watching the house, then what am I even doing?

When I open the door to the cabin, the fragrance of toasted bread assails me. I temporarily forget the exasperating block wall in my stalled investigation.

"Smells amazing!" I call, glancing around. The bathroom door is shut. There's a plate on the counter covered in plastic wrap. I lift the corner and find a stack of grilled cheese sandwiches. There's a covered pot of tomato soup on the stove. It's gone cold. I set the table, waiting for Ryne. I turn the stove back on. Tails starts pushing his nose into my hand. His butt wiggles and his forehead is wrinkled.

"What, bud?" He runs to the door. "You need to go out?" He wiggles again, and I open the door. He sprints toward the road, goes down it a little bit, then turns around and barks at me. Something's not right. I run back into the cabin.

"Ryne?" I knock on the bathroom door. I suddenly realize how quiet it is. "Ryne?" I open the unlocked door. Ryne isn't there. I climb the ladder to the loft. Empty. Back outside, I call Ryne's name over and over. They're gone. I look for any clues to a struggle. There's nothing. Everything is orderly. They finished making lunch and cleaned up. Their bag is gone. Back outside, the bike is gone too. Ryne left. It's only after a few minutes of sheer panic that I realize there's a note on top of the maps I've been studying.

Louisa, I'm so sorry. I know you're going to be worried. I promise I'm totally okay. I can take care of myself. Just trust me. I think I can get to the bottom of this.

Ryne signed the note in a neat cursive.
Fuck.

CHAPTER SEVENTEEN

Tails licks my face. I'm on the floor, my head resting between my knees. My heart pounds and sweat dampens my hairline, settling in my eyebrows. My breathing is hard and fast, like a dog who's run too far on a hot day. The room spins, swirling in my peripheral vision, the walls come in toward me. I squeeze my eyes shut. Images of Ryne appear, and always of Ryne in the worst possible scenario—dead. In some of them, he replaces the dead guard, lying there on the airstrip covered in blood.

Normally I'd force myself to picture somewhere serene—a wildflower meadow surrounded by mountain peaks. I can't get there now. My mind just won't go. My body is trembling, wanting to act, to go solve the problem, to jump up and run out of here, but my mind is paralyzed by this endless loop of images and fears. My skin tingles and my chest hurts. I wonder if I'm having a heart attack and have to remind myself that it's a panic attack. Naming it helps a little. Tails tries to lick the sliver of face that's not hidden by my legs. I raise my face and his wet tongue starts lapping the sweat around my ears.

"Gross." My voice is breathy. I slowly lift my arm and place it on his head. "You've made your point. Stop." He sits at my side, awaiting further instructions. I remember to check the heartrate tracker at my wrist. *130. 128. 127...* Heading in the right direction at least. I sit up straighter and take a deep breath in. Tails watches me closely. I hold the breath in for a four-count, then exhale until all the air has been pushed out of my diaphragm. *122. 120.* Ways to go still, but at least I'm getting there. I try to formulate next steps. Good, but I'm not ready yet. My therapist is in my head, reminding me that if I'm still in the panic attack when I try to formulate solutions, the solutions won't be rational, and I can easily fall back into the panic. I shake my head, picture my wildflower meadow, and focus on eye contact with Tails. It is ages before the heartrate monitor reads ninety. Still higher than my resting, but at least in a normal, healthy range. I slowly stand, and exhaustion hits me as I do. There's no time to rest, though.

I blink a few times. The room looks so innocuous, as if nothing just happened here. In a way, I guess it didn't. Ryne just left of their own accord.

"Okay, Louisa." I speak out loud. Tails listens. "Ryne is a smart kid. They're not going to do anything stupid." I find their letter on the floor, apparently crumpled by my fist. The letter offers no clues as to where they've gone, but *I know I can get to the bottom of this* has to be about Mr. Drew and that pilot.

Trust me, the letter reads. I do trust Ryne, though right now I'm not sure if I should. What are they doing? Why are they doing it? How do they think they can help? They don't know the whole situation— or what Mr. Drew does to people he deems untrustworthy. Maybe I should have told them about the guard. One thing is for certain—Dolly is going to kill me.

I think I'd rather face Mr. Drew.

Maybe Mr. Drew knows where Ryne is. Maybe he's got them trapped in that huge house right now. He controls these pilots, so if Ryne has gone to meet one of them, Mr. Drew will know. I can confront him. It will be risky without backup, but far less scary than telling Dolly I've lost her grandchild. Maybe Mikey can back me up. I grab the satellite phone and start dialing, but something feels off.

"Stop, Louisa. Think this through." My first reaction is to jump immediately to solving the problem, but one thing I've learned in my police work is that sometimes what might seem like the most *direct* route is absolutely not the *best* route. In trying to be too abrupt, sometimes I can make the situation worse and close people off to me entirely. Not that Mr. Drew has ever been an open book…

I breathe in and out slowly as I run through the possibilities of how a conversation with Mr. Drew could go. It's one of the perks of being an anxiety person and a massive overthinker—my mind naturally wants to rehearse conversations before they happen, and often that can alert me to possible minefields before I enter them. Mr. Drew won't try anything violent with me because he knows I'm connected to the Seward police force, and they're not in his pocket anymore. He would naturally deny knowing Ryne or having seen them. I can confront him with my knowledge of the pilots, but that will just close him off even more, and then I will never learn anything. The avenue of confronting Mr. Drew closes off before my eyes.

Damn. Until Ryne is guaranteed safe, I can't approach him. I slump into one of the dining chairs. I know what Mr. Drew does to people he thinks have betrayed him, and I cannot risk that happening to Ryne. I need to think of another route.

"Okay. The priority is Ryne's safety. Finding Ryne is the priority."

I look around the house. They must have left a clue somewhere. I reread the note. Then I search the cabin like I would a crime scene. I look for anything they left behind. Anything that's out of place. Then I look for anything that's missing. It's a tiny place, so this doesn't take long. Ryne hasn't taken the first aid kit. They haven't taken any sort of weapon—all the kitchen knives are accounted for. I sort through the maps and information I keep in the center of the kitchen table. The topographical map of the state park is there. Dolly's safety information is there. But something *is* missing.

It's the map where Mikey marked Mr. Drew's house and the airstrips.

I grab Ryne's pillowcase and hold it to Tails's nose. After he's gotten a good whiff, I shove the pillowcase in my bag. Ideally, we'd do this on foot, but we don't have time. Tails walks several yards down the driveway, tracking the scent. Then I call him into the ATV.

There's only one way Ryne could have gone from here on bike. They would have crossed the bridge at Exit Glacier. After that, they would have taken one route toward the secret airstrip and another toward Mr. Drew's house and the known airstrip. Mr. Drew's would be the far easier route—they could just follow the road toward Kolit's, then turn off onto the long gravel driveway that leads to his house and arrive right at the gate. The route to the secret airstrip would be harder—Ryne would need to stop periodically to check the map, and depending on their navigational skills, they could easily get lost because there's no clear path, except the occasional tracks in the mud and squashed-down foliage left by the ATV. There are ATV tracks all over this area left by loads of people, but if they can manage to find my marks, that will bring them within a fifteen-minute walk of the airstrip. I curse myself thoroughly, even as I remind myself that I couldn't have known.

At the parking lot to the Visitor Center, I stop. It's possible that Dolly is in there, but I don't want to barge in and make a scene. I need to tell her, though. As soon as I cross the bridge, I'll lose signal again indefinitely.

CHAPTER EIGHTEEN

Dolly is pissed. It barely matters that I didn't have the nerve to face her in person—I can almost see her glare coming through the phone. I'm not sure if anyone has ever been so pissed at me in my life. She's also stuck at work for three more hours, and she'll have to pretend everything is fine because she's working with a busload of summer camp kids today. I could not feel worse. I try to focus on what I'm doing instead of how Dolly feels about me right now.

Just over the bridge, I stop the ATV and let Tails hop out. I give him the pillowcase and he finds Ryne's scent again. We walk for a couple minutes, him following his new friend. Then we hop back in and continue following. At the point where Ryne would have to choose between the easy route to Mr. Drew's and the harder route to the airstrip, we stop again. Tails keeps his nose nearly touching the ground as he follows the scent into the woods. I let him go for a while just to be sure. Ryne is headed for the secret airstrip. Back in the ATV, we follow our old tracks as long as we can before the trees become too dense, then I throw it in park, and we proceed on foot. I follow Tails's lead even though I know where he's going. Ryne didn't take the most direct route—they apparently started and then doubled back several times if Tails is correct, and the track is so fresh that he probably is.

I pick up the marks of mountain bike tires in the mud a few times. There are shoe prints here and there, where Ryne stopped the bike and put a foot down, likely trying to figure out the best route. Finally, I spot the airstrip in the distance—we're at the opposite end than the one I usually approach by. I don't see tire marks on the flat expanse of the makeshift runway, and the bike would have pressed down the grass if Ryne had taken it out there. Maybe the bike is still here somewhere. I present Tails with the pillowcase again so he knows he's still searching.

It only takes him a few minutes to locate the bike, neatly propped up against a tree. Ryne has made no effort to obscure it. Did they know I'd track them here and want me to find it, or did they just leave it so they could easily retrieve it later? I take a picture of the bike as it is, then stand there examining its placement. I walk around the tree on which it's propped, careful not to expose myself. From the airstrip, the bike wouldn't be obvious, yet from the side of my approach, it was fairly easy to spot. Did Ryne place it like that so Mr. Drew's crew wouldn't see it, but I would? It's possible, but it's also easy to assume intention where there is none. I stare at the ground, following Ryne's footsteps.

Yet another young person's footprints disappearing onto this same airstrip. And, like Branden before them, it seems obvious Ryne has willingly taken off in an aircraft, and I can't follow.

I consider taking the bike with me, but in the end I don't. I leave it just in case Ryne didn't take off in a plane and will need it again soon.

Oh please, please just let Ryne be here doing their own investigation. Let them not have gotten on a plane. Let them be safe and just snooping around somewhere in the woods.

I consider calling out to them, but it's too risky to expose both of us if they're out here too. I head back to the ATV with Tails, then pull out the satellite phone.

First, I ring the FBI. The plane was back here just an hour ago. It departed again about twenty minutes after it landed. I ask Mensel to call me back as soon as it lands. I take a few breaths before I call Dolly. She says barely two words to me. I suspect she'll be waiting for me at the cabin, but I have no intention of going back there. Tails and I continue to canvass the area for other signs of Ryne. I only realize how much time I've spent walking in circles when my stomach begins to growl. I'm exhausted, and it's been a long time since I've eaten. The grilled cheese sandwiches Ryne made went untouched. There's no way I'm heading back while Ryne is still out here, though. What's taking Mensel so long?

The phone rings.

"Louisa. The plane just landed."

"Where?"

"I'm really hoping this is going to mean something to you. It's in Portlock."

I stop in my tracks, trying to figure out whether that name should mean anything to me. I'm coming up with nothing. "I don't know where that is."

"It's down at the tip of the peninsula. I'll pull everything I've got. In the meantime, can you get down there and check it out?"

"Yes, sir."

"Good. Get down there as soon as you can. Let me know what you find and if you need assistance."

"Thank you, sir."

I load Tails back into the ATV and we head back to the cabin.

CHAPTER NINETEEN

Dolly is at the cabin when I get there, and now I'm glad. When I tell her the plane is in Portlock, she stands up straight.

"Any idea what it could be doing down there?"

She shakes her head. "It's a ghost town."

"What?"

"It's been abandoned for decades. It was a canning town, but most people cleared out in the 40s, I think. There's nothing down there but some abandoned buildings. But I can tell you this…" Her face is full of concern. "Bad things happen in Portlock."

"Now? Or you mean before it was abandoned?"

"Both."

"What bad things happen now? It's totally empty, right?"

"Yes, but sometimes people hike there to see the ghost town. Bad things happen to them."

"Like what?"

"Death."

I blink at her. "Would you mind expanding?"

"Violent deaths. People torn limb from limb."

It's like pulling teeth. She's shut herself off, and I don't know if it's because she's upset about Ryne or because she's mad at me for letting them go. Probably both.

"Is there someone murdering them? Are these animal attacks? The more you can tell me, Dolly, the more I can help."

"I thought you were going to help before, but you've lost my grandchild. You were supposed to be keeping them safe. Now they're in danger because of you."

I sigh. "I know, and I'm sorry. But we are wasting time. We could be looking for them. They weren't anywhere near the airstrip, and Tails and I did a thorough search. We have to assume they got on that plane."

Dolly nods just once. "Then let's go." She starts toward the door, and Tails and I follow to her vehicle.

The Park Service plane is not far from Exit Glacier. Dolly tells me to wait in the car while she goes in to tell another ranger she's taking it. While she's inside, I call Mikey and inform him of where Dolly and I are going. He seems just as confused as I am as to why the plane is in Portlock. As far as he knows, there's nothing there except some abandoned buildings. He's never been there himself and says aside from a couple random search and rescue activities in the area, Portlock has seen pretty much no police action from the Seward force in years. He promises to call Homer, which is much closer and more likely to respond to any calls coming from that area. He echoes the FBI's offer of backup and resources if we need it.

Dolly's back, and we load into the plane. Getting Tails in there is a bit of a hassle, but he'll be useful for tracking Ryne once we arrive. Dolly fiddles with the GPS mounted between us. She cusses at it. It doesn't recognize Portlock as a destination. She ends up consulting several maps, then entering coordinates. Before long, we're airborne.

"You're lucky it's a safe day for flying."

I stare out the window as the trees grow smaller below us. Fine day for flying though it may be, the wind buffets the side of the plane, causing us to list temporarily to one side. Dolly corrects quickly.

"Dolly, I'm really sorry. I thought it would be okay to leave them for just a couple hours. I shouldn't have." She exhales heavily. "We'd been developing a good relationship. They seem so trustworthy."

"Even a trustworthy child is still a *child*. They can be manipulated by evil people. That's why we have to protect them."

"I know. I used to work in Social Services. I should have known." My mind goes back to the girl I lost in my last case as a social worker. We sit in silence for a while. "I should never have left."

Dolly is so focused on the instruments and the GPS, and for so long, that I think she's not going to say anything. "Ryne is of their own mind. If they wanted to go, they would have found a way."

I turn to her. "What do you think they meant by 'getting to the bottom of this'?"

"Ryne has always been a helpful child. When they see that I'm distressed, or that someone they care about is upset, their natural instinct is to try to solve the problem."

I grimace. That sounds all too familiar.

"But they are also seventeen years old. Teenagers are overconfident. They think they're indestructible."

"So, they're likely in over their head."

"Precisely."

We're flying over a seemingly endless plain of white with the occasional jagged black peak jutting up through its surface. Looking more closely, I see what looks like ripples in the ocean all across the expanse.

"Is this the ice field?"

Dolly nods. I whistle. It's impressive, but then Alaska never fails to impress. Having been here for nearly six years now, it's hard to imagine living anywhere else. I've gotten totally spoiled by having a stunning landscape right outside my window every day. It's easy to take Alaska's beauty for granted when you can go for a hike with breathtaking views pretty much any day. As long as you're well-prepared, that is.

"How big is it?"

"Eight hundred miles. Been here twenty-three thousand years. Hopefully be here plenty more...Scientists come out every fall and spring. Measuring accumulation and ablation. How much snow fell, how much is melting. Isn't looking good."

"What happens if it melts too fast?"

"Glaciers retreat, like Exit's doing. Whole landscape changes. Weather changes. Wildlife changes. Park changes. All of Alaska changes."

"Not in a good way."

She shrugs. "Not good for the wildlife, and that's not good for the people."

She fiddles with the GPS while I stare out the window and watch the ice field move past. It's hard to tell how close we are to its surface, and I keep looking at the surrounding peaks for reference. They rise on either side of our tiny plane. Despite the wind, we're flying smoothly. I'm guessing Dolly has flown over the ice field hundreds of times.

"And your ancestors used to travel over this?"

She nods. "All the time. If animals were moving across it, they were moving across it."

"It looks inhospitable."

"Wasn't to them. Still isn't to me. You just have to recognize its power and how it moves."

It's hard to imagine it moving at all, locked in place for tens of thousands of years as it has been. But ice is perpetually shifting, cracking, melting and refreezing. Overnight, crevasses can open and swallow climbers whole. Giant chunks can calve from glaciers or icebergs, plunging into the water and capsizing boats. Our lives depend on this ice, and it's disconcerting to think of it as impermanent.

We both fall back into silence, and after a while, the white below us narrows and gives way to jagged ridges of green.

"I have no idea where to land. Any ideas?"

"I don't know Portlock, so not really. If it's on the coast, though, I'd imagine there's a stretch of beach."

"No, I mean, do we want to be sure it's not seen?"

Good point. I don't even know what we're flying in to. I wish I'd had the patience to do a little research before this trip, but time is of the essence.

"We definitely want to be far from the other plane. I think, for the sake of caution, we want it as far from where we think whoever might be here with Ryne is." I give her the last location of the maroon and white plane, and she sends the NPS plane into a sweeping half-circle.

"We're not going to fly directly over Portlock. We'll cruise for a few minutes in case anyone on the ground sees us. We'll look like we're just joyriding." It's hard to think of anything that could be further from the truth. After she's sent us in a few meandering loops, she starts lowering the plane. The forest below us is densely packed, but if this was a thriving area once, there are old airstrips here, though they may be so overgrown as to be unrecognizable. Dolly tinkers with the radio until I hear a man's voice, crackling with static on the other end.

It must be another park ranger. Dolly asks if he knows a good, discreet place to park it near Portlock. She doesn't give him any details but gives just enough clues that he might guess she's not doing regular park work. He gives her a location and she thanks him.

"This is mostly national forest, so he'd know as well as anyone. We're going to trust his judgment."

I spot the bay in the distance, the trees marching almost clear up to the water, but we turn away from it as Dolly steers us through a narrow pass. I hold my breath—the trees and rocks seem near enough to scrape the windows. She sees something she likes under us and noses toward it. I close my eyes as the trees envelop us. When I open them, I swear I can touch the pinecones, but there is a pretty clear patch of land beneath us.

"Hang on, this is going to be tight."

That's an understatement. We're going fast and there's a rock wall at the other end of our landing strip. Dolly leans forward in her seat and adjusts our angle slightly. I grip the sides of my seat and lean back, wanting to close my eyes again but needing to see. It's almost like Dolly's landing a helicopter—it feels like we're coming straight down even though the forest speeding past says otherwise. That rock wall is coming in hot.

"Dolly—"

"I got this."

I grit my teeth. My mother might have said a prayer right now. Tails pokes his head between me and Dolly. "Tails, lay." He immediately curls up on the back seat, but when I turn, I can see that his head is still up and looking out the windshield.

"Brace."

I brace myself as best I can while also stretching my left arm to grip the back of Dolly's chair—a barrier in case Tails goes flying. I hope to hell my seat belt is in good working order.

The landing gear comes down and the wheels hit the ground. The brakes come on so fast that Tails bounces into my arm and lands on the floor behind me, where he thankfully stays. I take in the deepest breath I've possibly ever taken, hoping it won't be my last. We're still moving forward. Next to me, Dolly exudes calm confidence. Ahead of me, the rock wall approaches. I can see its full stratification, all the silver and copper and granite lines clear as day as the sunlight glints off them. Beautiful, but not what I want as my final view of the world. Dolly is pressing the brakes hard, and momentum is pulling me forward. I grip the seats, pressing my head into the rest.

"Come on!" Dolly shouts. The brakes suddenly catch, and the plane comes to an abrupt stop, sending our torsos lurching forward so hard my spirit temporarily leaves my body. There's complete silence, then we all seem to realize we're still alive.

Dolly landed mere feet from the rock wall.

"That'll be an interesting takeoff."

It's all she has to say about her genius piece of aviation work.

CHAPTER TWENTY

I clip a leash onto Tails's harness. He looks at me with slight indignation, but I have no idea where we are or who might be lurking. I prefer he be as close as possible by my side, and I want us to travel in complete silence. No voice commands.

Dolly leads the way, GPS in hand, using hand signals to indicate our movement through the trees. I reach down several times to carefully disentangle Devil's club from my hiking pants. Hard to believe this same vicious plant has been lessening the pain in my back for the past week or so. We hike through the forest for two miles, each of which takes most of an hour to cover as we fight through new growth and pick our way over stones covered in slick moss, around which frigid water rushes. At one point, we must cross a fallen tree to pass over a wide flow of unknown depth. I still feel the dizzying effects of the concussion as I concentrate on not falling. Tails crosses with ease just in front of me. On the other side, Dolly holds up a hand and we stop.

The town is there in front of us—or what used to be the town. There is one large building and several smaller ones between us and the bay water. The buildings sit in an area that was cleared at one time, but which is starting to become overgrown with vines and trees again. I'm glad—we're not as exposed as we would be if it was still nice and tidy. The only part of the landscape that's super exposed is a short expanse of beach and a pier. Along most of the shoreline, trees and boulders provide potential cover should it be needed. In the distance, mounds of rounded-top mountains await on the other side of the lagoon. There's no sound but chirping birds and the occasional rustle of a small animal in the brush.

We head toward the large building, keeping concealed as well as possible. I draw my weapon. To my surprise, Dolly pulls a handgun out of her waistband too. I have no doubt she's expertly trained to use it. Most rural Alaskans learn how to shoot a gun as soon as they're old enough to properly hold one. It's just basic safety here, given the wildlife.

We keep tight to the wall of the large building, sliding around the corner until we reach its front door. I go ahead of Dolly, listening for anything inside. After several minutes, I nod briskly. The door is unlocked, and I push it open without showing my body, listening again. Then I lead the way inside, my gun a hard barrier between me and anything that happens to be lurking.

There's light in the building. Part of the roof has collapsed in, and sunlight streams in, dust particles dancing in the green-gold beams. Leaves, pine needles, and twigs form a mound on the floor. Desks are lined up against the walls, and where the light shines on them, they look ready for a new class of pupils to come sit. I run my left hand over the surface of one, feeling where the name *Jack* has been carved into the surface.

This is exactly the kind of place that would draw people in.

Alaskans love adventure, and if there's one thing we love more than adventure, it's a mystery. Something in the landscape is conducive to imagining violent deaths, and many people here find that promise. This place should be crawling with ghost-hunters and game hunters alike, not to mention groups of teens on dares and random hikers. But there's no evidence of anyone at all now, at least not here in the biggest and most obvious building in the town. There's not even a beer can.

I look at Dolly and scowl. She's also frowning. She shakes her head quickly. Nothing here. No indication of Ryne. I lead the way back into the copious daylight. The next building we come to is a modest home right next to the school. There are pots outside like there was a container garden here at a point. When I enter the house in the same way I entered the school, I find furniture still in place. There's a plush sofa that's been eaten through in several places by wildlife, and a rug on the floor that, though covered in dust, looks to be in good shape. A large mirror hangs over the small fireplace. Something about it feels feminine.

This place, like the schoolhouse, seems oddly undisturbed. The roof is intact, though the windows are blocked off by shrubs, meaning little daylight is finding its way through the dirty panes. I crouch to examine the floor while Dolly stands by the door with her gun drawn. There's nothing out of place here, but I notice long streaks through the dust, as if someone hastily swept. It's hard to tell how long ago that would have been. The air isn't circulating despite one smashed-in window, but new dust also hasn't settled in the path.

Still, there are no signs of Ryne, or of anyone aside from the home's previous owner. Tails does a thorough investigation with his nose. The buildings all seem endlessly interesting for him, as his nose rarely leaves the floor, but he never alerts me to anything peculiar.

The next building shows the same broom marks, but in this one I can tell they're recent because the roof of this building is virtually gone, as are most of the windows. This building is closest to the harbor, and cool breezes reach us inside. Someone swept here recently. Who hikes or boats into a remote ghost town with a reputation for men meeting violent deaths and cleans up dilapidated houses?

I wave Dolly over to me. "Someone's cleaning up after themselves."

She frowns. "Why?"

I can't answer that, but I indicate the broom marks. She looks around and realizes the same thing I did. "No trash."

I nod. She shakes her head. Since neither of us voices a theory, I indicate that we should keep going. As we finish our search, I hear a distant plane, but by the time I get outside there's nothing to see. It's impossible to know whether it took off from our area or whether it's just one of the many low-altitude private flights moving around the peninsula passing by.

All of the buildings are empty, all clear of any hints of human occupation, and of Ryne in particular. We don't find a broom anywhere, or any bags of trash.

We retreat to the denser forest to plan our next move in a defensible position. Dolly pulls out a map of Portlock.

With our heads together and our voices low as possible, we decide to investigate along the water. The only logical ways to get here are by plane and boat, and often small craft land near harbors instead of trying to find space in the forest. As long as we steer clear of the area around the pier, we should be able to investigate the coastline without exposing ourselves too much.

CHAPTER TWENTY-ONE

We walk along the shoreline north of town, where a mist has gathered. The trees also start back up in that direction, so we won't need to be so exposed. It's a warm evening, and Tails wades into the cold water as we go, soaking his leash. I let him splash around a little as we walk along searching. We discover several new-looking fishing lures and hooks tangled in the trees near the water.

Suddenly the tug on the end of the leash stops.

"Tails?"

I squint at the sun on the water and see the ridge of his back. His head is beneath the surface. Suddenly his head pops up with water streaming off his fur, and he looks at me. I put my hand up so he won't bark. He refuses to budge even when I tug the leash, so I remove my footwear, roll my pants, and prepare to follow him out. Dolly's eyebrows are knit in confusion, but she just watches. I continue until the water is waist high, wondering how much I'm going to regret conducting the rest of this search in sopping-wet clothes. I remove my button-up camp shirt and throw it toward Dolly. I am now in just a tank top.

Tails is in the same spot, and he dips his head under again to show me what he found. I reach down and feel it immediately. Plastic. There's a black mass under the surface. I pull up a garbage bag, tied tight at the top. I half-drag, half-float it back to shore, where I tear it open. It's full of trash, including the wrapper for a peanut butter granola bar, which is likely what caught his canine attention. I sigh and glare at Tails. Not exactly what we're looking for.

I get my bag and extract Ryne's pillowcase, presenting it to Tails so he'll get back to business.

Dolly is at my side, speaking low. "Should we throw it back? If someone sees it, they'll know someone was here."

I nod and start to tie the bag back together. As I do, I note the trash more carefully. There are mostly soda cans, with the occasional beer thrown in. The contents all look pretty new though. There are some candy wrappers and a few sopping newspapers. The dates are sadly illegible. A magazine offers the clue I'm looking for. Its soaked spine still reads June 2009. This trash was dumped recently. I present the magazine to Dolly, who notes the date and nods. Back with the trash it goes, and then back into the water.

Tails still splashes along the edge of the water, but he doesn't seem to be tracking Ryne's scent. If he was tracking Ryne, his head would be down, and he'd be moving more deliberately. Instead, it looks like he's just having a nice time cooling off. He looks around, his eyes occasionally falling on me. At one point, we find ourselves in a secluded cove where the tree roots come right up to the rocks that line the water. The ground under my feet is marshy, and my boots sink into it enough that I indicate to Dolly it's time to turn around. We're far from town anyway. Tails is out in front of me, and I whistle low for him. The mud is halfway up his legs. He turns to look at me, then wags his nub. His single, sharp bark echoes before I can hold up my hand again for his silence.

"Tails, come," I growl. He wags his back end harder. I sigh deeply. If this is more trash, I swear…

I signal for Dolly to hang tight while I investigate. She's not into the muddiest bit yet, and there's no point in her joining me in potentially getting stuck. As I get closer to Tails, he starts digging in the mud, flinging slimy chunks of muck onto my still-damp shins. The mud stinks, so I keep my breaths short and shallow. It smells more foul the closer I am to Tails—a stench like decomposition—mushrooms, oakmoss, and something sour and not quite nameable.

To my horror, Tails sticks his muzzle straight into the mud.

When he pulls it back out, he's got a hand in his jaws. A human hand.

I turn my head to the side, away from the unexpected sight of my dog holding a severed human hand. As I regain my composure, I remind myself that maybe this discovery isn't all that unexpected. This isn't the first time the dog has presented me with the hand of a deceased person. Clearly, we need to talk about his matchmaking endeavors. I'm reluctant to leave the hand in the mud, where it can sink or shift.

"Louisa!" Dolly whispers as loudly as she dares. I wave her toward me. Dolly can handle this. She's seen animal attacks, which aren't pretty. Tails resumes his dig and alerts at several other spots in the muck. More body parts. The mud sucks at Dolly's boots with each step, trying to pull her down. When she is with me, I show her the hand. Her eyes grow huge, but she immediately draws the same conclusion I have.

"Not Ryne's."

"No, but also not good." I place the severed hand carefully at the base of a tree not far from where Tails found it. It should be easy to find again.

Dolly helps me and Tails sift through the mud, and soon we're all a uniform dark gray color and reeking. We do our best not to move anything while still trying to get an idea of what we're looking at. We're able to spot what looks like part of an arm and a likely torso. As we uncover new remains, I note their locations with coordinates.

Dolly stands up straight and wipes her hands on her pants. "I have to keep looking for Ryne." Her expression is stern.

"We will keep looking, I promise, but I have to get Anna and her team here as fast as possible. I need to notify the authorities for this area too."

Dolly is breathing hard. As worried as I am for Ryne, I can't imagine how she's feeling—especially having seen what we just saw. They're in extreme danger.

I put a muddy and disgusting hand on her muddy and disgusting forearm. "I promise. Just let me call and we'll get right back to it. I'll give her the coordinates so she can find it even if we're busy."

Dolly nods.

I keep the conversation with Anna as brief as possible, but I do tell her what she's in for. She will need her team's help this time. She promises me she's on it, and that it's nothing she hasn't seen before. I'm not so sure about that. I also let her know what led Dolly and me to Portlock. I ask her to wait for Mikey. I don't want her out here without official protection, and Dolly and I need to keep searching for Ryne. As soon as I hang up with her, I call Mikey. He promises he will have Anna flown out in the department's plane, and he plans to come along.

"Do you need to contact the Homer station?" Portlock is much closer to their jurisdiction, but I'm hoping that until Ryne is found, we can keep this as quiet as possible. We still don't know why the plane is here or what we're dealing with, and the larger the presence, the more likely the pilot is to catch on and disappear—with Ryne.

Mikey hesitates. "Technically, yes, I should call them…But

maybe it can wait until we have a little more information. I'm pretty sure Portlock isn't exactly their territory anyway. Besides, I'm guessing you'll be calling in the FBI."

"I will at least try to get them here. I'm not a real agent, so the best I can do is try to convince them that this is worth their while."

"Which you will. And if you tell them what you've found, you know they will barge in full force with helicopters and a million agents."

"Not necessarily. Remember, they do undercover well."

"But it's at least one additional plane landing there and likely boats coming in too."

"True."

"If anyone is out there—and if you're finding hidden trash and cleaned buildings and a bunch of body parts, clearly *someone* is camped out there—the FBI will scare them off immediately."

"Dolly and I will keep looking for Ryne. Maybe I should see what we discover first and then call them in. After all, I don't want to seem trigger happy. Mensel told me that I'd have to have something rock solid to get them involved." I squint into the sun, starting to doubt myself. "But then again, if Ryne is here and the FBI rolls in, they're going to find them. No question."

"Right. But if Ryne's not there, and if you haven't found them yet, then it's really likely they're not, and the FBI rolls in..." Mikey seems to be talking to himself more than me. "Well, if someone sees the FBI, they're going to know they've been found out. And if Ryne is their brand-new recruit...well, whoever has Ryne is going to want them dead on the spot for giving up the operation."

We don't even know what the operation down here *is* yet. I was just starting to get a handle on the Seward operation, but this may be something much different. And Mikey's right. If the FBI swoops in full force, which they'll want to do given what we've discovered, my odds of being able to learn more will be zero. I'm just a liaison. Mensel will take over the entire operation, and Ryne won't be his priority. Sure, the FBI will work to find them and keep them safe, but they'll also be busy dismantling this whole town trying to find more body parts.

Maybe subtle is better. Just for now.

"I'm just thinking, maybe it's better to call them in as soon as Ryne is found," Mikey concludes. "After all, you don't know that Ryne is there. You said their bike was at the airstrip. You don't know they got on the plane at all. Didn't they know you were tracking it?"

"Yeah."

"Then why would they bother getting on it?"

I pause. I wish I had time and space to think this through, but I don't, and Mikey is making me question what I've assumed. Mikey is good at that, and it's not always a bad thing. Like my challenging him, it's what made us good partners for each other.

"Louisa, my take, if you want to hear it, is that Ryne is back in Seward doing the same thing you're doing—spying on Mr. Drew's operation."

I'm flustered. I'm not sure what to say. I was so confident, but this whole Portlock situation is no answers, all new questions.

"Will you hold off on calling the FBI? Let me and Anna get down there, you and Dolly keep looking, and then we'll reconvene and decide what's next."

"I…" I make a decision before I waste more time overanalyzing it. "Okay, just hurry." I rush back to Dolly, who's practically bouncing in her agitation. She unfolds the map and points at a series of marks behind the buildings of the town.

"What's this?"

"A cave system."

We stare at each other. If someone wanted to hide here—really hide—caves would be where they'd do it. Not run-down buildings right on the water where any random boat could show up.

"They're on their way," I say. "Let's go."

CHAPTER TWENTY-TWO

The cave system around Portlock is extensive. There's an old mining cave that we explore first. Here, there are signs of human visits—lots of cigarette butts, a bunch of beer cans, and some food wrappers, as well as remnants of a bonfire. No sign of long-term use like clothing and sleeping bags. I'd guess this was kids out for an adventure. Whoever has been cleaning the buildings hasn't bothered with this cave, so I expect we'll find nothing in it.

Turns out my supposition is accurate.

We've just started exploring the first of the other caves when Dolly hears a plane. I'm not sure—the sound underground is tricky. But as soon as I step out with the satellite phone, it rings. Anna has arrived. When I tell Dolly, she curses. "There's not enough time."

"I know, but it's not safe to investigate alone. This place gives me the creeps."

She nods. "Me too. But I know there's something here. I can feel it."

"I think you're right about that."

"Did you call for the FBI?"

I scratch a spot on my neck that doesn't itch and pretend to examine the wall of the cave. I wondered when Dolly would ask. I don't want her to think I'm ignoring her needs. I'm still not sure if Mikey is right about my current course of action. I'm still considering how to address the question when Dolly continues.

"Maybe best not. They might just make things worse. If we can find Ryne without making a mess, that's best."

❖

Anna and Stan, her assistant, are by the water. Stan looks all business, as usual. When Anna sees me and Dolly, she grins. An environment like this creeps into my bones and infects my brain. It's hard for me to stay positive in a place where I know a crime has been committed, no matter how beautiful the natural setting. Knowing death has been there ruins it for me. It doesn't seem that way for Anna. I smile back at her.

Anna enters the mud. She's dressed for it at least. Everything she's wearing, from her ripstop hiking pants tucked into waders to her button-down, has that water-repellent sheen.

"Am I headed in the right direction?" Anna asks. She doesn't whisper or lower her voice. I put a finger to my lips.

"We're not sure if we're alone out here," I explain. She raises her eyebrows and nods.

Tails jumps to Anna's side like he's ready to join her. Stan pulls on a pair of latex gloves.

Anna turns to me. "Remind me. We've got a hand, a torso, and at least a few other body parts still buried in this stuff?"

"That's right. The hand is there." I point to the tree.

"Thinking they're all from the same person?"

Dolly shakes her head. "The skin color is different. The torso is darker than the hand. If it was just sun exposure, that would be opposite."

"Aaaah. Tricky. So, we could be looking at a mass grave." Her face looks neutral, but I see the glint in her eyes. Anna likes a challenge. "Well, we came bearing gifts." She reaches into her pack and pulls out what looks like a crowbar. "Lead the way!"

"Of course."

Dolly leads us to the marshy shoreline while I hang back with Anna. Despite the fact my hands are filthy, she grabs one briefly and gives me the most fleeting wink.

"Where's Mikey, by the way?"

"He's here too, but he wanted to catch some pictures of the general layout, give some context to your find when we're explaining it to people who have never been here. It's not exactly easy to get to."

"Only boat or plane is my understanding." I lift my legs high as we start into the deepest part of the mud.

"That's right. And depending on the weather, not either of those, either." Her boots make suction noises as she wades in.

"Geez. The families who lived here must have been so isolated."

"Do you think it was whole families? I always picture a bunch of men in these old towns." She crinkles her nose slightly as she speaks but says nothing about the putrid smell.

I nod south. "There's a pretty big schoolhouse in town."

"Oh wow. I'll have to check that out when we're done here."

When we arrive at the torso, Anna whistles and warns Stan not to touch it yet. She pokes at it with her gloved hands.

"There are gashes in it," she declares as she works a finger into one of the slits. "Certainly not nice, but also not fatal. Not unless these got real infected, and it's hard to tell with all this mud, but it doesn't look that way."

She crouches in the mud and puts her face closer to the body than I'm comfortable with. I wonder how long it will take for me to get over wanting to protect Anna from gruesome sights. She's been doing this much longer than me, and in a much more intimate way. No job is more up-close-and-personal than hers. Still, she's such a sweet person I only want her to see other sweet things. I can't deny it, though—she takes obvious pleasure in her job.

"Animal?" Dolly says. "Bear?"

There's a glint in Anna's eyes. "I'm not going to say for sure until I get this back to the hospital." I'm guessing she already has a theory.

Anna gives Stan the go-ahead, and he starts helping her pull the body up. There's more than we initially thought. Part of the neck is still attached, though it was well covered. The shoulders are there, severed just below the rotator cuffs. There are hips, but only the top of one leg. The places where the limbs have been severed are not clean. The flesh, muscle, and bone at these spots are extremely ragged. It's hard to tell at first glance if the limbs were removed by a human hand or by an animal, but Anna will know, I'm sure. She's already moved on for now, digging around in the mud with her tool.

"We've got something else here." She reaches down and pulls up part of a tree root. "Nope. Not unless that's decomposed in a way I'm not yet familiar with." Before long, she makes another legitimate hit.

"What have you got?" Tails and I have paused at a new find.

"Another torso. Same kinds of marks."

"I've got a thigh. At least I think it's a thigh. Few sets of puncture wounds."

Before I can finish the sentence, Anna's assistant rushes over to pull it out as gently as possible. He carefully places it in a plastic bag and pulls out a marker to label it.

Dolly yells before he's even finished. She's got a pair of hands and part of a leg.

"Doctor, I'm not sure we can transport all of this...all of these parts. We've going to run out of bags if we keep them all separated." Stan's brows are pulled into a tight scowl.

"I've got some with me too." Mikey's familiar voice comes from just behind me and I jump. "Why? What have you got?" I smile when I see him. He's already losing his balance in the mud, and I pull my boots out carefully so as to not lose my own balance as I greet him. Tails bounds over to him too, temporarily distracted from his sniffing duties.

"Hey, buddy!" Mikey reaches down to pet Tails and nearly falls face-first. "Geez, this is something else."

"Yeah, there's a bunch of roots buried in here too. Real death trap." Anna smiles even though no one else laughs.

Mikey rolls his eyes. "Oh, well, there's the Anna pun, so my day is complete." Anna just giggles. Mikey turns to Dolly. "Hello, ma'am. Thanks so much for flying Linebach out, and I'm really sorry to hear about Ryne. We'll find him—don't worry."

Dolly corrects Ryne's pronouns tersely, and Mikey blushes and apologizes. His body language is strange around Dolly. I've never seen Mikey physically back away from someone who doesn't have a weapon trained on him, but he does with her. She can be blunt, sure, but it still strikes me as odd. Dolly's a good person. Mikey is usually quick to recognize the good in people. I want to analyze their interactions, but there are still people here, under my feet, waiting to be recovered. I call Tails to me.

"Mikey, if you want to help me, I'll fill you in."

He follows me to where I last searched. As we work, following Tails's ever-intelligent nose, I tell Mikey about the caves and our hunch that Ryne is here and not near Seward. Out of the corner of my eye, I see Dolly lingering within earshot.

"Dolly, do you want to tell Chief about Ryne's conversation with the pilot?"

She eyes me like she might be a little pissed off, but she tromps through the mud and joins us. She repeats most of our conversation, but she leaves out her conclusions about the types of young people the pilots are targeting. I fill this gap in carefully, looking at Dolly for any sign that she doesn't want me to reveal something. She doesn't give one.

"Okay. So, we believe Ryne is here, that they were flown here by one of Mr. Drew's pilots. We know Ryne had been approached about a job that makes a lot of money, but he—*they*—I'm sorry, Dolly...*Ryne* doesn't fit the profile of the young men Mr. Drew normally uses to run drugs. So, there could be another operation that Ryne has been drawn into. But we don't know what it is yet."

"Right." Dolly nods.

"And now we have a pile of body parts. And I'm guessing that you'd really rather be trying to find Ryne than digging up limbs."

"Yes." Dolly exhales.

"Body recovery isn't exactly my specialty either. How about if you and I check out some of these caves? Louisa, you mind covering Anna and Stan?" He nods toward Anna and her assistant, who are working yet another body part out of the mud.

"Of course not." I raise an eyebrow at Dolly, who nods to indicate that it's fine. *Huh.* She doesn't mind Mikey joining her instead of me. I look at Mikey. I'm surprised he doesn't send me with her too. After all, missing persons is my specialty. Maybe he sees an opportunity to clear the air of whatever's between them. I hope he can. This investigation is complicated enough without tensions I don't understand.

"Dolly, do you have something Tails can use to come find you when we're finished here, if you don't have reception?" She pulls off the bandana that's keeping the sweat out of her eyes. As Mikey and Dolly walk away, Tails looks at them, and then at me. His lack of exuberance is noticeable as he joins me in assisting the medical team. *Yeah, I'd rather be walking the beach too, buddy.*

By the end of the hour, we have twenty-three body parts. There are five torsos, so at least five distinct men. After Anna pulls her gloves off, she rubs her hands together.

"Anxious to get back to the morgue?" I ask.

"Definitely ready to start piecing this all together."

I crinkle my nose. "Can your puns get any worse?"

Anna's eyes get big. "Oh, I didn't even mean to do that! That's perfect!"

I shake my head.

As Stan loads the body parts and the pilot prepares for the flight home, Anna and I stand next to one another, looking out toward the water. It *is* a beautiful place. I sigh.

"You know, I could use a nice sightseeing trip that doesn't involve death or drugs."

She winks at me. "Sounds like just what the doctor ordered!"

"*Are* you ordering it?"

"Yup. At least three days' rest, a whale watching tour, and two hikes. Minimum. Preferably with someone charming and cute."

"Oh shit, I'll have to find someone." She scowls and drops her beautiful mouth into a fake pout that makes me laugh.

Stan clears his throat. He looks as if he'd rather be anywhere else. My experiences with him five years ago indicate he has little to no sense of humor. I empathize now. I used to be like that too. All work, no play. Louisa was certainly a dull girl.

"Dr. Fenway, I've got some small animal tracks. Rodent, I think. Would you like me to photograph them?"

"Absolutely. We're also going to need to do a little digging around to see what bugs have been getting at these guys. I know that's your favorite part."

Stan's face doesn't change at all. "It is," he says.

Anna explains that entomology was his specialty in grad school.

"That's awesome." I'm not lying. You can tell so much about a dead body by which bugs have taken up residence and which have been nibbling at it.

"We have another half hour, tops. The wind is supposed to pick up tonight. Louisa, you might want to go find Mikey and Dolly."

I agree. Stan whips out a mason jar and starts digging through the mud, turning his back to us. I lean my head into Anna's. I don't want to touch her and leave grime in her hair.

"I'm going to start planning that trip," she says softly.

I smile at Anna as I head off to find my friends.

CHAPTER TWENTY-THREE

Tails needs Dolly's bandana to track her and Mikey. They're deep in a cave when we find them, and Mikey looks concerned. I'm not sure I've ever seen him scowl so deeply. He keeps running his hand over the shadow of a beard. Dolly is well ahead of him and shines a small flashlight over what look like metal filing cabinets.

"What is all this?" I whisper. Noise bounces off the walls of these caves.

"I'm almost positive someone is making drugs here."

"What like, cooking in a cave?" His *mm-hmm* is vague and he keeps rubbing his beard. "Wow. But that makes sense though, right? With as many men as Mr. Drew has running drugs, it would make sense that he's producing them too. Or at least that his guys are getting them straight from the source…and that source is here."

Dolly's light bounces off metallic surfaces. I catch fragments of metal tables like the ones Anna works on. Dolly opens and closes the metal cabinets and glass clinks.

"Careful, Dolly. We don't want them to know we've been here." I speak as loudly as I dare. Dolly returns to me and Mikey.

"Meth. They're making a lot of meth." I raise an eyebrow at her. "What? I raised children. I keep myself informed on what to look for."

"Fair. Mikey?" I look at Mikey. I know he knows and can corroborate. Drug busts were his specialty in Anchorage—not to mention the family connections.

He sighs. "Yes, meth."

"Fuck." Meth is popular in Alaska, and it messes people up faster than almost any other drug I've seen with the possible exception of heroin.

"My guess is we will find this setup in other caves too."

"I need to call in the FBI, Mikey. Just as soon as we find Ryne." Mikey doesn't make eye contact with me. "I know you want to get Mr. Drew just like I do, but this is bigger than us. There are dozens of people involved in this, if not hundreds."

He lowers his head. "I know. Just let me get in touch with Homer first, okay?" I scowl. "Seward and Whittier are trying to develop better connections with the other forces. This is Homer territory." I'm still looking at him. That means he stretched the truth, if not outright lied to me earlier. Mikey starts to wander back out of the cave. Maybe I need a word alone with him.

For now, we all head back to Anna and Stan.

The pair have done their best to make the site look undisturbed. There are still some boot tracks in the mud, but as the tide comes in, they will disappear.

"Thanks, Anna and Stan," I say. "It's worrisome that we didn't find Ryne today, but we will. Mikey, as soon as you have the conversations you need to have, I can get the FBI in here to search those caves thoroughly. Oh, and have you gotten that list of missing men?"

"Yup. I'll send it to you as soon as I'm back at the station."

Anna grabs Dolly into a hug and promises she'll see her again soon. "We're going to find Ryne, Dolly. They're a smart kid. I know they're fine. Okay?" Dolly hugs Anna back for a long time. I feel awful about how the focus shifted from Ryne to these bodies. There just needs to be more of us. I'm so tempted to just call the FBI as soon as Mikey is out of earshot, but I have to trust him.

Dolly and I leave the others to head back to our plane.

"Dolly—"

"I'll drop you back at the cabin." She's already on her phone. As we walk, she has a quick conversation that I can't hear, she's walking so far ahead of me. After she ends the call, she makes another announcement. "A friend from Nanwalek is going to meet me and bring me back with him."

"You're not just going to stay at the cabin tonight?"

"No. I have to return the park's plane. This isn't Park duty."

"Would it make sense for me to go with you, since Nanwalek is so close?"

She shakes her head. "You need to be at the cabin, in case Ryne—"

"Of course." *In case Ryne shows back up.*

"And I need to be in Nanwalek in case Ryne…"

"I understand. They could show up there any time. Maybe they're already at the house waiting for you."

Dolly makes a sign that must be a prayer of some sort.

"Yes. But there are also some things I want to check on tonight."

I don't ask her to elaborate. It surprises me to find that I already trust Dolly's instincts. Besides, the stakes are highest for her. Her family is on the line.

We fly in silence after some very careful maneuvering of the plane into a safe takeoff position. The wind has picked up, and it tosses the light aircraft around. Tails keeps his head down like he's trying to ignore the rocking. I try not to think about that statistic of Alaska being one of the most dangerous places to fly in the world.

Dolly lands us at Exit Glacier. Within minutes, another plane touches down alongside us. Dolly's friend. He looks a few years older than her, his face heavily lined. His dark skin contrasts with pristine white, close-cut hair. When he shakes my hand, he wishes me good luck and thanks me for helping to search for Ryne. I guess he and Dolly will not sleep tonight, and I'm relieved that she'll have someone with her to help in her own search.

"You can use the park ATV there. Key should already be in it."

I thank Dolly, but I am unsettled, just as I'm sure she is.

"Call me as soon as you find anything, okay?"

"You too." I wonder what I could possibly find in the cabin, so far away from Portlock. But then I remember that I am at least close to Mr. Drew, and that could come in handy. I'm not going to sleep, anyway.

Maybe I need to make a little pit stop.

Chapter Twenty-four

The path to the cabin looks entirely different in civil twilight, and I have to take it slow. The trip eats up over half an hour, but I need to eat something more than the granola bar Dolly gave me if I'm going to spend the night out in the woods near Mr. Drew's place.

And I need to figure out a plan that's more than watching passively as he hides.

I draw my gun before I open the door. My nose tells me someone is already here. Freshly brewed Earl Gray and milk. Yet there's no growl or bark from Tails, and no rush of sound as someone moves to defend themselves. Anyone I know would be cautious about startling cops who are already on edge. I lower my weapon as soon as I see who's standing at the stove, cracking eggs into a pan of butter.

"Holy fucking hell, Ryne!" I'm part shocked, part terrified, part relieved, and part an emotion I can't even identify. Whatever it is, no string of cuss words will be long enough to express it. Nonetheless, I swear a few more times as I put the gun on the table and hug the kid, who looks just as surprised as I am to see them. As soon as I let them go, I pull out the phone to call Dolly. Ryne starts to speak, but I interrupt.

"I've gotta call your grandma. She's terrified for you." Ryne tries to object, but I step outside. I don't even hear a complete ring when she picks up. I don't bother with a hello.

"Ryne's here! They're safe."

"What? Here where? The cabin? What…" The airplane drones in the background.

"Yes, the cabin. I came in and they're just standing there making eggs like nothing happened."

Dolly releases a barrage of curses, prayers, and words in English, then in her other language. When she's let it out, she asks where Ryne has been, what they were doing, how they got back, and exactly why the hell they're intent on giving their poor grandmother a heart attack and putting her in a grave before her time. None of which I can answer yet.

"I'm outside. I don't—"

"Well, why are you outside talking to me? Get in there and find out!" I promise to update her soon. "Don't you let that child out of your sight again. I'll be there as soon as I can be, but we're almost to Nanwalek now and we don't have the fuel to turn back. I'll see both of you tomorrow."

When I get back in, Ryne holds the spatula in the air and stares at me like they haven't moved since I walked out the door.

"How much trouble am I in?" they ask, still frozen in place.

"Oh my God, *so much*! Where were you? We were worried sick!"

"Whoa. Are you like, channeling my grandmother right now?"

"Far as you're concerned, *yes*. Answers, please!" I pull out a chair and sit, crossing my arms over my chest.

Ryne is in slow motion as they turn off the stove and slide eggs onto two plates, as if I'm some sort of wild animal and sudden movement might startle me. They settle into a chair, then glance up at me from under those long lashes.

"Guess there's no chance you'll promise not to be mad."

"No chance." I squeeze my arms tighter.

Ryne sighs and looks down, poking at their eggs with a fork but not eating. I'm ravenous and I want to devour mine, but I'm not moving until Ryne starts talking. Normally I don't mind the long pauses before they speak, but right now my patience is thin.

"Okay. I was at Mr. Drew's." The breath leaves my lungs. So, Mikey was right, and Dolly and I were totally off-base. I don't say anything, though—I just stare at them. More information better be forthcoming, though I can't imagine anything Ryne would say that would make this situation all right. They sigh deeply, then push their eggs to the side and lean back, examining their hands and fidgeting for a moment before placing them in their lap.

"Okay. So, you know I talked to the pilot when he came to Nanwalek. And I did tell you pretty much everything we talked about. But there was also something they said that wouldn't have meant much to you, but it seemed like something to me, and I wanted to know more. The pilot made this weird reference to Jeannie. They were trying to bait me, and it would be easy for them to find out she'd gone missing, but I couldn't pass up hearing more. So, I pretended I was really interested. I agreed to the stupid envelope thing. But then Dolly intervened, of course, and I totally understand why she brought me here, I really do." They make eye contact with me and wait until I nod. "But I thought, well, what's the best way to find out what's really going on?" I raise my eyebrows. *Infiltrate*, but I wait for Ryne. They lean forward. "Have someone on the inside, right? Someone who can get access just to see what's going on and report back."

"And that's what you were doing." I try to sound and look as skeptical as possible, though any anger I had is already gone. Now I'm just relieved that Ryne is safe again.

"Right. So, the envelopes were taken, but the pilot didn't know that, right? He would have just known they didn't make it to the recipients. So, I took a chance. I knew about the airstrips from the maps I saw here in the cabin So, I went to the airstrip. There was no plane or pilot, but the guard saw me, so I talked to him."

"Ryne, that was incredibly dangerous! I was attacked by the other guard! The same thing could have happened to you."

"I"—they blink rapidly—"didn't know that." Of course they didn't, because I didn't tell them. That's what I get for withholding important information, I suppose. "But I just approached him all innocent. I told him the pilot had been down in Nanwalek and that I really was interested in working with them." Now they lean forward, smiling a sneaky smile. "But I told them I saw the envelope thing for what it was—some test to weed out people who weren't actually serious. I told the guard I wasn't doing any silly tests, that I was serious, and I wanted to be all in."

I want to scold them for being so very reckless, but I'm too fascinated.

"And then?"

They grin, and their face lights with a mix of pride and amusement. "The guard took me right up to see Mr. Drew."

"Holy hell."

"Yeah. That house!" Ryne whistles. "The guard patted me down and all, which was okay. I don't carry weapons." I shake my head. "He took me upstairs to Mr. Drew's office and we had a whole, like, meeting. I think he was impressed that I took the initiative to come all the way to Seward just to see him."

I'm still shaking my head. How long have I been doing that? My stomach is growling but the eggs are not compelling right now.

"And Mr. Drew said?"

"Well, first of all, what a dick. I mean, I'm sorry. Grams wouldn't like me talking like that. Really, though. That guy's a total jerk. And pretentious too, which just makes it worse. He gave me shit about… well, being me. Said usually only *men* work with him, but that he guessed I wouldn't be the first exception." They snort indignantly. "But anyway, he asked me a lot about my grades in science and the chemistry competitions I've won. I started to realize when we were talking what he wanted me for."

"To cook meth."

Ryne's eyes get big, and they nearly fall out of their seat as they lean forward. "Exactly!"

"Dolly found the caves where they're cooking in Portlock."

Now it's Ryne's turn to look terrified.

"Grams was in Portlock? Is she okay? What was she doing there? She could have gotten hurt!" Ryne stops and then looks ashamed.

I lean forward and put my hand on theirs. "She's fine, Ryne. But we were in Portlock because we tracked the plane there. We thought you were on it because I found the bike near the airstrip."

"Shit. Oh. Yeah, that's where I found the guard. He drove me to the house. I didn't even think about the bike until after I talked to Mr. Drew, and you must have been well gone by then. I knew the plane had come and gone, but I didn't think that you'd think…"

"Ryne, you just disappeared."

Ryne rounds their shoulders as if they'd like to retreat into a turtle shell to avoid looking at me. They pull the plate of eggs back in front of them, but just so they can poke at the food.

"I know. I didn't think it through. I just felt like I had to do something. I'm really sorry."

I exhale slowly. "Well, it's all right now that you're back, but please don't ever do anything like that again. You scared us half to death. And you're in for a full round from your grandmother."

"Oh, I know. Totally deserved." Ryne focuses on me again. "But it was worth it."

I lean forward. "Why? What else did you learn?"

"Well, when he was telling me about what I'd have to do for him, he said all the guys I'd be working with are required to live in one place where they do their work. I'd have to leave Nanwalek and my family, and they would never be able to know where I was or what I was doing. No contact. Ever."

"And people agree to this?"

"Yeah." They lean forward and rub the fingers on one hand together. "For money. Mr. Drew offered me two hundred thousand dollars *up front* to move, cut off contact with everyone else, and start training under someone called the Scientist. He said every year I'd get more money the better I got. He'd just hand me cash, every single year. Or store it for me if I was worried about it getting stolen. Then when I finished working for him, I'd have all that money to send to my family or to start a new life. I wouldn't have any expenses. He supplies food and housing and everything."

"Except if you sent it to your family, Dolly would never get to know where it came from."

"Right." Ryne scowls. "I had a lot of questions about how that works exactly, but I wanted to seem like some gullible kid who just wants a bunch of money and doesn't care how."

"That's smart." I correct myself. "I mean, nothing about what you did is *smart* per se. It was a *dangerous* thing to do. But if you wanted him to buy what you were selling, it was smart to not ask a lot of questions. He's an intelligent, albeit evil, man. He would have caught on."

"Right." Ryne leans back, looking wound up. "So, these... *chemists*, I guess—they live together, make drugs, and Mr. Drew pays them a bunch to do it. But they can't stay in Alaska when they retire."

"That's a hell of a trade-off."

"Yeah. But that explains why he's preying on people he thinks have shitty lives. And talking to him, he obviously thinks my community is shitty." Ryne's expression clouds over. I can't imagine how hard it was to hear that and not react. "He's wrong, you know." I can see the emotion in Ryne's gaze. "I love my community. I love Grams and all my cousins and friends. I wouldn't trade them for any money Mr. Drew could give me."

"I know that, Ryne. But do you think Mr. Drew knows that?"

"Nope. He totally bought it. He's planning to fly me to the secret location on Saturday. Even promises there will be cash waiting when I get there."

"What?" I stand up, upsetting the chair as I do. Tails jumps and looks at me as if he expects an order. "You're not going anywhere, Ryne. No way."

"Louisa, this is your chance to bust him! You could catch him red-handed! The Scientist is supposed to be there and I'm going to meet with them in person. You could follow me. If they're going to show me some drug operation, it'll be all laid out right there for you."

"Ryne, I'm not using you as bait. We already saw the operation. There's no need to endanger you."

Ryne stands too. "But you have to! If I don't now, Mr. Drew will know he's been compromised. And besides, how else will you tie what you and Grams saw to him?"

"Or he'll just think you got cold feet, which would be totally understandable given what you've told me."

"Well…" Ryne looks doubtful for only a second. "Maybe. But this is too good an opportunity to pass up. He said I'd learn how the entire operation works."

"And then he'd expect you to stay down there for the rest of your life."

"Well, for a while. Yeah. He'd expect me to have all my clothes and stuff I need. I wouldn't be allowed to leave after Saturday, just in case I chickened out and then told people about it." Ryne looks at me and uncharacteristically rushes to speak. "But that would never happen because you and the police would sweep in and bust the whole thing and arrest the Scientist *and* Mr. Drew, and bam! The whole operation's done, and we've got hard evidence of what he's been doing."

It's hard not to get caught up in Ryne's excitement, and as much as I don't want to admit it right now, they have a point. The only way to bring Mr. Drew down will be to catch him in the act. But this is too risky.

"But would Mr. Drew even be there? Wouldn't he just have a pilot fly you down there and leave you?"

Ryne sits back down, looking contemplative. "Maybe. I didn't ask. It would make sense that he wouldn't go. He obviously doesn't want to be directly connected. He even took my phone away and all to make sure I wasn't recording him. No notes. No nothing. You might be right about that."

"So, this scientist would just take the fall."

"But with me to testify? To say *his* pilot flew me to the location? There'd be evidence of that."

"I don't think those pilots are exactly formal employees."

"Maybe. But it would be so much easier, Louisa! If you bust the operation, one of those guys is bound to take a deal to rat him out."

Ryne is likely right. Some of these workers must be desperate to get back to their families, money or not. And I know the FBI is sometimes willing to make deals—hefty and expensive deals if it gets them what they want. I rub my temples. The exhaustion is setting in, and now I'm wishing I hadn't abandoned those eggs.

I pull the plate back toward me. Stone cold. *Yuck.*

"Grilled cheese while you think about it?"

I sigh. "We really both need some sleep."

Ryne scoffs. "You really think you'll be able to sleep?"

"No." I shake my head. "Grilled cheese sounds great. But, Ryne, listen. And I want no objection." They look at me, eyes wide. "We have to run this by Dolly. Whether I or the police or anyone else thinks this is a good idea doesn't matter. You're not eighteen yet. We're not doing anything without Dolly's blessing. Understood?"

Ryne bites their bottom lip, carefully groomed eyebrows pulled together, but then finally looks at their feet as they nod. "Deal."

Deal. *Right.* I'm talking to a teenager about using them as bait and praying I can figure out a way to keep them from ending up cut up on the marshy beach of Portlock. They have no idea all they don't know, and how dangerous this really is. There's a lot of details to work out before I can convince myself that this is a viable option, never mind convincing Dolly.

I step outside to make the necessary phone calls to Mensel and Mikey.

CHAPTER TWENTY-FIVE

Mensel and Mikey both agree to the basic plan with restrictions, contingencies, warnings and so on. Overnight, I consider and plan for those as best I can without being near Portlock. Everything is almost easy if the maroon and white plane is used, if Mr. Drew is there, if Ryne's debrief happens in the open or near the beach. But there's no reason to expect this sting operation will go easy. I look over at Ryne asleep on the sofa. We're not even one hundred percent sure this will go down in Portlock, or the caves. It's the most logical guess, but...We found evidence of drug-making, not drug-makers.

I shake Ryne awake early and fill them in on the rough plan as well as some of the details of Mr. Drew they didn't know. I secure their understanding of the additional dangers I see—plus the unknown others I may discover on location. They are still enthusiastic about going forward, so Ryne and I talk through how to deliver the pitch to Dolly.

When I hear Dolly parking, I remind myself that she's going to need a little time alone with Ryne. They are surely in for a stern talking-to, and I might be in a little trouble myself. I briefly greet her and duck out quickly when Dolly comes inside, taking a seat on the porch while Tails runs around the cabin's perimeter. I glance again through the missing persons list Mikey sent to bide the time. I promptly shared the names on it with Dolly, but I doubt she's even looked at it, given how focused she's been on Ryne.

Ryne gets a full round of talking-to. Dolly's voice gets loud at points, though I never hear Ryne talk back. Smart on their part. After about half an hour of a stern voice from Dolly, punctuated by periods of silence that I suspect are either Ryne responding or hugs, Dolly calls for me. I stick my head in.

"All clear. And no, I don't plan to give you trouble." I call Tails and we go back inside.

"I took the missing persons list Chief Harper gave you to Council. They cross-checked it with their own records. They also reached out to the councils of other tribes around the peninsula. No one feels confident that this is comprehensive, but there are still a lot of people here that weren't on Seward's list."

She removes papers from folders. There are photos on some of the pages with basic physical descriptions. Some of the people pictured look Native Alaskan, but many do not. They are a diverse group in terms of gender, physical attributes, height, and weight—but they are all young. The oldest looks maybe mid-twenties if that. They don't meet the description for Mr. Drew's pilots or drug runners. But they may qualify as chemists.

"Thank you, Dolly. Before we do anything else, I think we need to chat through everything Ryne learned at Mr. Drew's."

"You're going to want to call Anna too."

"I doubt she'll have much yet, but I can try."

"No, *I* need to talk to her. About one of the bodies." I raise a brow. Dolly sits. "One of the leg pieces had a long burn scar. There was a young man in Nanwalek who had a similar scar. He got it riding on a friend's motorcycle. He came to me for salve. When I saw that leg, I had a feeling that was the same young man." She shifts the folders and loose papers on the table, finding the one she wants. She looks at it herself for a long moment, then slides it to me. "This is him."

The boy has a bowl-style haircut with long sleek black bangs stopping just before his eyebrows. His dark eyes are slightly wrinkled at the edges like he's already smiled more than most adults have. His smile lights his whole face. I swallow a lump in my throat. He went missing at seventeen. He would be twenty-five now.

"Is that Timothy?" Ryne asks. They lean in to look at the face. Dolly nods.

"You knew him?" I ask, and Ryne nods.

"He was ahead of me in school, but I know his little sister. She graduated a couple years ago. We were both in school when he disappeared. I remember that she missed him for a long time."

I go outside to call Anna. She's already been at work for hours, trying to match the parts first. She wants to ID everyone before she looks into who or what killed them. When I tell her Dolly may be able to help, she sighs in relief.

"I was worried I wouldn't be able to get anywhere with any of them. The decomp on some is advanced, and so few have distinguishing marks. Other than these bizarre cuts."

"Any idea of what caused those cuts?"

"Not an animal, I can tell you that, and I've barely even scratched the surface of examining the wounds yet. There's always four cuts together, spaced evenly, which means a blade. Inflicted with different levels of force, and usually after death. In a couple cases it would be enough to kill, but not in most."

"Why?"

"I keep trying *not* to ask myself the same thing. I really want to know who these men are so we can notify their families. Some of them have been missing for a very long time." She pauses. "Would you mind putting Dolly on?"

When Dolly comes out, I go inside to Ryne. Ryne sits transfixed, staring with their large eyes at several of the file papers in their hands. They are crying and not bothering to wipe the tears away.

"I know. It's a lot to process. Especially if some of these were people you knew."

They slide a paper across the table. The face is of a young woman. It looks like one of those professional high school graduation pictures proud parents shell out money for. This young woman poses casually, leaning against a tree, with her legs crossed. She wears a pale sundress, and her long dark hair spills over her shoulders, landing nearly at where her belly button would be. She has generous hips and full legs. Her lips are pulled into a wide smile, her cheeks round. Her eyes are so familiar. I look at Ryne, who now stares at me. They're the same eyes.

"This is Dolly's niece. Your...cousin?"

Ryne nods. "I called her my sister, though. She was like a sister."

"She went missing when she was eighteen." Another nod. "I'm so sorry. It was a long time ago, but I know that the hurt doesn't get any better."

"Just worse."

I study the picture for a long time. She looks so happy. She's pretty. My mind automatically questions whether she was seeing someone dangerous. Sadly, domestic violence often turns out to be to blame for disappearances among young women.

"What was she like, Ryne?" Ryne shrugs fast. My impression is they'd rather not talk about it. But they continue.

"She was fun. She was always smiling, like she is there. Carefree,

I guess. She never worried." They pause for a long while, flipping the photo back toward them. Tears form again, and their tone shifts. Maybe they really do want to talk about it.

"I used to worry all the time as a kid. I was really anxious, you know?" I nod. *I* definitely *know*. "I'd always go to her when I was upset because I didn't want to worry Dolly. Jeannie always took me seriously. She never minimized my feelings. She always knew how to reassure me and comfort me. And after we talked, she'd always put her hands right on the side of my head"—they place their own hands on their temples—"and she'd pull me forward to give me a kiss right on the top of the head. She was so much taller than me then." Ryne smiles. "She was like that for everyone, I think. She was the person people went to when they needed to talk. You could tell her the most terrible thing and she'd find a way to make it seem all right."

"She sounds wonderful." We both sit looking at the picture. I glance up to see if there's any sign of Dolly, but she's apparently still talking to Anna. "Ryne, was she dating anyone when she disappeared? Maybe someone Dolly didn't know about? Any new friends? Anyone new in her life, really."

Ryne shakes their head slowly. "I thought and thought and thought about anything that might have made her go missing like that. But there's nothing. She was looking forward to getting a job and helping Dolly around the house. She loved Dolly. She loved me."

The door opens and Dolly sits back down next to us. She catches her breath when she sees Jeannie's picture. She quickly slides it back into a folder marked *Jeannie Agapov*.

"I'm going to help Anna identify these remains if I can." She turns to her grandchild. "There was something you said you wanted to talk to me about, Ryne."

Ryne and I look at each other. *Here goes nothing.*

CHAPTER TWENTY-SIX

Through the entire pitch, which Ryne delivers beautifully—I suspect they've rehearsed it in their head several times—I'm convinced that Dolly's going to say no. I'm prepared to intervene if need be, but I think this will be an easier sell coming from Ryne. I remind myself to breathe as I wait for her answer, and it's a good thing, cause I'd suffocate in the amount of time it takes her to say something. She gets up from the table, makes a pot of coffee, does a thorough scan of the fridge—though she pulls out nothing—then waits for the coffee to brew and pours three mugs at a speed that is painful. I twitch my foot up and down, trying to channel my impatience.

Ryne sneaks me a cross-eyed snarl that almost makes me burst out laughing. Dolly glares at us. Maybe we aren't so sneaky. Finally, she settles into her chair and opens her mouth. But she closes it again and starts spooning sugar into her coffee. Since when does she take sugar? I swear she's just drawing this out to torture us. That, or she's waffling on her decision. At least it's not an outright no, then…

She takes a sip of coffee, grimaces, and sets the cup down gently. Then she folds her arms and looks at both of us steadily, one then the other. She holds her gaze on Ryne.

"Fine."

Ryne squeals, quickly restraining themselves.

I almost fall backward in my chair.

"I don't like it at all. And I better not end up regretting this. But fine. Ryne, you'll go to Portlock to meet with this scientist. Louisa will follow you. But Louisa," she turns to me, "I need to know that the FBI will have reinforcements there at the ready. We'll need a signal. If Ryne is in danger, there needs to be backup there right away. Louisa, I want you as armed as you can get. And we're leaving this cabin today. We're getting down close to Portlock. I want as good a feel for the place as possible before Ryne goes in there. And I want to be there."

"Dolly, the FBI is already on alert, and we've talked through escape routes and plans. But if this is a full FBI operation, you can't be there. At least not right there for the meeting."

"Yes, I figured. That's why we're staying right outside of the town. One of my neighbors knows about the place. It's abandoned."

"You already have a place? How—"

"If Ryne hadn't turned up, I was going to move down there so I could look 24-7. Apparently, it's far enough out of Portlock that the people working there may not know it exists. Or if they do, they've ignored it. No running water. No electric. We can deal with it for a couple days."

I nod. "Thank you, Dolly." She's certainly saved me and Mensel some work, which he'll be glad to know. "We'll make this as safe as humanly possible for Ryne."

"Are you absolutely sure, Ryne?" Dolly's face says she hopes Ryne will change their mind.

"I am." Ryne reaches over and grabs Dolly's hands.

"I don't want to say yes. Just know that."

"Can I ask why you have?"

Dolly turns to me. "Because if any of those bodies are members of our community, then Ryne and I can help end this. We have a responsibility to. And besides"—she looks down—"that pilot mentioned Jeannie…"

I wait for her to continue.

"Well, if someone knows something and Ryne can get it out of them…"

"Of course." I pause. "I suspect you're going to help a lot of people get answers about their loved ones. Hopefully you can get some too."

"You two better get packing." She doesn't say anything else. She looks at Tails as if he might have bags to get together too. He can feel the energy in the room, and he bounces up, following me and Ryne around the cabin as we get our things together. Dolly washes the dishes and tidies while we pack.

❖

Before we head to the new place, we drop Ryne in Nanwalek, so I get a glimpse of where they and Dolly live. That's where Mr. Drew will expect Ryne to be coming from, and the pilot is supposed to meet them a couple miles outside of town. Dolly assures me that the entire village will be keeping an eye on Ryne until the appointed meeting time. Nanwalek is a cute town on the water; the homes are small but comfortable looking. The views of the Alaskan landscape are astounding. Still, it's a tiny village, and entirely removed from everything around it. As idyllic as it seems to me as an outsider, I can see where growing up there would foster a desire to leave and see something else. That desire likely makes Mr. Drew's recruiting job easy.

Ryne will bring a couple bags to make the whole thing look authentic. They've given me the appointed time on Saturday. I have no idea whether the tracker is still on that maroon and white plane. Mensel reported its last location as Portlock the day we found the body parts, and then nothing. I'll keep an eye out just in case Mr. Drew is still using it—assuming they're going to fly. Dolly also helps map the route they could take by boat. She will be out on the water at the appointed time while I have eyes on the air. Thankfully, those are the only options for accessing Portlock. It's only about twelve miles between Nanwalek and Portlock, but it's not possible to traverse by car. From what Dolly says, it wouldn't be easy even by ATV.

As Ryne gets ready to leave the plane, they lean over and give me a hug.

"I've got your back, kiddo. I'll be close behind you."

"I know. I'm not scared."

"Well, you're braver than me."

Ryne grins and steps out. Dolly waits, watching as they walk toward the pale blue house we saw from the air. When they're out of sight, Dolly takes off again. She tracks Ryne even when we're airborne. She circles slightly, and the small figure below us waves and disappears inside the house.

"I hope this isn't a mistake," she says, possibly to me, possibly to herself.

❖

Dolly was certainly right about the lodge. It's a hunting cabin and it's…basic. It looks like one of the hundreds of small hunting structures that dot the peninsula's wilderness. It would have been a much-loved weekend home for people needing to get away from their weekday lives to just soak in the forest, maybe shoot at a couple animals here and there, cook over the fire, and sit outside enjoying the great outdoors. There's an outhouse with a compost toilet, though no wood chips to throw in after use. There's an outdoor shower and sink, but when I turn the taps on, nothing happens. The kitchen is of little use without electricity. That's all right. We're just over a mile from Portlock, so smoke from a cooking fire shouldn't be too obvious.

Dolly and I settle in, and I cook some beans and hot dogs over the campfire. We sit on the porch steps to eat.

"Who owns this place anyway?" Something about the lodge is comfortable, like it was so well loved that the echo of it can still be felt. Though I'm guessing it's been a decade or more since someone was last here.

"Not sure. No deed or anything on record. Not too surprising. Used to be people just built where they wanted. You built it, it was yours. It's not park land."

"I guess that would make it hard to sell."

She shrugs. "Just left it when they were done. Or when they died."

"It's a shame. It's beautiful here." We both stare out into the seemingly impenetrable line of pine trees, standing like an advancing army against the tiny cabin. "I hope someday someone will give this place some care again." I knock crumbs off my lips as I finish my hot dog.

"We're using it now, aren't we?"

"True." I wipe my hands on my pants and sigh. Why does food cooked outside always taste so much better?

After dinner, we take a walk to get to know the area and find the best route to Portlock. Circumstances aside, walking with Dolly is nice. It's almost as if we're just friends going for a hike in the woods, except that we're moving quickly and checking our time periodically. If the pace was more casual, it would be easy to forget that we're two *friends* planning to bust up a major drug operation and identify the remains of several missing men. Working with the right people can make even the grimmest task bearable. But I have it easy—I don't know the people we're identifying.

A couple rusted-out pickup trucks mark the edge of Portlock's remains. Dolly and I duck behind them to check that we're alone. She marks her map to indicate where our path led us and whispers that it took us thirty-two minutes to arrive here from the cabin. Not bad. I glance toward the caves. I want badly to explore them more, but we can't risk getting caught and foiling the plan with Ryne, so Dolly and I back away. We leave via a different route, hoping it will be even faster.

CHAPTER TWENTY-SEVEN

S o, tell me more about the Portlock rumors." Dolly and I have settled in for the evening with a pot of green tea. Dolly makes a clicking noise with her tongue and scowls.

"It's a bunch of silliness."

"Yeah...but humor me? Sometimes there's a grain of truth in what seems like nonsense. Besides, I could use a good story."

She shakes her head but proceeds with a sigh. "It was a cannery town, of course. Didn't last long. I think they also tried to mine there. Port Graham has good mining, so they thought maybe Portlock would too. Mostly men for a while, then they brought their families and opened that school. The residents reported seeing a monster, what we call Aula'aq—like Bigfoot. They blamed it for everything went wrong."

"And what went wrong?"

"Strange noises, ransacked buildings at first from what my grandfather said, but then disappearances. The men started to vanish from the town, and some of them were found dead with deep cuts all over their bodies, or with parts missing. It could not be a bear, they said, so it must be Aula'aq. That scared more people away. The attacks kept happening, and eventually everyone in town moved away." Dolly frowns into her tea. "They just weren't equipped to live so remote. Some people hate it. It's not for everyone."

"For sure. But all of them at once like that? This was a mass exodus."

"It is strange. But Aula'aq?" She snorts. "And Mr. Drew wasn't around in the 1930s and 40s. It can't have been related to what's going on now."

I sip my tea, enjoying the view from the porch. The late-night sun is finally starting to drop, filtering through the leaves, causing their edges to turn yellow and lime green. The patterns of the trees' bark tells complicated stories about natural history. The bark of a paper birch unfolds around its base like layers of an onion, perpetually revealing and concealing. Where the light hits the dried pine needles on the forest floor, they glow in a color that makes people call this *the golden hour*. The birds are still singing. Like I do every summer, I wonder if the long hours of daylight affect them just as much as us. Nearly all Alaskan homes have a couple sets of blackout curtains for sleeping, but I can't imagine how that works when you live in the trees.

Dolly picks the thread of our conversation back up.

"Every so often there's a hiker or a documentary maker or just someone nosy who comes down here and reports seeing this same sort of creature." Dolly still looks thoroughly skeptical. "People just want these stories to post on the internet, to get attention."

"Maybe." She's right about that—Alaska is wildly popular for people who want to post outlandish stories with little chance of anyone trying to verify them. And for people on very misguided adventures in general.

"So, if Portlock has this reputation, why would Mr. Drew pick the place to undertake a major drug operation?"

"What if he picked it *because* of its reputation?"

Dolly looks at me steadily.

"I mean, what if he knew people were afraid of the area, so no one would want to build or try to live out here again? Portlock is so far removed, and with the reputation…who's going to go exploring the caves if they think they're going to get mauled?"

"What if there really is a creature?" Dolly's voice is quiet.

"I guess there could be. It seems unwise to assume we know everything that lives."

We're quiet for a long time. I mull over how little we actually know about the world—especially about the Alaskan wildlands. Absent the gruesome deaths, I secretly root for any life form that can survive humankind. The sky is streaked with apricot and lilac, fading to a pale gray.

"I guess it's time we check in with Mikey. I wonder if he's got anything to add."

When I call, Mikey is oddly quiet. He tells me Homer couldn't offer any additional information on activities in Portlock—just that they get occasional rumors and reports about humanesque forms prowling the woods and the coast in the area. I think about the strange gashes on the remains we found. Maybe Anna has some news.

Anna still sounds bright and energetic when she answers. *Good.* I definitely didn't wake her. I fill her in on the conversation.

"Well, you ladies may be on to something." I flip the phone into speaker mode, though the volume is still low.

"We're both here. What did you find?"

"Well, thanks to the Council's files, I was able to identify a couple of the men. One of them is from Nanwalek—Timothy." Dolly looks crestfallen even though she knew—she was the one who identified his burn mark. "Another is from Tatitlek. He'd had his nipples pierced, and the missing persons report mentioned it."

"Both tribal members?" Dolly asks.

"No. The one you identified, yes, but not the other."

"Okay."

"I'm still working on IDs for the others, but I keep getting hung up on those claw marks. I believe they were created by a custom-made weapon placed on a human hand."

"Hang on. What now?" I'm having trouble picturing what such a thing could look like. Dolly is curling and uncurling her own hand like she's trying to imagine it too.

"Think like, Wolverine. Four long, curved pieces of metal attached that can be worn on the hand."

I'm disgusted, and I know my face shows it. Dolly's lip curls.

"How did you figure that out?"

"Consistency. The space between the cuts is uniform, and the cuts are smoother than what you'd get from an animal claw. The pressure is even too. If you've got an animal swiping and a victim moving around, it's not going to look like that. Someone used this weapon after the person was already still. Already dead, given the absence of blood."

"So, you think someone kills people, and then cuts them with this fake claw to make it look like an animal attack?"

"Oh, that would be too easy, Officer!" she chirps.

"You have a strange idea of easy, Doctor."

"You're not wrong about that. But you're wrong to say *someone.* It's *someones.* Multiple people."

"Seriously?"

"Yup. There are at least three of these weapons in the mix. I think they're customized to fit. On some of them, the metal claws are set closer together than on others. And the pressure used to make the wounds varies. Now that by itself doesn't necessarily mean different people—one person can stab at different intensities and whatnot depending on several factors. But given the size difference in the weapons, it just furthers my theory that it's not just one person."

"You always tell such sweet stories."

"Only to you."

"And Dolly." Dolly still makes a face.

"And Dolly!" Anna echoes extra loud so that her friend can hear.

"Okay. So, we have meth made in Portlock, which has a reputation for some sort of Sasquatch killing people in gruesome ways. Mr. Drew picks this location knowing the history and legend. He has his pilots—delivery men—kill people when they mess up, and the bodies are dumped here in Portlock if there's a body to dump at all. Cutting the victims up makes them harder to identify—"

"And ups the chances of parts being carried away by animals or going out to sea—"

"Right, Anna. And then they're giving them fake animal wounds and burying them in the mud?"

"Or giving them fake animal wounds and tossing them in the water."

"Then they wash up into the mud?"

"I'm guessing no one is taking care to see where what they throw in the water ends up. But they've covered their asses anyway by making it look like victims of an animal attack."

"So, if someone did stumble upon a body part, they'd be convinced that the legends are true and there's something in Portlock killing men in brutal ways. That would scare them straight out." Dolly speaks so quietly that I have to repeat her words for Anna.

Anna whistles. "It's perfectly diabolical."

"Gruesome."

"That sounds like Mr. Drew to me," I conclude.

"So, who is disposing of the dead?" Anna asks.

"Great question. Whoever it is, is on the line for even more serious charges than drugs."

I glance at Dolly, whose eyes have gone wide. She stares at the tree line. She holds a finger to her lips. Anna still chats, but I'm no longer focused on what she's saying. I hear it now, what Dolly hears. A rustling in the trees.

"Anna, I gotta go," I whisper and then I hang up. Dolly is still frozen in place. The rustling persists, but now it's coming from three separate locations.

"How did they know we were here?" I half-whisper, half-growl. Dolly just shakes her head. "You cover the left; I've got the right."

"Should we cover in the house?" Dolly sounds remarkably collected.

"Go to the door." I position myself behind one of the thick pieces of lumber holding up the porch roof. Dolly slides just into the cabin without a sound, her gun arm out and half of her face peering around the doorframe. When she's in position, I clear my throat. "Show yourselves." Nothing happens. The rustling continues. "We know you're there, and we're armed."

Slowly, the first tuft of light brown hair appears above a clutch of teaberries. My breath is controlled and even. I keep my entire body behind the post. I glance out again. The brown hair isn't moving, but the other two figures are rustling the leaves, drawing closer. I aim my gun at the hair in my view.

"I will shoot."

Finally, it pushes through the plants, towering, muscled, and intimidating...

And a fucking moose.

"Oh, for the love—" I lower my gun arm.

"Louisa?"

"Moose!" I yell, and Dolly emerges. A calf pushes through the shrubbery to join its mother. The female moose stares at me. It is maybe twenty yards away.

"Best get back inside. They're not friendly."

Dolly is right. Moose can be extremely aggressive—especially mothers with their young. I start to turn, but it's hard to take my eyes off the creatures. The baby now looks at me with pure curiosity. Such awkward, strange creations that inhabit Alaska with us. They are dangerous and massive animals. But I respect anything that can survive outdoors in Alaska year in and out.

Dolly is next to me now, her gun still out. "We should be getting to bed anyway."

I nod and head into the cabin. She backs in behind me, not lowering her gun until the door is shut. I push aside the gingham curtains and continue watching the moose until they disappear into the forest. I will them to stay away from Portlock.

CHAPTER TWENTY-EIGHT

When Saturday morning arrives, I'm feeling pretty confident in my ability to navigate quickly and efficiently to Portlock to follow Ryne. I've seen a few planes pass overhead, but none were maroon and white. Dolly has done a thorough investigation of the shoreline and found a few prime lookout points for spotting boats headed to Portlock from different directions. This morning, the water is choppy and unsettled, though the sun is shining, and a light breeze rustles the leaves. Maybe a storm will arrive tonight, but for today, it's hard to imagine Alaska ever being anything but gorgeous and shimmering.

Ryne's meeting with the Scientist is set for two p.m. I guess there's no point in saving clandestine meetings for night when it doesn't really get dark anyway. Or if they take place in caves. I pull out the radio, adjusting the dials until I get a weather report. There are storms around Seward. Dolly confirms that the wind currents over the area of the icefield have drawn a warning from the Park Service not to fly over Kenai Fjords for the next several hours. That doesn't mean Mr. Drew's men will heed the warning, of course. Still, I'm glad Dolly is here to watch out for boats. By noon, we're each at our selected posts. I'm at the top of a rocky hill not far from the cabin, just high enough to be able to see out over the thickest of the canopy but not high enough to be obvious to anyone flying low. My bulletproof rests firmly around my torso beneath my light jacket. The view behind me is obscured by peaks and forest, but the view toward Seward and Kolit's is clear. Dolly calls to let me know she's got eyes on the water. In theory, nothing should be able to get to Portlock from Seward without one of us noticing.

It was not my favorite decision to make, but Tails is back at the hunting lodge. I'm not exactly sure what I'll be walking into when I follow Ryne, and I don't want to endanger him. Besides, he doesn't have a bulletproof vest. Hopefully there will be no need for his tracking skills. I already know my way thanks to our advance scouting.

My binoculars are trained toward Seward. At one point, my arms get tired from holding them to my eyes. It's easy to get distracted by the birds of prey that fly past the lenses. I follow an eagle to its nest high in a cedar, then get back to staring for planes.

It's over an hour before a pure white plane appears on the horizon, coming in low. I immediately call Dolly. She'll keep an eye on the coast just to be sure we shouldn't expect additional visitors. I call in to the FBI as I start jogging parallel to the plane's course, keeping my eyes on it at all times. I want to see where they land it even though I believe that Ryne's ultimate destination will be the caves. It's important to spot them entering, though—I don't want to spend time wandering through the wrong one.

Mensel is breaking up as he speaks. I'm guessing he's out in the field. I definitely hear the word *delayed*.

"Delayed? No. The plane is here now. I need them to be ready in Portlock."

"Close...by water. Air currents..."

"I'm losing you, sir. They're coming by water?"

"Yes."

"How long?"

"...be maybe twenty. You hold off?"

"I can't hold off, sir. I'm going after them. As soon as they land, tell them to get to the caves."

The call drops.

I hope he's not pissed at me, but there's no way I can leave Ryne in there alone. It's worth losing my position as a liaison to keep my promise to Dolly and Ryne that I'll be right there, as close as possible, waiting for Ryne to give the long whistle that signals it's time to get them out of there.

The plane lowers into what is presumably a clearing back behind the caves, as far as possible from the shoreline. I lose sight of it as it descends, but I know they'll approach from the bluff behind the town then, coming down it to enter the cave system at one of its many openings. I swing around so I can enter from the town side. We won't accidentally cross paths that way, and they'll have to cross my line of vision, so I can see where they enter. I sprint when I can, ignoring the underbrush that reaches out for my black ripstop pants. My hiking boot tangles occasionally, and I rip it free, temporarily carrying a trail of vines and dead foliage with me like a jellyfish trailing tentacles. I run through alternating shafts of white light and darkness, the shade cast by towering trees. My eyes don't have time to adjust as I go, so I slow and speed up again, covering the mile by the route Dolly and I identified as the fastest. When I arrive at the deserted trucks, I stop and train my eyes on the spot where the caves begin. I nearly immediately pick out Ryne and the pilot—the pilot is wearing a bright red windbreaker. Ryne is in a navy-blue tunic and black leggings. They are both standing at the top of the bluff. Ryne is scanning the town in front of them. I wonder if they're looking for me. They won't see me hidden behind a rusty pickup, but I'm sure they know I'm here. The pilot is casually scanning the horizon too. I'm surprised by how long they stand there—they're so obvious. I guess that's the confidence that comes with doing something highly illegal in a place that terrifies most people.

After a couple minutes, they head down a steep slope over the bluff. The pilot points to one of the cave entrances and I lose sight of Ryne as they enter, which makes my breath catch. It was inevitable that I'd lose visual on them temporarily, but it still fills me with panic for just a moment. The pilot stands at the cave entrance for another minute, scanning, then follows. I can't see a weapon on them, which is surprising. Of course, that doesn't mean it isn't there.

After the pilot has disappeared, I do a quick scan around me to make sure no one else has shown up. Silence. Nothing moves—not a single squirrel. I keep myself hidden as well as possible as I move toward the cave where Ryne vanished.

When I get to the cave mouth, I draw my weapon and peer inside. I can see the first several yards in. There's nothing there—just a thin stream of water trickling down a wall, forming a small pool that I'll need to avoid splashing in. Given how loud the dripping of the water is, I'm going to have to be extraordinarily silent. The echo is something serious. There's algae and slick moss covering some of the rocks. Otherwise, there's nothing extraordinary about the mouth of this cave, but I can also see that it narrows quickly. The darkness further on looks very complete, and I can't use a flashlight. I listen, and I hear what sounds like a low hum of muffled voices in the distance. At least they'll give me something to follow if the cave splits.

I keep my left hand on the rock wall, which alternates between smooth and slick, and jagged enough to cut my finger if I press down too hard. The stone is cool to the touch, and the temperature has dropped at least fifteen degrees from outside. It would be a fine place to explore on a hot summer day—if it wasn't full of criminals. Then again, I would probably never bother to come somewhere like this if it wasn't.

I can hear Ryne's voice, and that means I'm very close. I stop and look behind me, listening for the footfalls of the agents who are supposed to be out there, backing me up. I hear nothing. It's been twenty minutes, surely. *Are they down by the water?* I need to go back out to show them where I am, but Ryne is here, and I don't want to leave them. For a second, the decision of whether to go back out paralyzes me. I listen to the voices inside. Ryne is asking questions. The person answering sounds like a woman. *The Scientist?* The pilot seems to be saying nothing. Perhaps they're standing guard. There are no other voices. There are three of them, then. Two against two, but I have no intention of allowing Ryne to fight anyone if it comes to that. Still, I don't mind these odds, though it's hard to say how they're armed in there. What kind of equipment is in there with them is another big question. If this is where production of meth actually happens, there are seriously volatile chemicals in there, and we'll all need to be mindful of where we're shooting. I take a few deep breaths. Ryne's voice is calm and even, asking about who they would be working with on a daily basis and what their role would be. They're doing an amazing job sounding casual but excited about the prospect of making money.

The voice that answers is even, unhurried, seemingly unbothered. Ryne seems to be in no relative danger at the moment, so I make the quick trip back to the cave entrance, careful to go the right way at the one split I encountered on the way in and poke my head back out into the sunlight. I see no one, even down by the water. I check my satellite phone. Nothing. I can't risk stepping far enough away to make a phone call to Mensel. I listen for the sounds of boat motors, but there's nothing. I'm alone here except for Ryne, the pilot, this scientist, and whatever other of Mr. Drew's team occupies the rest of the cave system. As far as the forest and the birds and the abandoned town are concerned, I'm alone entirely.

I stay out there watching for my backup for as long as I dare, which is only a couple minutes. Then I'm back in the cave, navigating my way back toward Ryne's voice.

I can just start to make out their words when I get to the split. I'm hurrying as fast as I dare toward them when another voice, directly in my right ear, stops me dead in my tracks.

"Hello, Officer Linebach. Kind of you to join us." It's Mr. Drew.

CHAPTER TWENTY-NINE

My gun is still pointed straight ahead of me when he speaks, but as soon as I go to turn, I feel a cold barrel press against my temple.

"I think you should drop your weapon. Don't you?" I let the gun clang against the stone at my feet. There's another gun in my waistband next to the PLB, but it would be unwise to reach for it while Mr. Drew's full attention is on me. I slowly raise my hands and turn toward him.

"Hello again." I try to keep my voice as even as possible as I squint into the darkness. I can just make out the lines of his face—the cheekbones and distinct eyebrow ridge. The voices in the other direction—Ryne and the woman he was talking to—have stopped.

Mr. Drew raises his voice. "You can drop the act, my dear—she's arrived."

"Oh good. I was getting bored." I can't see the woman who has stepped behind me, but I can feel her presence.

"Hello, Ryne." I can hear Ryne's breathing behind me, hard and fast. "Thank you for luring Louisa to me. That was quite kind of you."

"Louisa, I didn't know." I can hear Ryne's breath catching as if they're trying hard not to cry.

"I know, Ryne. It's all right." I keep my eyes on Mr. Drew. I'm able to make out his eyes now—and that cocky smile. "Let Ryne go."

"We both know there's no chance of that. Thanks to your little expedition, Ryne knows far too much to let him go." At that, several men appear from behind Mr. Drew. Two of them push past me like I'm nothing and grab Ryne by the arms.

Where the fuck is my backup? They might be there right now, standing on the beach, looking around and wondering where the hell I am. My location beacon will be totally worthless in this cave—it needs clear sky for a signal. And I didn't think to leave a trail for them to follow. Son of a bitch. Why didn't I drop something—leave something out there for them to find? I slowly turn to look at Ryne, and glance at the entrance of the cave. I can see the opening, though anyone out there would have a hard time seeing me in the dark. They wouldn't see Mr. Drew or most of his men, but they would see Ryne and the two holding them. The woman is obscured by a cave wall, hidden in the dark.

"You know, I'm glad you're here, Louisa," Mr. Drew is saying, still uncomfortably close. His breath is hot against my face. It smells like coffee and maybe a trace of bourbon.

"Is that so?" *Keep him talking.* Mr. Drew is an egotist. *He'll want to revel in the fact that he's got you where he wants you.*

"Shame you couldn't bring your friend Harper with you. I guess he's too busy to assist an old pal."

Where is Mikey? He knew all about today. He'd said he was going to alert the Homer force but that he'd be here whether they were going to be involved or not. Why isn't he here?

"He's a busy guy. You know, there seems to be quite a drug problem in Seward these days." I keep my voice conversational. There's no chance I'm showing this asshole fear, though I'm absolutely feeling it. Less for myself, and more for Ryne. *Honestly.* I can't believe I let us walk into this. Hopefully Ryne will have a chance to forgive me, but it's not looking promising right now. Maybe I can cut a bargain to get them out of this. I think through how I can negotiate when I have no leverage.

"I've heard something about that." Mr. Drew forces a dry laugh that sounds like the crackling of brush fire. "And yet that problem doesn't seem to have gotten any better since Chief Harper took over. How interesting."

I'm sure he can't see me scowl in the dark, but I do it anyway.

"What is that supposed to mean?" If I can keep us talking, gradually increase the volume of my own voice, anyone looking for me might hear.

"Oh, come on. It's never struck you as odd that Chief Harper lives in Seward, runs the Seward Police Department, knows everything you know, yet he and I manage to peacefully coexist?"

It has struck me as odd. It's been five years that Mikey has been here, and I assumed he would have brought Mr. Drew in within a year or two. But Mikey said the missing men problem had gotten better. And I know for a fact that Mr. Drew has been mostly barricading himself in his house, so there'd be little to catch him at.

"Are you saying you've bought off the police chief?"

"Oh, bought off sounds so…*common*. Give us both a little credit, Louisa. Chief Harper knows what's good for his community. He doesn't need to resort to accepting cash to turn a blind eye."

He's making shit up to piss me off, because that's how Mr. Drew operates. He wants me confused and off my game.

"He knows you had Branden Halifax and Kyle Calderon killed. And how you did it."

"It's a great system, isn't it? They kill each other and I don't have to dirty my hands."

"Did you kill Lee Stanton?" I know he didn't, but I need him to keep talking until help gets here.

He sighs. "That was a real shame. He could have been such an asset. I suppose some people just aren't equipped for this line of work. So sadly, no. I never got the chance. He made his own decision."

"He made his own decision because he felt horrible about what you made him do."

"Oh, my dear"—I grit my teeth—"I don't *make* anyone do anything. I simply offer them an opportunity that will improve their lives. They have the choice of whether to take it or leave it."

These assholes always find a way to rationalize it. "You offered Ryne a choice too. Do they still get to make that choice? If you get me, Ryne is still valuable to you if you allow them to stay here and work with…your scientist." I turn slowly toward the woman I know is behind me. She stays absolutely silent, still hiding in the darkness. *Coward.*

"Trying to cut a bargain for your friend, I see. I'm sure you made his grandmother some promises about his safety. What would she think?"

I inhale audibly. Does he know where Dolly is right now? Is she in danger? I hear Ryne breathing just as hard as I am.

"You didn't answer the question," I snarl.

"That will be a discussion between me and my, as you called her, scientist. Ryne has betrayed our operation. That is not taken lightly, as you very well know. For now, I believe we've discussed everything we need to discuss." I see him nod in the dark, and two men step toward me. One secures my wrist, and as I watch, the other spreads plastic across the cave floor. Neat and tidy. Mr. Drew wouldn't want my blood giving away what happens here.

No, not yet. I have to buy more time. The FBI has to be out there. I say something I know will get his attention.

"Don't you want to know what happened to your guard?"

The outline of him goes still. "Ah. Frederick. I had my suspicions. Should I assume you somehow managed to kill him?"

That's certainly not a story I want to tell, but I can draw this out at least. And I have a name now for the man.

"I did. I've been watching you, you know. For weeks now. You have those nice cameras set up on the property, but you don't have enough of them at the airstrip. I watched Frederick for days. Every time he went behind that dumpster to smoke a cigarette, I took note. You might want to put a camera there, by the way." Mr. Drew chuckles. If he's upset by Frederick's death, it's impossible to tell. "I watched him check the security system, so I knew where everything was. But I took my chances so that I could work on your plane. Frederick came out and tried to pick a fight. Something about private property, which you and I both know is a lie."

"Well, it *is* private property. It's simply not mine." I can tell by the flash of white in the dark that he's grinning broadly. "And so?"

"So, your guy thought it was a great idea to tackle me. Now, granted, he was a big dude. What, ex-military?" Might as well learn as much as I can in case I get out of this and actually have a chance to find Frederick's family.

"Oh, nothing so dull. He was in fact the much more interesting of my guards. Gus is rather boring company, I'm afraid." He steps slightly forward while he speaks, revealing a bit more of his face. He's still far enough away that I couldn't reliably spit on him. "My lovely Frederick was a boxer. He was very well respected in his native Croatia on the underground circuit. Sadly, his fortunes in the US were not as great. I picked him up at seedy rink in Philadelphia." I wish I could punch him in the face for talking about the man like he was some sort of trash he plucked off the floor. "He was so desperate he was willing to throw fights for cash." He makes a *tsk tsk* sound with his mouth.

"And you swooped in and *saved* him, I suppose. Gave him the nice high life working for you in Alaska, hmm?" My tone is taunting. Mr. Drew likes an adversary, and as long as he's entertained, he'll go on all day.

"Why yes, I suppose I did. I'm a real Prince Charming, you know. Too bad you're not...of an orientation that allows you to see that." He grin stretches grotesquely back toward his ears. "He was undocumented, no family, no bank accounts. Just perfect for me. A man who can disappear with barely anyone noticing. And if someone did notice, they'd surely just assume he'd gotten himself killed, which makes him even better in my book. So, I hired him as my guard. I got him out of his shitty little apartment and made sure he was well taken care of. He made a fine salary." Mr. Drew doesn't say anything about what the man's actual life was like. That wouldn't matter to him.

"Why is it that you seem to think you can buy anyone you want at any time?" I squint at him in the darkness.

When he laughs this time, it's rich and deep—not the perfunctory chuckle he usually gives. "Because I can, of course! I learned a long time ago that people can be bought and sold just as easy as candy in a shop. I was bought myself, and I've been buying others ever since I managed to free myself."

"What do you mean you were bought yourself?"

"Ah, I don't like to belabor that story, it's so dull."

"Humor me. A girl should know her enemies, don't you think?" I say with as much sickening sweetness as I can muster.

"Ah yes, I suppose a sad little person like you would want a sad little story right before her end."

"So, indulge me." I may be buying time, but I am genuinely curious.

"Oh, the same old boring story. Grew up poor, yadda yadda, mother died when I was young, blah blah, father didn't know what to do with me, et cetera, sold me off to a life of servitude."

"Sold you! Like *literally* sold you?"

"Why yes! Don't sound so surprised. You used to work in Child Services, didn't you? You know about the trade in children, especially near the border."

"The Canadian border?" Unfortunately, there is a trade in children running over nearly every border this world has to offer.

He scoffs. "Mexico. I'm sure you already know I'm not a native of Alaska. This was in Texas."

"He sold you to a Mexican cartel?"

"Ah, there we go. She's getting her wits back about her." He turns to the men behind him, who smile as if required to do so.

"That's shitty."

"Oh, come now, there's no need to pretend to be sad for me. Besides, it led me to where I am today. I worked hard for them for years. I worked my way up until I was part of the cartel too. Made myself a name selling drugs, and then got into the trafficking business myself."

"Girls?"

"Oh no. I've never had much interest in that part of the trade. I was much more interested in recruiting young men, then selling them off to the cartels at a very nice profit."

"Jesus. After that had been done to you?"

He takes a step closer. *Come on, Mr. Drew.* Get close enough for me to draw my other gun and shoot. Even if the asshole behind me shoots me too, at least I'll die happy when you drop dead in front of me.

I'm sure I hear shuffling outside, but Ryne starts into a coughing fit. I hear them shout as one of their guards prompts them to stop with violence.

"I was offering those young men an opportunity. Sure, there would be a few years of not having free will, but they were coming from the worst possible backgrounds. Abusive families. Molestation. Child prostitution. They had nothing to lose. Once the cartels had them, they'd be moved all over the country. They could start whole new lives, move up in the organization. Become like me if they were savvy enough."

I raise my voice a notch to cover the sound of footsteps. "Oh yes, Lord knows the world needs more of you!"

There's a long, shrill whistle behind me, and then the entrance to the cave explodes in sound. There are dozens of shouts. Mr. Drew suddenly retreats from my view. The man gripping my arms shifts and the cold of the barrel leaves my head. When I turn, I see that he's pointing it at the mouth of the cave. When my eyes adjust, I see five figures silhouetted against the bright light and one rushing toward me.

"Drop it!" Mikey yells.

Tails leaves the ground, and he latches on to the arm of the man holding me.

CHAPTER THIRTY

My second gun is now pointed at the man who was just holding me, who is totally distracted by Tails. I don't even have to fight him to grab the gun out of his hand. I keep his own gun on him and switch the focus of my weapon to the men holding Ryne. As soon as I do, the men point their weapons back at Ryne.

A standoff.

I call Tails, and he releases his teeth. I resist setting him on the men with Ryne—I can't risk them accidentally or intentionally shooting them when Tails latches on to their gun arm. The dog sits tense at my side. The man whose arm he mangled retreats toward Mr. Drew, who doesn't acknowledge him.

Mikey steps forward, and so does Dolly. Both of them have guns pointed at the pair holding Ryne. Mr. Drew's voice betrays no emotion.

"Shoot the boy."

Shots are fired and Dolly screams, but it's not Ryne who falls to the ground. My shot hit one of the men holding them in the forehead, and before he's even down, the other guard is slumping forward with Mikey's bullet buried in his chest. Dolly springs forward and pulls Ryne with her toward the mouth of the cave. Shrapnel explodes near my ear and I'm temporarily deaf as the cave wall sends splinters of stone into my body. I duck back behind the wall of the tunnel that leads to where the Scientist was meeting with Ryne. I don't see her, though she has to be here somewhere. I'll need to risk it. I'm glad my vest is covering my back, though I'm anticipating the barrel of a gun at my head again any second now. The volley of gunfire quickly stops as bullets bounce chaotically off the cave walls. It's impossible for anyone to see where they're shooting between the dark and the smoke. When it dissipates, it looks as if one of Mr. Drew's men is clutching his shoulder, but he keeps his weapon pointed at Mikey.

"Get far clear, Dolly," I yell, unable to hear myself, but I don't need to tell her. She's already disappeared with her grandchild. As the smoke clears, three other figures step further into the cave, and I can see now that they're Mikey's officers. They're still evenly matched—two men now stand where Mr. Drew stood, though I know he's still there, hiding. The men covering him are both pilots—I can tell because their brunette heads are almost perfectly level with one another.

"Ah, Chief Harper, nice of you to join us."

"Mr. Drew." Mikey sounds cooler than I've ever heard him. "Have your men drop their weapons and come out so no one else will get hurt."

"Oh, I think not. Perhaps you should come in here with us."

"That's not happening."

"Well then, perhaps we can once again negotiate." *Once again?* "How about if you leave me Ms. Linebach, and your team can head back to Seward like nothing happened. I'll even forgive you killing my guards."

"No. This has gone on long enough, Randolph."

Mr. Drew sighs, his face and body just showing behind his two remaining men. When I study their faces, I see fear. They may have killed in the past, but they certainly don't look comfortable now.

"Then I suppose we'll both need to resign ourselves to losing some good men—and perhaps a woman too. Fire at will, my friends."

My gun is aimed at what I can see of Mr. Drew, but before I can fire, I'm being pulled backward by a force I cannot see. I'm suddenly on the ground with my gun pointed at the ceiling.

"Stay down!" a female voice barks above me.

There's heat. Intense, blinding, horrible heat. I feel it on the soles of my feet through the thick hiking boots. There's a burst of light— white, then orange, red then a rusty brown. The sound is so incredible I'm not sure I will ever hear again. Something heavy is on top of me. There's movement and confusion. I can't tell what's happening, but it's catastrophic—I sense that all around me.

A few seconds pass, or maybe it's minutes. The weight comes off me and I'm coughing, rolling onto my side. I'm covered in soot or dust. I can't see anything. As my hearing returns, there's screaming over a piercing ringing. The screaming sounds like it's coming from multiple sources.

"Come on." The voice sounds far away, but there's a hand on my arm, trying to pull me up off the ground. I don't know where my weapon is. I fumble for it, find it, and get to my feet. The hand is still gripping my arm, pulling me. My eyes start to focus, spots of bright light interrupting my field of vision. There are bodies littering the floor of the cave, and behind the place where Mr. Drew and his men stood, there's fire. As I'm pulled out into the sunlight, I can see two men writhing on the melted plastic underneath them, desperately trying to put themselves out.

I can't see Mikey. I can't see Mr. Drew. The sunlight is blinding.

"I need to…"

"No. Stay out here. There will be more explosions."

"What…" But she's already gone. I have to get back into the cave. Mikey is still in there.

I shake my head, wipe the dust out of my eyes, and check my weapon.

"Tails!" He's at my side, a patch of fur gone from his neck but otherwise moving and seemingly fine. "Stay!"

I go back into the cave. I can see more clearly, and it's a horror. The dying men are severely burned, their skin blistered and peeling off. Some of their faces look like melting candle wax. The smell is sickening. I cover my mouth. One of the men who was on fire lies lifeless on what was the plastic tarp. There are still screams—one of them is coming from ahead of me. There is a thick coating of dust covering everything, and large chunks of rock and what looks like glass litter the ground. I pick my way through it all, looking for the source of the screaming.

I find Mr. Drew further back in the cave than where I last saw him, lying flat on his back. He's burned horribly, but I would recognize Mr. Drew no matter what state he was in. He's still screaming as he looks up at me, his eyes wild.

"You fuckin'…" He utters slurred words from a mouth that's been torn open by shrapnel and glass. There's blood all around him and oozing from his head and chest. Mr. Drew tries to move his limbs like a swimmer. There's a gun close to him. I kick it away. Mr. Drew is going to die. There's no doubt in my mind about that. I could put him out of his misery, but he's not the man I'm looking for.

"Mikey?" I scream. A shout answers me from the opposite direction, close to where I was when the explosion happened.

I find him against the wall. The Scientist was lying on top of me, but Mikey must have been blown back by the blast. Part of the cave has come down and now has Mikey pinned to the ground. Light streams in from above us where there was no light before. His hair is singed—his eyebrows totally gone—but otherwise, the top half of his body looks relatively unharmed.

It's the bottom half—

I look away instinctively. The boulder that has him pinned is far more than I can possibly move. His legs are somewhere underneath it. His torso is covered in blood. I bend and try to lift the rock, but it's no use.

"We'll get you out of here, Mikey. I just need some—" I turn toward the cave entrance and scream. "Help! I need some help! The chief is down!"

There's movement around me. A man has risen from the cave floor and is crawling toward me. Several figures are rushing past him now.

"Get that side!" The Scientist is across from me. She's gripping the rock from underneath and yelling. "Ryne!" Then Ryne is at her side, working their fingers under the boulder near hers. Dolly appears suddenly near Mikey's head, waving smoke out of her eyes. It's still so hard to see—an orange haze lingers in the air.

"Dolly, when we lift, pull him free!" She nods at my instructions. The man who was crawling toward us has worked into a crouch next to me. He looks half-dead himself, but he grips a flat part of rock.

"On three!" I shout. "One…" I make sure my grip is solid, my legs ready to lift. "Two…" I take a deep breath in. "Three!" At once, we all lift. The side the officer and I are on comes up higher than the other, but it's enough. As soon as Dolly pulls Mikey clear, we let the boulder drop.

And that's when I finally get a look at my former partner.

From the hips down, his legs have been effectively obliterated.

CHAPTER THIRTY-ONE

Ryne screams as the FBI rushes into the cave.

"We need medical!"

Dolly is already on the phone.

The FBI agents swarm around me. Someone lifts Mikey into the air in a fireman's carry.

"Out of the cave. Now! Now! Now!" someone barks. I recognize the voice as Mensel. We're all rushed outside. Less than a minute later, a series of smaller explosions sound from inside. The fire has reached something volatile. Tails stands firmly by my side as if he's trying to protect me from the chaos surrounding us. I try to follow the man who lifted Mikey, but I lose them in the confusion. I turn to Dolly, who is staring straight ahead like she's entirely dazed. When I follow her glance, I see that she's staring at Ryne, who has their arms around the Scientist. She's hugging them back. They're both sobbing.

"Dolly?"

She opens her mouth, but she doesn't look at me.

She walks away from me, toward them.

"Jeannie?"

The Scientist unburies her face from Ryne's shoulder and looks at Dolly. She keeps one arm around Ryne but opens the other for her aunt, who crashes into her.

Her niece. I'm processing slowly. The Scientist is Dolly's niece, Jeannie. A million questions try to crowd into my mind, but I kick them all out.

Mikey. I need to go with Mikey.

I find him laid flat on the beach. There are several officers surrounding him. One of them is binding the remnants of his legs.

There are tourniquets pulled tight high up on his thighs. Mikey's calves and the entire area above both knees is a pulpy pink mash. There is bone poking through his left leg. His right leg is bound tight in gauze.

"How bad…" It's all I can get out before I'm silent. The agent… the medical personnel…working on him doesn't look at me as he responds.

"He needs amputation."

"There's no way to save them?" I know looking at him that there's no way he'll keep his legs, but I have to ask. The medical officer shakes his head. "Is he awake?"

"No. I drugged him. Medevac is on the way."

"Is he going to live?"

"If he can make it till they get here, maybe."

I crouch at Mikey's side. I take his hand in mine and speak to him even though I know he's far away.

"Stay with us, Mikey." I push what Mr. Drew said out of my head. If Mikey makes it, I'll have so many questions for him, but now, this is Mikey, my friend, and there's a very good chance that he's dying. Now is not the time to question his deeds or motives.

As I sit there holding my former partner's hand and talking to Mikey about all the reasons he needs to stick around, I see the teams carry the last of the bodies from the cave.

"Linebach, we need you." Mensel is at my side. "We need you to identify Mr. Drew."

"I'll be right back," I say to Mikey as I reluctantly let his hand go. Dolly appears at my side and picks his hand up just after I've dropped it.

"Go ahead," she says.

There are five men laid out on the beach, all of them badly burned, most with missing limbs and shrapnel embedded in their skin. One of them wears the uniform of an Alaska State Trooper. He was one of Mikey's team. I close my eyes briefly in acknowledgment of him. One of the men is unrecognizable. One I identify by the damage to his arm, inflicted by Tails. One is the man I killed before the explosion happened; I can tell by the bullet hole in his head. Given the condition of the bodies, perhaps I spared him.

That leaves only Mr. Drew. It's clear as soon as I reach him that he's dead. I wonder how long he hung in there after I left him. It's sickening, but part of me hopes he suffered for a little while at least. He certainly deserved to suffer. I let Mensel know that it's him.

"Dr. Anna Fenway is the medical examiner in Seward. Will they go to her?"

"Yes. She'll have the best chance of identifying them if they're all from Seward. Besides, we don't need the bodies. We just need to understand the extent of what was going on here."

"They were cooking meth in the caves here, Mr. Drew's team." I scan the crowd of uniforms and pick out the Scientist, crouched next to Dolly, who is still holding Mikey's hand.

"You'll want to talk to her. I believe she was the person running the operation here." Mensel turns swiftly toward me.

"Is there a reason you didn't arrest her?"

"She saved my life. And Mikey's. I don't know why, but I think she caused the explosion that killed Mr. Drew and his men."

"And one of Chief Harper's men and possibly Chief Harper."

"Yes. Like I said, you'll want to talk to her. I know about as much as you do at this point."

He nods and strides off to the Scientist—Jeannie—who slowly rises, placing a hand on Dolly's shoulder as if reassuring her. Then she puts her hands up, making clear to Mensel that she doesn't plan to resist or run.

"Is there anyone else in the caves?" Mensel yells his question to her.

"About two dozen people, but they won't try to fight if you let me call them out." Jeannie's voice sounds calm. There are at least six guns pointed at her, but she doesn't seem anxious. I watch in wonder as she calmly turns to each agent, spinning in a slow circle. "They respond to me. I'm their boss. If you'll come with me, there are three operational caves. I promise, you'll be safe."

It's clear no one trusts her, and why would they? Still, as I watch, she very slowly begins walking back from the beach and through the town. The agents follow her, with one going ahead to sweep each building before they pass it. When they draw near the first of the caves, I can no longer hear their conversation, but I see Jeannie go first, hands still in the air. The agents cover against the cave walls. I watch in wonder as slowly—very slowly—a line of men in burnt-orange jumpsuits emerge, hands in the air, eyes wide. There aren't enough handcuffs for all of them, but there's no fight, just as Jeannie promised.

Tomorrow I'll be anxious to get into a room with her while she's interrogated. But for now, men are filing out of the next cave, the medevac is landing on the beach, and I want to be there with Mikey.

CHAPTER THIRTY-TWO

Mikey's surgery lasts twenty-four hours. Every time the doctor emerges with an update, he's in a heightened state of agitation and increasingly sweaty around the temples. Trying to save the life of a police chief must add an extra layer of horrible stress. Either a death or a miraculous survival thanks to the hands of a talented surgeon will be a major news story on the Alaskan news networks. No one wants *Doctors were unable...* to lead that broadcast.

Sitting in the waiting room in those uncomfortable chairs, Mikey's mother tells me how she feels guilty, like it's her fault he went into law enforcement. She'd been an addict when Mikey was a little kid—a fact he never mentioned to me, though I knew a lot of his family was in the drug trade. She'd been in and out of rehab for years and missed a lot of Mikey's childhood. Her husband had been supportive of her recovery, but he couldn't keep her clean, and neither could her kids. Eventually, after years of work and a couple near-death encounters, she'd gotten herself off the drugs and turned her life around. But by the time she did, many of her children had gotten into bad habits themselves. Mikey had gone reactionary, but that decision, she is sure, was still the result of her actions.

Now look where law enforcement has gotten him.

Anna calls every couple hours to check in on both me and Mikey. Dolly calls every few hours to check in and to let me know that Tails is just fine. She and Ryne volunteered to watch him since he couldn't go in the medevac. They are currently in Seward at the police station with Jeannie. She's been arrested, of course, but no one is ready to question her. The FBI is still in Portlock, cataloguing every single thing in those caves. One officer is dead, Mikey is gravely injured, and the officer who helped me get Mikey out of there is being treated at the Seward hospital for burns and a couple broken bones.

When I call the Seward station, Valeria answers. She assures me she's holding down the fort.

"Are you sure? I know that it is a lot with the FBI there and Mikey gone. I'm sure one of the agents can step in to help if need be."

She laughs. "You know I'm a trained officer, right? More years of experience than anyone here."

I shake the fog around in my head. "Wait, what?"

"I went through the training decades ago. I worked the beat for years. I was good too. Real good. If I had stayed on track, I would have been chief when Willington left, no questions asked."

"So, what happened?" Maybe that's a rude question, but I'm too exhausted to think too much about it.

"I had my twins. I got divorced. For a while I thought, you know, *women can have it all*, right? But you know how consuming this work is. I was short-changing my kids, but I was also short-changing myself. I was exhausted. So, I asked Willington to put me on the desk nights. Before he left, he tried to convince me to go back to regular duty, but it didn't seem worth it. My kids were in school, and I loved being able to go to their after-school stuff, you know?"

I blink, trying to bring the hospital walls around me into focus, but it's hard because they're just white on white on white. There's nothing for my vision to grab hold of.

"Oh, I'm sorry. I didn't know."

"That's because I'm careful not to tell people. They'll just rope me back in."

"Like what's happening now?" I sigh and slump forward in the tiny blue waiting room seat. I'm so tired. The bruises I sustained in the cave are purple and black, and I can't turn without my ribs screaming, though I've been assured nothing is broken.

"Yeah, but that's different because it's an emergency." She sounds perfectly calm about it.

"Valeria, it might be a while. Mikey is…not in great condition."

"I know. That's okay. He's been a good boss, and Joe was a good colleague too. I'll help out as long as I'm needed."

"Thank you. If you need anything, though, please just say something." I finally manage to focus on the vending machine across the room. A package of peanut M&M's hangs preciously over the edge of the spiral device that holds the candy back. If I gave the glass a hard knock, maybe I could get myself a free late lunch.

"Well, now that you mention it, I've got a whole bunch of arrested men running around the station. Your people are going to question them, of course, but a lot of these guys they're bringing in now are Seward men. These are guys we all knew when they were kids, before they disappeared. They're family. What kind of deal can we cut with the FBI to get these guys released so they can go home?"

I lean my elbows on my knees and cradle my head with my free hand.

"That might be a tough sell. They were cooking drugs that killed people." I saw a lot of deaths from meth in Anchorage. So did Mikey. "But if they can give us information about who else was involved in the operation, maybe something can be worked out. Probation maybe. House arrest. Something like that."

"Some of them were just kids when they left."

"That's true. That will help make a case." Movement near the double doors catches my eye. The doctor is coming back out. "Tell you what. I'll talk with my FBI contact and see what we can do. There's an update on Mikey. I'll call you back soon."

The update is that Mikey is finally stable enough for short visits. His parents go in first, and they emerge after only twenty minutes, looking shaken. The nurse waves me back with a warning that I don't have long. He needs his rest.

When I get into the room, there's a whole series of tubes coming out of Mikey's arms. The sight makes me cringe. I'm terrified of needles, and I can't look at the PICC lines embedded in his hands and inner elbows. Mikey's head rolls to the side as he catches my movement. His eyes look glassy and unfocused. I wonder what they have him on. The pain must be terrible, not just from having his two biggest limbs removed, but from the burns. I imagine there are few types of pain worse.

"Mikey?" A dry croaking noise comes from his throat, like he's trying to speak. "Need some water?" He nods. There's a glass and a pitcher on his bedstand, so I pour him a glass. It takes him a minute to be able to grip it, but he gets it and raises it to his own lips. "No need to talk. I just wanted to check in and see with my own eyes that you're okay."

"My legs."

I glance at the empty space under the covers. "I know. I'm so sorry."

"What happened?"

"You don't remember?" I'm afraid to touch him, but I place a hand on the edge of the bed so that I'm close. He shakes his head, spills a little of the water. He glances at the cup as if he has to concentrate to hold it. When he's finished the water, I set it back down for him. The drugs must be strong. "You came to the cave. Dolly had followed me from the cabin. She brought Tails to track me down. She said she ran into you near the buildings, and you and your officers went with her to find me and Ryne. You came in and Mr. Drew was there. He'd been waiting for me. I still don't know how he knew."

"The guard."

"You're probably right. He probably knew I was around as soon as the guard went missing. But he was there, with his guys. And he would have killed me and Ryne, but you and your officers and Dolly showed up with Tails. You shot one of the men who was holding Ryne. Do you remember?"

He nods. "It's the last thing."

"Well, after that, Mr. Drew told his men to fire on us. But they never got a chance. Dolly's niece was behind me. She's the Scientist, Mikey. Dolly's niece who went missing was the Scientist." I can't see much of a reaction on his face; his muscles seem slack. "I think she must have thrown something, because there was an explosion right behind where Mr. Drew was. It killed all of his men, and..." I stop myself. He might not realize one of his officers is gone. Mikey catches the hesitation, though.

"Joe and Coop?"

Coop. That must be the man who helped us get Mikey out from under that rock.

"Coop is going to be okay. Couple broken bones and burns. He helped us get you out."

"Joe?" He tries to focus on my face, though his eyes keep closing in longer and longer blinks. Still, he must see what he needs to see. He sinks back into the pillow.

"I'm sorry. It was fast. I don't think he knew what hit him."

"Ryne?"

"Ryne is totally okay. Dolly got them out of there right after you and I killed the guys holding them."

"Dolly's niece..."

"I know. I'm still getting my head around that too. Dolly's niece was the Scientist."

Mikey blinks up at the ceiling, then closes his eyes. I think he's dozed off, and I think of the story I just recounted.

"I don't know why she killed Mr. Drew," I say aloud.

Mikey forces his eyes open. "Find out."

"I will. I'm going to head back to Seward and question her. I'll let you know exactly what she says." I start to retreat, but then step back toward the bed, a thought hitting me. "Unless you don't want me to. You're recovering. You've been through a ton. Valeria is covering the station, and a million FBI agents will be there with her as soon as they're finished in Portlock. Anna is IDing all the bodies. If you want to just rest and recover, you absolutely earned it. I'll come visit as much as I can, but I don't need to tell you about the investigation if you don't want to know."

"I do."

I nod. I figured he would say that. Hopefully it will also keep his mind occupied. I can't imagine how I'd feel knowing I had months lying in a hospital bed ahead of me. I make a mental note to bring him a big stack of those crime novels he loves next time I visit. Or maybe not crime novels. Maybe some cheesy romances. Or fantasy. Something light and happy. Or will that seem insensitive? I shake my head. I'll ask Anna's opinion. "Okay. Then I'll be back soon with news. I'll see if they'll let Tails visit."

"He's okay?"

"Missing some fur, like you, but he's all right."

Mikey slowly raises a hand to his shaved head. He reaches for his eyebrows, which are mostly gone. He makes a face.

"It'll grow back."

His face falls and he looks at the blankets. "That will at least."

I approach the bed and put my hand on his shoulder. He looks at me. There are tears forming in his eyes. Mikey sighs deeply. He looks so tired. I should go.

"I'll see you again soon, okay?"

He nods and closes his eyes. I shut the door behind me and nod to the nurse as I leave.

CHAPTER THIRTY-THREE

Valeria gives me the conference room. It looks like it's just me and Jeannie, but I know there's a whole team of agents watching, including Mensel, who will be ready to step in if he feels it's necessary. Jeannie looks oddly comfortable sitting there in the police station. She almost looks relaxed. It makes me wonder what her life has been like for the past decade.

Time to find out.

"Hello again." I'm interviewing her as an Alaska State Trooper with one colleague dead and two injured, one maimed for life. And I'm interviewing her as Special Liaison to the FBI who is the lead on the Mr. Drew investigation. In theory, Jeannie is a bad guy. She's been his lead chemist, creating incredibly dangerous drugs and allowing this whole operation to run for ten years. And yet she also killed Mr. Drew and saved my life, as well as Ryne's, Mikey's, and Joe's. I want to remind the agents watching us of that, since they weren't there.

"Before we start, I wanted to let you know that Chief Harper is going to survive. He's lost his legs, and it'll be a long recovery, but he will be okay. So, thank you for helping me get him out of that cave." She just nods and smiles. "I'm sure you know that I have a lot of questions for you." I smooth the top sheet of a fresh notepad.

"Am I going to go to prison?" She sounds merely curious when she asks it. She's not crying or shaking like most people in her situation. She's not angry. She looks perfectly serene.

"That's very likely. You were making drugs. You were fully aware that Mr. Drew was recruiting vulnerable young people to make and distribute them. You knew people were being murdered and dumped in Portlock."

She closes her eyes for a second. "I know. I was one of those young people."

"Why don't you start from there? How did you get involved?"

She pulls a plastic cup of water toward her, takes a sip. "How long do we have?"

"As long as we need."

"Oh, good."

❖

The story Jeannie tells flows with everything Ryne learned about how Mr. Drew and his recruiters operate. She was offered a lot of money—enough to keep her family more than comfortable. One hundred thousand dollars up front, and more every year. She has it stashed away in the cabin Mr. Drew set her up in. I make a note that Mensel will want to search the place. Mr. Drew promised her she'd be queen of the hive and that after ten or fifteen years, she could retire.

She brushes her dark hair off her round cheeks, leans back. She keeps eye contact with me while she talks—not like most people in her situation. It's hard to think of this woman as a villain, especially because the longer I look at her, the more I can see the resemblance to Dolly.

"The thing is, I was good at it. I knew within days what we were making. I knew it could kill people. I knew it ruined people's lives. But I was really good at the science, and I was a good leader. Morale was great. The guys were pretty happy, overall. And I thought..." She sighs. "At first, I thought Mr. Drew really respected me. He didn't seem misogynistic or racist at first. I didn't realize how awful he was until I realized how he was preying on people he thought didn't have other options."

"None of the men you worked with ever gave you trouble? Mr. Drew didn't?"

She thinks, shakes her head slowly. "Mr. Drew? No. I've never known him to be with a woman or talk about one, and he certainly never hit on me. The guys on the team—some of them would get restless. These were young men. They should have been dating. I knew they snuck off sometimes, but I didn't live with them, so I pretended I was oblivious. None of them were bold enough to try anything with me." She laughs. "I just tried to keep them happy in their work. Because I knew what would happen to them if they stopped working."

"Mr. Drew would have them killed."

She nods. "There were a couple…" She shakes her head, once again displacing the hair she keeps trying to push behind her ears.

"Go on." I pour myself some water and refill her cup.

"There were a couple who wanted to try to fight Mr. Drew. They realized too late what they'd gotten into, and they wanted to go back to their families and their towns. They started to argue about the work. One of them started showing up high and getting belligerent. He was a recovered addict, but he was so stressed out he started sampling the product."

"What did you do?"

"I sent him away with the cash he'd gotten up front."

"What do you mean you sent one of the men away?"

She repositions herself in the metal chair, which was meant to be uncomfortable. "More than one of them. I couldn't send them back home, of course. He'd just find them there. I told them to get as far away as they could go. Then I told Mr. Drew they'd died in lab accidents. Or, one of them, I told Mr. Drew he'd killed himself."

"And he never suspected?"

"I don't know. If he sent men after them, I'd never know. He could have snooped around, I guess, but I don't think he did. The men were gone. He didn't have to give them money anymore. None of them ever turned back up as far as I know, so what did he have to worry about? Hopefully, they just went off and started new lives. But who knows. He could have been paying attention all along and found them, killed them." She shakes her head slowly, as if picturing it.

"You never heard from any of them again?"

"No, but how would they get in touch? I didn't even have an address. It's just a little cabin in the woods. Most of the men lived in the caves around Portlock, so not exactly easy to give them a call or drop them an email, right?"

"Some of them lived in caves for years?"

"Yeah. It sounds worse than it was. I mean, it was bad. Obviously. But at a point, I think…you know how sailors can either fight like hell or just become a big family?" Not really, but I nod. "It was kind of like that. They'd fight initially, but once they'd been there long enough, it was like family. And they left the caves sometimes in the evening to hang out in the houses around Portlock. I understood. We all needed some fresh air. The only rule was they had to clean up after themselves."

That explains the tidying of the buildings and the trash disposal. I lean back in my seat. It's a lot to digest.

"Did you ever try to fight Mr. Drew about what you were doing?"

"I *did* fight him. He just didn't know it until the very end."

"Tell me." I lean my elbows on the table, temporarily forgetting about my notes. The whole thing is being recorded anyway.

"About a year ago, the team was getting really restless. The kids coming in were getting younger and younger. Some of them saw their family members coming in. They realized that Mr. Drew was targeting kids from the tribes, but also kids who were kind of outsiders. Loners. Kids with no parents. And it pissed them off. When he recruited us, it had at least felt…I don't know. I won't say *fair*. But we were getting ready to graduate. We were at least legally adults. We could make a choice. But then there were sixteen-year-olds coming in who were literally getting ready to go to foster care. That's just taking advantage."

"Yes, it is."

"So, I started feeling out the guys on my team, chatting with them. Listening to their conversations while we worked. And I realized it was time."

"For?"

"Time to make a plan. We wanted to get Mr. Drew, but he'd started going full reclusive. We never saw him anymore. I knew all of us together, we could kill him if I could get him to Portlock, but I didn't know how. Still, we started working on weapons. We had the advantage—we knew those caves so well. We had all those chemicals. We outnumbered him even with his guards and those pilots. The nice thing about him not visiting is that he never knew that we were planning a full-fledged revolt." She smiles to herself.

In a way, I wonder if it's a good memory, that camaraderie with her team, that shared mission. It's a bit like the FBI seems, and it's why I'd like to be part of it.

"It was a bomb you threw."

"Yeah. Homemade. The tunnel he was standing in has a lab in it too, so I knew if I could throw it far enough, it would set off other explosions. And that's what happened."

"You could have killed us all."

She nods. "I know. I'm sorry. And I'm especially sorry about the officer who was killed. But once Ryne was out, I figured it was worth the risk. He was going to kill Ryne, and he would have killed you and Dolly and Chief Harper's team too."

I nod. She's right.

"I still can't get over Ryne trying to catch Mr. Drew out. That kid's gotten bold." She grins, and I stifle a laugh. Clearly Ryne gets it honestly.

"How much did you already know when the pilot brought Ryne to you?"

She shakes her head, and her long black hair makes a sound like beach grass blowing in the wind.

"I knew someone was coming to meet me, but that's normal for the new recruits once Mr. Drew has vetted them and they've signed on. Mr. Drew showed up with a bunch of guys in the morning—now that was unusual. The last few newbies, he's had pilots bring them to meet me. He didn't join us. But this time, he showed up unannounced and told me to get the kid they were bringing talking, then they were going to ambush him. I had no idea why, or what he'd done. Or who it was. As you might imagine, I was distracted trying to figure out whether we were ready to take out Mr. Drew."

"You didn't know it was Ryne he was bringing?"

The way her eyes go wide, and she puts her hands flat on the table as she leans back makes it look like she's still somewhat in shock.

"I had no idea. As soon as I saw him, them, I had the pilot go out to guard the entrance so we could talk. Ryne was great. He," she pauses. "Sorry, I have to get used to the change. I knew Ryne as a boy." She sighs, finally looking regretful. "That's what I get for leaving, I guess. I don't know my own family." I give her a moment, and she gets herself composed again. "Ryne didn't let on that we had any connection to each other until the pilot was gone. Though once I thought about it, I wonder if maybe Mr. Drew knew Ryne and I were connected. Maybe that's why he recruited them."

I'd been wondering the same thing. If Mr. Drew was making such an effort to identify potential recruits, how could he have missed the fact that Jeannie and Ryne were related? Did he recruit Ryne thinking it would keep Jeannie around? It's likely I'll never know, unless I can get the other pilots talking.

"Did Ryne tell you about me?"

"Yeah. Right away. Ryne told me you were staying in the park because you were investigating the pilots that were showing up in Nanwalek, and their connection to Mr. Drew. I told Ryne I was planning to go after Mr. Drew too, and that's when we realized we were on the same side."

CHAPTER THIRTY-FOUR

She'd disappeared into the tunnel and grabbed the bomb as soon as she realized Mr. Drew would kill Ryne. She'd wanted to wait until her team was assembled and could attack Mr. Drew together, but that's not how it happened. She'd had to make up her mind to do it alone. Mr. Drew was so distracted by me that he never even noticed.

I can't tell her before I leave that I'm going to try to convince the FBI to cut her a deal—she can identify nearly every single person in Mr. Drew's operation. If she'll do so, they might be willing to keep her out of prison, though she'll forever be on their radar. I do, however, ask her to write down the names of the men she sent away and anything she can think of that might indicate where they went. She doesn't hesitate or stop to think at all. These men are clearly on her mind often. When she's written everything she can remember, I glance at the list. A name strikes me immediately. *Marty Gussido*. I met his parents five years ago when they came to see if one of the bodies found was his. It seems they will have to wait a bit longer to learn where he is. I take the list and slip it into my bag. I'll try to track down these men as soon as I can. I'll let them know they can come home, though they won't be able to avoid questioning.

I don't realize how long Jeannie and I talk until I emerge into the lobby of the police station. There's a warm, amber-colored light seeping through the windows, cast by the late-setting sun. Yet despite the fact this should be a quiet part of the evening in the station, I'm surrounded by people, all seemingly talking at the same time. Mensel and several other agents stood there and watched the entire interview. But it's not their energy that permeates the room. When I step into the main lobby, there are dozens more people there. The building is packed. We're surely violating the fire code. The air is charged, and the excitement is contagious, even though I don't know what's going on.

The crowd is overwhelming, but as I start to adjust and see individual people, I realize some of them are familiar. There's a journalist I've met before from the Seward paper, as well as his cameraman. There's Mr. Stanley Gussido, a veteran in a wheelchair who has grown a long beard since last I saw him. I'll need to go talk with him. At least I can tell him that Marty's been seen alive recently, even if we don't know where he is, and even if he's likely back to using. I scan the room and see his wife, Lena, deep in conversation with another pair. Several of the others in the crowd I remember from that same time. They'd told me the stories of their loved ones' disappearances. Some of them had even given me photos.

I fight through the warm bodies to Valeria, who stands near the front desk and tries to hold three conversations at once. I add a conversation to her plate.

"Valeria, are these all the families?"

"That's right. As the men from the mines came in, they all gave me their names and the names of their families. I looked them all up and called." She looks at me like she's daring me to challenge her. "Don't worry. I got your FBI guy's permission. Not that I should need to." I wasn't going to challenge her. I would have done the same thing. These families have been worried sick.

"The Gussidos are here, but their son left the mines."

"Yeah, one of the men mentioned that Marty had been there. I told the parents he hadn't been recovered, but they wanted to come anyway. Friends of theirs have kids who were."

"Are the men even here?"

"Oh, yeah. Your people have got them in every room we could spare, questioning them. Who knows how long that will take." They must have all filtered past the room where I was interviewing Jeannie.

"They haven't said when the families will be able to see them?"

She shakes her head. "But I don't think they're going anywhere anytime soon. If they don't hurry up, I'm thinking about pulling out some army cots."

"I'll check in and see what we're looking at." Before I head back down the hallway, I return to Stanley Gussido. He puts his hand on my arm and thanks me for what I've done. When I explain what Jeannie told me about sending Marty away, he gives a faint smile.

"It's more than we've heard in years, and it's something to cling to."

I pull out the notes Jeannie made about the men she sent away. Next to Marty's name she's written that they'd talked about Hawaii.

"He was obsessed with Hawaii, even as a kid. Always wanted to see it. That's a start, and Lena and I will go out there if we need to."

"Well, hopefully it won't come to that. I'm going to do everything in my power to track him down. It might take a while—I'm sure he's changed his name—but we'll find him. I'll be in touch soon, okay?"

Stanley nods as Lena returns to him, looking at me inquisitively. I wish I could stay and repeat what I've said to her, but there's so much to do right now.

I turn down the hall, passing the room where I left Jeannie, who is now talking with another FBI agent. I pop my head in to ask the agent where Mensel is.

"In the break room," she says.

When he sees me, Mensel inclines his head in the way he does when he approves of something or someone. "Linebach. Yes, come in. We're almost finished here."

"Yes, sir. Sir, can I have just a moment?"

He nods and motions with his hand to a young agent who looks unsure of where to go. The agent stands still while Mensel follows me to the other end of the room.

"Sir, were you aware that their families are here?"

"Linebach, I've been aware of nothing for the past"—he looks at his watch—"seven hours. The agents"—he nods toward the one who is pretending not to listen—"have interrogated every single man. Twenty-seven of them came out of those mines."

"Any trouble, sir?"

"Oddly, no. Your scientist demanded their full cooperation. Seems they listen to her."

"Sir, I'm not sure what procedure normally is. They haven't been formally charged, have they?"

"No. We'll need to regroup and consider what we want to do."

"In that case, sir, will it be possible for them to see their families? Some of the people out there thought these men were dead. You can imagine how they're feeling."

He looks thoughtful for a moment, then nods slowly. "Hmm. I suppose so. We can release them to their families, but they all need to understand that they will be charged, and if they disappear, there'll be hell to pay if we have to go tracking them down. Make sure we've got addresses and phone numbers for where every single one of them is going. And no one goes out of state. Pat them all down before they go. Anything they had with them in those mines stays with us, and nobody leaves with a firearm. Got it?"

I stand straighter but remind myself that I'm not a soldier and he's not my drill sergeant. "Yes, sir." I start for the door, then turn around.

"And Jeannie, sir?"

"She stays in Seward." My face must betray my secret wish for her to be able to go home to Dolly and Ryne. "I'll arrange a hotel for her and her family. It will be helpful to have Dolly and Ryne here too."

"Excellent, sir. May I suggest Mr. Land's cabins? They offer a bit of privacy, but they'll still be readily accessible to your team." He nods. "The press is here too. Are we giving any statements?"

"You may do so, Linebach, but as a trooper. The FBI will be giving no statements."

Oh, how I wish Mikey was here. I'd happily pass media relations duty on to him. Mikey has no qualms about talking to people without advance preparation. I hate it.

It eases my nerves a little when I go back into the lobby and spot Anna's wavy auburn bob. As I approach, I reach out and lightly touch her arm. She turns to me with a grin.

"The families!" she exclaims, and I nod.

"The families," I confirm.

"This is wonderful."

It really is. It's so wonderful that I intentionally put aside the thought of the other families we'll need to contact as soon as Anna has identified the parts of the missing men still in the morgue. If she's even able to.

"Oh, I wish Mikey was here to see this!"

I smile at her. I wish he was too. The thought occurs to me to record the reunion just in time. As I pull my phone out, the door to the back hallway opens, and Valeria steps out. The FBI officers are nowhere to be seen. I'm guessing they've left out the back entrance, whether because they don't want to deal with the families or because they want this to be a happy reunion, I don't know. It's likely they don't want to be peppered with questions. For once, I'm glad I'm not joining them. In the moment, this is where I want to be. I hold up my phone, trying to be as discreet as possible.

"All right, everyone. Thank you for waiting so patiently." Valeria stops for a minute. The room is stone silent. "We're letting them out now." There's a collective murmur of excitement. "Just make sure…" She repeats louder as the families begin to shuffle around. "Make sure that before you leave, I have your name and your contact info." There's another loud rush of murmurs, and more shifting of feet.

The first of the men has appeared behind Valeria. He's so young—a teenager—and he's grinning out at the crowd like an absolute fool. A sobbing woman is pushing forward.

"And no leaving the—"

"That's my—"

The boy rushes toward her, and they fall into each other, hugging. *My son*, I mentally finish for her.

"No leaving the state," Valeria says.

But it's hopeless. The other men are pouring out of the door now, the families shifting away from me and Anna like a tide ready to break on the sand. As each new head appears in the doorway, it's swept out to sea, lost in a crowd of arms and sobs and exclamations. There's the dull roar of reunion noises like the crashing of waves, and before long, the room seems like nothing but salt—a sea of joyful tears.

I stop recording and send the video to Mikey's mom with a note.

Please share this with him. He'll want to know some of our missing men found their way home.

CHAPTER THIRTY-FIVE

Anna certainly has her work cut out for her. When I visit her the next day with Dolly, most of the body parts found in Portlock still haven't been identified. That certainly hasn't darkened her mood, though. We're both still feeling good after yesterday's reunions. The FBI is surely checking in on all the men, but I'm guessing it hardly matters. They all have a lot of catching up to do, and hopefully they're enjoying this time with their families. I haven't spoken to Senior Special Agent Mensel yet about what happens with the money that was recovered from safes in Portlock. It just seems secondary now that the men are home.

Anna is wearing a long white lab coat over a pair of gray slacks, her tortoiseshell glasses sliding slowly down her nose as she bends over one of the bodies she's partially reassembled.

"I'm afraid the other arm and the feet are still somewhere at sea, and if that's the case, we don't have much hope of recovering them. The mud offered a little protection from sea life, but out there...Well, you know how those bodies end up looking."

Dolly nods. The body at which she's staring is the young man from Nanwalek. He, at least, has a known identity.

"Does his family know, Dolly?"

"Not yet. Anna, do you think there's any chance we'll find heads to go with these bodies?"

Anna gazes at the body too as she sighs. "I'm afraid it's unlikely. In all these pieces there were none. There's feet and hands and legs and torsos, but no skulls. I'm guessing they were very careful to dispose of them. After all, a head is the easiest way to identify a body. Especially if the teeth are intact."

"You think they dumped them in the water, weighted down maybe?"

"Who knows. I suspect our best option is to question the hell out of those pilots, since they were the ones doing the killing. Louisa, did Jeannie and the men in Portlock tell you who was disposing of the bodies?"

"Yes. All of them said, in separate interviews, that the pilots were flying in bodies that they had killed elsewhere. The people in Portlock knew it was happening, but they tried to stay out of it. Get this, though…" I fumble in my bag and pull out my notebook, where I had Jeannie make a sketch. Dolly comes around to my left side, and Anna presses into my right trying to get a good look.

"Oh. That's the tool that made those gashes." She touches the paper as if it might yield more solutions if she can absorb them through her skin.

"Exactly. She said one of the pilots asked her to make several of these."

"So, there was one for each pilot. I knew it!" Anna, as usual, sounds oddly excited about her work.

Dolly turns to Anna. "Jeannie told me that the pilots wanted to cut the bodies because everyone thinks Portlock has a monster and they thought it would be…I don't know. Funny or something."

Dolly and I have already talked about this. I nod. "And it had the bonus of making any accidental finding of bodies extra gruesome. No one finding a body with those gashes on it was going to stick around Portlock to learn more."

"Unless they're us!" Anna exclaims. Fair.

"So, the pilots were killing their own, taking the dead bodies to Portlock, cutting them up, making these gashes either before or after the limbs were severed to scare people, and then dumping them in the water."

"Sounds like a good summary. I'm guessing your people aren't going to be as willing to cut a deal with the pilots," Dolly says.

She's right. What the chemists were doing was wrong on a lot of levels, but they weren't involved in any first-degree murder, or in the desecration of bodies. What the pilots did was just sinister. I shake my head, struck by the contrast between the fact that these men were recruited to the lowest-level job in the operation—deliveries—and yet somehow, they also ended up performing the most grisly and highly punishable task for Mr. Drew. All while he kept his hands relatively clean.

What Mr. Drew said about Mikey comes back to me unbidden. *Make* another *deal*. He had said it only to throw me, of course. But why? Surely to give me that brief moment of questioning, because a moment was all he would have needed. I try to distract myself by turning back to Anna.

"The Seward office and the FBI are already identifying and bringing in the pilots. I can't imagine it will be long before I can question them. We'll find out who these men are. We just have to hang tight."

Dolly lightly touches the arm of the young man who grew up with her children. "These aren't all of them, are they?"

Anna snakes an arm around Dolly's shoulder. "There are five confirmed here, but there could be more, you're right."

"The FBI did a thorough search of Portlock?"

"They did. They even searched the waters around it. If there was anything else to find there, they would have. But we all know how it goes when bodies get out into the water."

Those who were killed long ago will likely never be recovered.

Dolly looks at the floor, then nods. I watch her closely as a range of facial expressions play across her face in such rapid succession that it's like someone is projecting movie stills of other people's faces onto her at fast speeds. I can't imagine her feelings toward Jeannie right now. Then I remind myself that, as Dolly's friend, I can just ask.

"Dolly, how are you doing with all this? It's a lot."

Dolly reaches up to grab Anna's hand. "I'm not even sure, honestly. It's kind of a shock. Having Jeannie back…well, of course I'm so happy. And Ryne is safe, and so brave. But what Jeannie was doing. The reasons she was doing it." She shakes her head quickly as if there's too much in there and she needs to clear it out. She pauses for a long time. Her face settles back into a look of peace. "It will take our family a long time, but we'll be okay. Jeannie is back, so we'll be okay." She looks at me. "But if she goes to jail…I don't know if I can lose her again, mad as I am with her."

"I know, Dolly. She gave us the names of the men she sent away from the mines, and that helps. The fact that she sent them away like she did to prevent them from being killed helps too. She was doing some awful things, but she was also trying hard to protect people she thought were innocent. The FBI has a lot to consider, but they will look at all that carefully."

"Does it come down to whether she was trying to be a good person, or whether she can help?"

Dolly's tone sounds harsh, but I know she's just feeling defensive of Jeannie. I raise my eyebrows. I do appreciate Dolly's candor. I am just as honest with her.

"Probably the latter. And Jeannie can be a big help. She knows more than anyone about what Mr. Drew was doing. With the exception maybe of the guard I killed: Frederick. She's an asset, and if she…" I think carefully about my wording, trusting that Dolly will read between the lines. "If the FBI thinks the only way to get all the information they want is to make a deal to keep her out of jail, they may well make that deal."

Dolly gives me a single nod.

"How is Ryne doing?"

Dolly assures me that Ryne may be faring better than anyone, given the situation. They are apparently really enjoying having Tails around too. I've missed my dog while I'm spending all my time at the station. I'm hoping to pick him up before I head back to Anchorage to see how Mikey is progressing in his recovery.

Dolly, Anna, and I all say nothing for a while, just standing close to one another. The quiet of the moment is a relief. The station has been an overcrowded, overstimulating buzz ever since we got back from Portlock. I'm guessing Anna has been just as overwhelmed trying to put together these unidentified bodies, and Dolly has been through the Class IV rapids of emotional rides. It's nice to just stand here together, all understanding one another and how our roles in this fit together. Even if we are hanging out in a morgue.

Dolly finally breaks the silence. "Afraid I can't help more, Anna. I don't recognize anything from any of these other bodies, and I should get back to Ryne, and Jeannie if they've released her from the station for the day."

"That's all right, Dolly. Thanks for trying." Anna gives her a long hug. I'm slightly surprised when Dolly turns to me for one too.

"Tell Ryne to give that dog a long belly scratch for me."

"I just have to watch they don't give that dog half their dinner."

I laugh. Tails is a bottomless pit. Speaking of food, as Dolly sees herself out, my stomach growls and Anna laughs.

"Is that a sign that we need a late dinner?"

"Oh, geez you heard that?" I place my hands on my stomach, embarrassed. "I was just trying to remember the last time I ate." We both turn to the clock on the wall.

"Well, hooray for tourist season—some of the restaurants on the water will still be open." She studies me for several moments. "Unless you don't feel like dealing with a bunch of people. I'm pretty sure I've got the makings for tacos at home."

I fall against her side in a fake swoon. "You sure know how to talk to a lady."

She laughs those sweet windchimes again.

"Tacos it is." She cleans up quickly, then puts her hand on my lower back and steers me toward the door, locking up behind us.

CHAPTER THIRTY-SIX

It's impossible not to smile stepping into Anna's pale-yellow cottage on the quiet block. The cabin in Kenai was nice enough, and the hunting lodge near Portlock was great despite the lack of electricity, but it's hard to imagine anywhere more warm and inviting than Anna's home in Seward with its dark woodwork, cozy rooms, and pocket doors. As soon as I've removed my boots and she's pulled off her black pumps, she puts her hands on my shoulders and points me toward the living room.

"You go sit."

"Are you sure? I'm happy to help."

"No, no. You're exhausted, and dinner'll be ready in a jiff." She goes to a small curio in the corner and pulls out a stack of records, setting them on the coffee table. Then she produces a small olive-green record player from underneath. "Pick a record. Any record."

She floats into the kitchen, her steps so light the hems of her gray trousers barely touch the ground. I spread the records out before me, taking my time in getting more of a feel for Anna's musical taste.

Astrud Gilberto. Tori Amos. Mazzy Star. Portishead. I chuckle lightly when I encounter Jewel. I'm tempted by Tori, but I end up putting on Billie Holiday after carefully reviewing her impressive collection of classic jazz. This is where our tastes really overlap. She might not have any 90s grunge, but she has Louis and Ella.

I lean back into the sofa, head against the plush back, and let Billie's expressive voice flow over me. Even from decades away, she seems to know exactly how I'm feeling. Like I'm groping in a dark room, but there's a light not far away, and it's bringing the edges of everything into view so I won't stumble. I train my eyes on the ceiling, where a small chandelier casts flickers of light around the space. My eyes are open and I'm awake, but I guess Billie lulls me into some sort of trance, because I startle when Anna enters the room to clear the coffee table, replacing the stack of records with a plate of warm flour tortillas.

"Excellent choice." She hums along with one of the more upbeat songs as she brings in bowls of shredded cheese and chopped tomatoes, beans and shredded chicken speckled with spices. Anna settles next to me, hands me a plate, and grins.

"Sorry, but I only offer the table for *first* at-home dinners. After that, it's sofa or bust." She slaps a tortilla onto her plate, draws parallel lines of guac and hot sauce down its center, and then proceeds to load it up.

I laugh as I plop a blob of sour cream onto my tortilla, with guac and hot sauce directly on top of it. There's already barely enough room for the meat and beans.

"Don't worry. I don't even have an actual dining table. I've got a little rectangle that folds down from the wall and one chair, and that little rectangle is perpetually covered in paperwork."

"Are you still in the apartment you told me about last time?"

I nod. "I keep saying I'm going to find a house."

She tilts her head to the side in an accidental impression of Tails. "Keep saying—but why haven't you done it yet, do you think?" She doesn't sound judgmental—just genuinely curious.

"You can't ask a big question when I've got a mouth full of shredded cheese!" I say once I have slightly less than a mouthful of shredded cheese.

"Oh, sorry. Former waitress. That's a built-in skill."

"I should have known." I can absolutely see Anna as a waitress in a nice restaurant like the Bake, raking in loads of tips. Her sunny personality would be perfect. It's a rare woman who can take care of people on a nice date and then take care of their bodies when they die in a horrible accident—but that's Anna.

Once I've downed another bite of taco, I attempt to answer her.

"I'm not sure there's a real reason per se. I know Anchorage well enough now that I know which neighborhoods I'd like to live in. And my income is stable enough. Tails and I could certainly use the space, that's for sure. It's just…there's this sort of lurking feeling in the back of my head that Anchorage isn't where I'm going to be long term."

She laughs. "You make it sound like you don't have a choice in the matter. Is Anchorage where you *want* to be long term?"

I smile sheepishly. She sure got to that very quickly. "No. No, I guess it's not."

"So, where *do* you want to be?"

"Honestly? I'd love to be around here, in Seward. Or maybe even somewhere like where Dolly lives, in Nanwalek. When we were staying at the hunting lodge, even though it was just for a couple days, or the cabin…I don't know. I hadn't realized how much I'd love that."

"You grew up in the city, right? In Seattle?"

"Yeah. But the woman I've told you about who raised me—Anneke—she had a farm way outside the city, and that was my favorite place to be."

"Interesting!" Anna pulls another tortilla onto her plate and commences to load it. "So, tell me what a Louisa dream home looks like."

"Oh, geez. I don't really even know. Does that make me not a true adult?"

"I think you're all right. Besides, you're going to tell me about it now!"

"Oh, okay then." I laugh and try to imagine my dream home. The first thing to spring to mind is the home I'm in, but I certainly won't say that. "I've never been super-imaginative, so creating places just in my mind isn't something I usually do. But let's see. It would be surrounded by a lot of trees. No neighbors close by."

"So, Alaska still, huh?" She laughs.

"Oh, definitely."

"Near the water? On top of a mountain? Do I need sled dogs to get to it?"

"Nah. Tails wouldn't like pulling a sled. Near water would be nice, but I'm not picky about whether it's the beach or a lake or a river. Close enough to town that I could get take-out."

"All right, I'm getting the picture. And how big is this house?"

I look around at Anna's home. "About the size of this one, I guess. I could probably go a little smaller. Hell, I'm used to tiny now."

"Dream big! Or dream thirteen hundred square feet, I guess." She laughs. "That's what this one is." I make a mental note of that in case I ever do start looking.

I'm slowly starting to get a picture in my mind. It's some combination of Anna's house and the hunting lodge. "A log cabin maybe. Something that looks like summer camp."

"But without the plaid curtains, right?"

I make a face at her. "What's wrong with plaid curtains?"

She winks. "Okay, lumberjack."

I push my lower lip into a pout. "Look, I'm not exactly an interior designer. How about I get the log cabin and I turn over decorating duties to you." Once it's out of my mouth, I wonder if the implications of that are a little too much. No walking it back now.

Anna just raises her eyebrows. "Deal! So, a small log cabin in the woods near some water, not too far from town. That kind of thing exists near Seward, you know."

I nod. *I know.*

"Lots of property?" Anna adds hot sauce to her taco.

"As long as I don't have to mow it."

She throws her head back and laughs.

"That's my least favorite chore too. So, lots of acreage so no one can build next to you, but all wooded so no mowing. And lots of space for Tails to run around."

"Perfect!"

She polishes off the second taco. We listen to the strains of the haunting last song on the album, then Anna gets up and puts on another. The cheerful opening of "The Girl from Ipanema" plays, then Astrud Gilberto's voice begins to flow over it, light as linen and smooth as fine rum. Anna leans back into the sofa, watching me make another taco. As if that's renewed her appetite, she picks her plate back up.

"You've been in Anchorage over five years. Think Quint would let you put in for a transfer?" She frowns. "Or…what about the FBI? They're based in Anchorage."

I nod. "I've thought about that too. They are based in Anchorage, but of course they handle cases all over the state, so agents are out and about all the time. I don't know the agency well enough to know if they have people living outside the city."

"Couldn't hurt to ask, right? It seems like it would be a good thing to have agents local to different towns. As you and Dolly have proven, a close connection to other organizations around Alaska can be a great thing. And if they'd get it together and work more closely with the tribes, that would be even better."

"That's true. And even with all the people we found in Portlock, it doesn't answer the question of what's happening to all those Native Alaskan women."

"Exactly. That puzzle requires all hands on deck."

"I wonder if all the tribes would want the FBI involved."

She jumps up and heads back to the kitchen, speaking over her shoulder.

"That's a big question." She returns with two Mexican beers, hands one to me. The bottle is nice and cold in my hand. "But that's why it's important to have agents living in different places, making those connections, and building trust. Or at least trying. They need to make the effort. If the tribes choose not to play, that's up to them and I wouldn't blame them for declining. But as far as I see it, it's up to the FBI to make that first effort. Especially since so many of the local police departments won't. Or can't, if they're on the reservation."

Mikey and the Seward department spring to mind. And as soon as I think of Mikey, I think of what Mr. Drew said about them striking some sort of deal. When Anna asks what I'm thinking, I know I must have been scowling.

I wonder if I should talk to Anna about this. She and Mikey have been living in the same town for five years now. They've gotten close. Does she know something about what Mr. Drew referenced? If she does, will she tell me? And if she does, will I still be able to trust her? I start to overprocess these questions, but I stop myself. My instinct is to talk to Anna about it, and my gut tends to lead me in the right direction—if I don't let my brain nullify its recommendations.

"Anna, when we were in that cave, before Jeannie threw the bomb and killed Mr. Drew, he said…he said something to Mikey. He asked if he and Mikey could reach *another deal.* Like they'd already had one. Do you have any idea what he was talking about?" I rush my speech, trying to clarify when there's a good chance I don't need to. "I'm not saying he was telling the truth. I know he was a liar. He was likely saying it to throw me off my game. Maybe he didn't mean—"

"Louisa, I think there may be something to what he said." It's the first time she's cut me off, albeit gently. She leans close to me and puts a hand on my forearm. I put my plate down on the coffee table and look her in the eyes.

"You think Mr. Drew and Mikey had a deal? A deal to what?"

She shakes her red waves.

"I don't know exactly, and I'm just saying this based on my feelings and what I've observed. But I've kind of wondered, since Mikey became chief, if maybe there was something going on."

I don't have to look at the fitness tracker on my wrist to know my heart is racing. "Like what?"

She scowls so hard the skin between her eyebrows puckers. "Like

I said, it's just a feeling, and I never saw or heard anything definite. But I know that right after Mikey got here, he went to meet with Mr. Drew. He told me he was going to end everything. He had lots to say about how he was going to put a stop to what Mr. Drew was doing. You know how new folks in charge are—totally ambitious. Sometimes kind of naïve."

"Did he tell you what happened in the meeting?"

"That's the thing. After it happened, he got really cagey about it. He told me they'd met at Mr. Drew's, that they'd had a long conversation. He said we wouldn't need to worry about Mr. Drew. But he wouldn't give any details about what was said. And the thing is, the drug running didn't really change."

"Mikey said fewer men went missing."

"From Seward. Fewer men went missing *from Seward*." She holds my gaze.

"Oh no…"

"I work with the other MEs a lot, and we talk, of course. I started hearing about more and more men going missing in other towns. Even Whittier lost one. When I asked Fritz about it, you'll never guess how he described their missing man."

"Shit."

"Yup. Five-ten. White. Early twenties. Brown hair…"

"Brown eyes," I add. She nods. "No obvious distinguishing characteristics."

"Exactly. So, I started asking around. I talked to the ME in Fairbanks, the one in Homer, Juneau…and I was right. The missing persons cases had gone down here—and increased everywhere else."

"Does Mikey know this?"

She takes a long sip of her beer. Her normally happy gaze is now turned downward and somehow clouded over. "He does. Because I told him."

I let out a long whistle. "How did that conversation go?"

"Frustratingly. I told him I'd talked to the other MEs, and about what I'd learned. I thought he'd be really concerned. I mean, that *should* concern him. And he listened attentively and all, like Mikey always does. He told me he'd look into it. And then, nothing."

"Nothing?"

"Not a word. It was like the conversation had never happened."

"Did you follow up with him?"

She sets her plate down, her taco half finished, tomatoes spilling all over the plate. "I had this feeling. It's irrational, but I had this feeling that he was ignoring me on purpose. He even stopped calling me for our weekly lunch. So, I went to Valeria instead. I asked her if she had any news on the missing men Mikey was supposed to be looking into."

"And she said?"

"She had no idea what I was talking about."

I worry my bottom lip, biting lightly down on it, then releasing it over and again. I'm ruining what's left of the raisin-colored lipstick I put on for the occasion.

"Well, it's possible that he didn't tell anyone else because he wanted to investigate privately."

"Oh, definitely a possibility. But I was the one who raised it. Why wouldn't he talk to me?"

That I can't answer.

"And he never brought it back up again?"

"Never. But when you say what Mr. Drew mentioned…Well, I'm not saying one way or the other because I don't know. I'm just saying it…*feels* like it makes sense."

I cover her right hand with my left. Her eyes look worried, as if she might have offended me by raising questions about my friend. Our friend.

"I think you're right. Something about the whole thing seems… off." I reassure her.

"I'm sorry. I feel like I've brought down the mood. And you were supposed to be relaxing." She picks up my beer, notes that it's empty, and heads back to the kitchen to replace it.

When she returns, I take a sip, then set it down carefully and draw Anna to me.

"There's no need to try to maintain any certain mood. I like being able to talk to you about all kinds of things. Work or personal or… dream home."

She leans into me, wraps both her arms around my neck, curling herself around me. I know I just said maintaining a mood isn't important, but I want to get us back to happy topics.

"And what about the Anna dream home, anyway? Are we currently in it?"

She lifts her head up and grins.

"Oh no. Are you sure you're ready for this?"

I laugh. "Do we need some drafting paper and colored pencils?"

"They'd be helpful, but for now, just picture this…"

CHAPTER THIRTY-SEVEN

The next day is spent interrogating the pilots. We talk to seventeen of them, including Eliyah, a friend of Branden Halifax who gives us a few more names. The longest-serving pilots are from the Seward area, but many of the newer ones are from elsewhere in the southern part of Alaska. Their origins are further evidence that Mr. Drew cast his net wider after Mikey became chief of police.

The interviews are long, and I'm glad the FBI is putting its full force behind this case now. I only do one interview because I'm more focused on finding the men Jeannie sent away and bringing them home. Besides, I can't talk for long without coughing. I inhaled a lot of smoke during the explosion, and my lungs are still healing. I'm in all the briefings, though. They're all looking at jail sentences, and a lot of them have young families that will be on their own. Mensel has offered all of them deals for sharing anything the FBI might want to know about drug operations on the peninsula, and that gets most of them talking.

Six of them admit to killing men for Mr. Drew, and two of them implicate four others. Once we inform the newer crew that the Seward men have admitted to murder, one of them fesses up and admits that the new guys were initiated by accompanying a seasoned pilot to dispose of a body. These men were watching as the pilots who had committed murder hacked-up bodies, then dumped them in the water. *Learning how it's done*, the newest recruit said. He admits that he's relieved we broke up the operation. He didn't think he could kill anyone, and he was worried that he would be killed because of it.

One of the Seward pilots informs us that dumping the bodies in Portlock became procedure after I identified Branden, Kyle, and Lee. Before, the pilots had been able to use their own discretion in killing and disposing of bodies, as long as it wasn't done in Seward or on Mr.

Drew's property. After I solved those cases, the deaths became tightly regulated. Apparently, my discoveries spooked Mr. Drew. Hearing this made me grin.

All of the men who admit to killing for Mr. Drew are charged and taken to jail. The men who watched the disposal of bodies weren't there for the actual deaths, and though the FBI threatens them with accessory charges, they are released to go home after their passports, pilot's licenses and anything else enabling their travel are secured. Regardless of what happens to them, they'll remain on watch lists for the rest of their lives.

I'm exhausted by the time the killers are led away and the rest of the pilots, thoroughly spooked, go home. A few members of the FBI team invite me out for a drink, which I appreciate, but I decline and let them know I'm headed to the morgue to assist the medical examiner with the identities of the men in the hospital drawers. I don't tell them that first I'll be bringing in one last person I need to talk to.

AJ looks like he's aged years since I saw him at Branden's funeral. Deep lines crease his forehead even more than before, and something keeps tugging the corners of his mouth down. I don't want to stress him out more than I need to, so I get straight to the point.

"AJ, there was a guard of Mr. Drew's, a big blond ex-boxer, at least from what Mr. Drew said. I think he was staying in Kolit's. Do you happen to know who I'm talking about?"

His face answers before he says anything. He knows the guard. "Oh yeah, Frederick. What happened to that guy? He was staying above the hardware store, but I haven't seen him in weeks."

"He was staying above your hardware store?"

"Yeah." AJ twists his face into a strange expression. "Not my choice, exactly. Mr. Drew showed up at the bar one evening, asked if I had a place to rent out. The way he asked *if*, it was pretty clear I had to say yes."

"What was he like?"

"Frederick? I mean, scary as shit." He laughs uncomfortably. "I didn't have to see him much, though. I left a tray at his door with breakfast and then one at dinner; always knocked and then just took off. He never came down to the bar, and I really never saw him out and around. Just figured Mr. Drew kept him busy all day."

"Is his stuff still in the apartment?"

"I'm sure it is. I haven't gone in there."

"Would you be able to let me in to the apartment?"

He blinks rapidly. "Mr. Drew's dead, so I guess that's all right."

"Thank you, AJ. Mind taking me there now?"

He nods and stands.

Kolit's Hole is quiet when I arrive, following AJ's truck. It's already a tiny town—just a few houses clustered around a gravel road with the hardware shop/bar/convenience store at their center. A few deer bound between homes. The bell above the door tinkles as I follow AJ into the hardware store. The selection of souvenirs AJ keeps near the front—decorative knives with dull edges, baseball caps and snow globes—is covered in a layer of dust. Tourists would have little reason to visit Kolit's unless they're lost.

"You ready to go up?" He grabs a set of keys off a hook at the back of the building and doesn't wait for a response before he waves for me to follow him.

He leads me up the back stairs and unlocks the apartment. "Take however long you need. Just leave the key on the table." He heads back downstairs.

It's a spacious apartment with large windows, though there are dark red cotton curtains drawn closed over them. The few pieces of furniture are large and occupy the space nicely. The place looks dated, but comfortable. It's hard to say how long Frederick lived here—there's very little in the way of what looks like personal articles in the living room and kitchen area. The stove is dusty, but there's not a speck of food or a drop of liquid on it. The pots and pans are stacked neatly in a lower cabinet. The sink contains only a single cup. The dining room table holds a few hardcover books in a foreign language. They look well worn, but they aren't library books. I wonder if they traveled to the US with Frederick. They must be special if he took them each time he moved.

I leaf through them, looking for any markings. One of them, bound in what looks like a dark green canvas, has a name and date scrawled in a beautiful script on the inside cover. The first name could be Lara or Lada. Lasa, even. The last name is Nikolic. The year is marked as '53. Frederick could have come by this book any number of ways, of course, including picking it up at a secondhand bookstore. But my hope is that L. Nikolic is one of his relatives. A grandmother, perhaps, judging by the year. I slide the book carefully into my bag.

The other books contain no handwritten names, so I leave them be for now. There's a surprisingly extensive collection of movies stacked in the entertainment cabinet beneath the TV. It's a mix of foreign language and English films, and they span a variety of genres, from Westerns and biopics to *The Maltese Falcon*. I study them for a long time. More than the books I cannot read, they give me a picture of Frederick and his taste. All of it drives home the fact that he was a human being, even if he'd made some bad choices.

The bedroom contains a little more in the way of personal belongings. Frederick's clothing hangs in the closet. He was neat with his clothing, though it's clear the smell of cigarette smoke would never quite come out. It's present here in the small closet, though I see no indication that Frederick smoked inside the apartment. Maybe those cigarettes at Mr. Drew's were his treat for the day. Two pairs of boots sit neatly beside a pair of running shoes. One drawer of the dresser contains six pairs of identical black athletic socks and three pairs of wool alongside some underwear. The bed is made. Frederick may not have been military, but he clearly liked an orderly home.

The nightstand yields the more important information of anywhere in the apartment. There's no passport or driver's license as I had hoped— no birth certificate or any kind of ID card. I wonder if Mr. Drew forced his men to get lock boxes or stored their identification in his own home. I'll be able to search that soon enough. There is, however, a planner. There's little written on the individual days. I suspect Frederick's days were about as uniform as his closet. I notice a small stack of folded papers. When I smooth them out, they're printed off e-tickets for flights meant to take place in October. The lone passenger is listed as Jonah Nikolic. He was meant to fly out October 13, Anchorage to Seattle, then several stops before landing in Zagreb the following day. He would have returned on Halloween. So, Zagreb is where his family is, and I know we're looking for Nikolics. I tuck away the flight information.

There's another book on the nightstand, and underneath it there's a Polaroid picture of a young family standing outside a building that looks like a church, though the top of it has been cut off. The family is smiling, a young man and woman crouched down on either side of a blond-haired boy of maybe eight or nine. Studying his face, it could be Frederick. Or Jonah. If these are his parents, he looks like neither of them. Both are darker complected, with dark hair and eyes. The way they have his arms around him, they were close and likely family regardless. Nothing is written on the back of the photo, but I slide it between the pages of the book in my bag.

I have everything useful I can find. I could go now, but I don't. Instead, I sit down in the rocking chair next to the bed. There's a fluffy buffalo plaid cushion on its seat. I lean back into it, feeling short and small. It's a large chair, and it would have accommodated Jonah—if those are indeed his tickets and that is in fact his name—quite well. I wonder if he often sat in this chair. I breath in, catching the faint whiff of smoke, and am assured that he did. The view from the seat is simple: the bed, the dresser, the closet and the door to the rest of the apartment, but there's a picture of a horse in a winter landscape on the wall, and a braided red and black rug on the floor. It's homey. Maybe this was where he could feel at ease.

I sit there for a long time, thinking about Jonah and his family in Croatia, imagining what his homecoming would have been like and wondering if there were many homecomings. Did he fly back every year, or would this have been his first time seeing his family in decades? I will be able to get answers now, thanks to those airline tickets. I silently thank Jonah Nikolic for letting me find his family here.

CHAPTER THIRTY-EIGHT

Though she went home hours ago, Anna invites me to come over and tell her what I've learned from the pilots. I volunteer to pick up Chinese take-out on the way, and she doesn't object to a second dinner.

When I tell her the names of the men the pilots admitted to killing and dumping in Portlock, she writes them down carefully. There are eight names on the list, and she already has five bodies mostly complete. Tomorrow, she'll call the families to see if anyone can make a positive identification, but it's unlikely.

"So, what will happen? If they can't ID…part of their loved one."

"My suggestion would be to have a funeral ceremony and a burial for all of them. Individual caskets for the five who are mostly whole, or whatever the families agree on. Cremation for the parts that can't be identified, maybe."

I rest my chin on my hand. "That's sad. People going into the ground without anyone even being able to say who they were."

"I know. It happens a lot, and it's always sad. But at least they'll receive a proper service instead of being out there in the mud."

"True." I start in for another bite of fried rice before I realize I'm not even hungry anymore. I ate the majority of my sweet and sour pork without even noticing what I was doing. I'm on a sort of sleep-deprived autopilot.

Anna puts a hand on my knee. We're sitting on the sofa, Frank Sinatra serenading us from the little record player.

"Louisa, what are you going to do about Mikey? About what you learned from Mr. Drew?"

I sigh. It's probably time I thought that through. I've been so busy with these pilots and chemists and unidentified bodies and men sent away that I've conveniently put off thinking about it.

"I think I need to have a conversation with Quint and Mensel. I don't want to bring it up with Mikey while he's still recovering, and I want to be here in Seward so that I can investigate properly."

"Do you think he'll lose his job?"

I push the remains of the food away from me as if it's the problem.

"I don't know. But I don't…with his injury, do you think he could continue?"

"I've been thinking about that a lot. I mean, I'd certainly hope so. The department would just have to accommodate him. Add a ramp, re-think his office. The question is whether he'll want to. What happened to him…he might want to get out of police work entirely."

"Maybe. But I have a feeling he might not have a choice. If he made a deal with Mr. Drew…that's…" I shake my head. I don't even know how to finish that sentence.

"Yeah. That's bad." Anna pushes her plate up against mine and reaches for a bottle of red wine, pouring us each a small glass. "If he did have some sort of deal, I hope…" She turns away. "I mean, Mikey's going to need his friends. No matter what happened with Mr. Drew." She looks at me.

"He has a lot of friends here in Seward, right? And his parents will likely come out to help at first."

"I know. Yeah, Mikey has a lot of support. But I mean, *you're* important to him, Louisa."

"Am I? I wasn't important enough for him to be honest with me about whatever was going on. In fact, if there was something there, then he intentionally lied to me."

"I know. And I'm not saying you shouldn't be mad. I would be too, for sure. I *am* mad if he reached a deal with that bastard. It's just, you're special to Mikey. I hope that eventually…"

"I can't make any promises about how I'll feel if I find out he cut a deal. If it's an asshole move to be mad at someone who nearly died, well…I don't know. Maybe I'll be an asshole. I can't say yet. I'm sorry. I wish I could promise I'd be here for him. But there's a good chance I'll be here and investigating him."

She nods, looking sympathetic. "If you are…if you are here investigating him, will it be a problem if I'm still friends with him? If I'm actively trying to help him? Not with the job or anything. Just with…life stuff. Adapting and all."

I hold eye contact with her as I grab her hand and squeeze.

Her hand is warm. The breeze that comes in through the open

windows, carrying the scent of salt and pine, feels good as it passes over our joined fingers. There's a hint of coolness foretelling the coming of fall.

"You and Mikey are friends. Whatever I need to do, I don't want you to think you have to change how you act with him. You should follow your own conscience. It won't change anything between you and me."

She smiles and squeezes my hand back. We sit like that for a few minutes, listening to Frank sing about his love watching the water for him. Anna must be listening to the lyrics too.

"Hey. If the FBI agrees to keep you here for a while, maybe you could take that little break we talked about." She turns her head sideways so she can give me a sly glance from the side of her eye. "Remember? The one with someone charming?"

I grin. "How could I forget? I think that might certainly be in order."

She smiles the whole time we clean up the food, and we're both smiling when she walks me to the door, where we both hover, half in and half out. The sun is setting, and it will be down by ten o'clock now. Mid-August—a time when we can start going back to our normal rhythms. When I look at her, Anna has her eyes on the horizon too.

"You could stay, you know. Unless there's something else you need to do." She flutters her eyelashes at me, and I smile.

"You know, I think it's time you had my full, undivided attention." I take her hand, and she leads me back into the house.

CHAPTER THIRTY-NINE

Mensel informs me the next morning that most of his FBI agents will be leaving that afternoon. There are only three men left to question, and I'm still trying to locate them. He wants me to finish tracking them down, bring them back to Seward, and interrogate them. He and I will consult on how to proceed from there. Since he's left the net of me staying in Seward empty, I go ahead and take the shot.

"Sir, when I recounted my conversation with Mr. Drew to you, right before he was killed, do you remember my saying he referred to some sort of deal between him and Chief Harper?" He nods. "I have reason to think there might be some grain of truth there." His thick gray eyebrows dart up. "You know that Mr. Drew was good friends with Chief Willington, and that they had arrangements that kept Mr. Drew operating without intervention." He nods. "I think Mr. Drew and Mikey—Chief Harper—might have reached a similar deal."

"That's quite a claim. Are you hoping to investigate that relationship?"

"With permission, sir."

"And you'd like to do that from here in Seward?"

"I think that would be easiest."

He sends his gaze upward while he thinks, then looks at me. "Well, it makes sense for you to stay here for the time being anyway, until the missing three are back. I can arrange for your debriefs and evals to take place here. Then you can launch into your investigations. If he's going to be in Anchorage for a while still, that might give you some freedom."

"Debriefs and evals, sir?"

"Afraid so, Linebach. They're standard procedure after an operation where an agent experienced violence or anything that could be considered traumatic. And I think it's safe to say that's you."

I can't argue with that.

"What's that process like, sir?"

He smiles in a way that's about as reassuring as his face gets. "Not to worry. Just a series of visits with a psychologist to make sure you're processing things. The debrief just has you go through all the details again. For the record."

"I see."

"If you like...well, I was going to set a formal meeting to speak with you about this, but I'll be leaving with the rest of the crew, and if you're staying, we might as well talk now."

"Sir?"

He motions for me to sit, and he does too.

"Linebach, I like your work. You've done an excellent job on this case. I'd like you to consider going through the process to become a full agent."

I straighten my back and try to keep my face neutral, but I'm struggling. I shift my weight in my chair, then shift it back again. I don't want him to see my excitement, so I tap my foot rapidly instead.

"I would like that, sir. I'll need to talk with Chief Quint, of course."

"No worry there. I've already spoken with him."

My eyebrows fly up and I pull them back down. I should be used to conversations going on around me by now, but it's always jarring to know people were talking about me behind my back.

"And he was all right with it, sir?"

"Well, he knows it's a long process. You've already gone through a lot of the background checks and training, but there's more of that, and you'll need the full psych evaluation. But since you'll be going through sessions anyway, I thought maybe we could continue onto the formal eval with the same psychologist here in Seward."

I don't want to push my luck—he's just told me he'd like me to join. *Still.*

"Sir, are all agents based in Anchorage? Do they have the option to live elsewhere if it's...beneficial?"

This time, it's his eyebrows that rise.

"I've really enjoyed my time in Seward, sir. And I think there are some beneficial connections to be made here. With the Park Service, maybe. And with the tribes of the peninsula."

"Ah yes. Your work with Ranger Agapov was commendable. We would need to speak in more detail about how...collaboration...works with the agency." He says *collaboration* as if it's not a word he says often. I still have a lot to learn about how the FBI forges relationships—or doesn't, if that's the case. "I suspect we could work something out, so long as you would be able to come to Anchorage as needed."

"Of course, sir. It would be an honor." *An honor?* I bite my tongue before I say something else that sounds goofy. He sees my scowl and chuckles, standing.

"As always, it's been a pleasure, Linebach. You and that knack for missing persons…It's really something quite special. I hope you know that."

I just smile because I'm too flustered to form words and I shake his extended hand. He about-faces on the heel of his polished oxford and is gone. I still stand there, looking after him. My first thought is to go tell Anna the news, but I need to pay Dolly and Ryne a visit. There's a dog waiting for me.

❖

Mr. Land requires all visitors to his cabins to check in with him at the office. I'm glad to see he's still just as cautious as he was five years ago when I met him investigating the disappearance of Kyle Calderon. I guess having a person go missing from your hotel has an impact for life.

It's obvious Mr. Land recognizes me as soon as he opens the screen door and steps out of the cabin that functions as his office. The last time I met him, the man barely said five words. This time, he sticks out his hand immediately.

"Good to see you again."

I shake it firmly. "And you."

"Been following the story about all those folks in Portlock. Hell of a thing."

"It is. I'm glad I was able to help get them back to their families."

He does a sort of forward rock of the head that must be Mr. Land's version of a slow nod. "Be better off without Mr. Drew around here."

My laugh sounds hesitant to my ears. "I'm not sure the whole town will agree with you there. It'll be a blow to the Seward economy, that's for sure."

"We'll live. Better to restart than to go on with him doing what he was."

"I happen to agree with you."

"Well, thanks. Lived in Seward my entire life, first time there's been a cleanup of that sort."

I smile. That means a lot coming from someone who is Seward through and through. Now that he's finished what he wanted to say, he seems unsure of how to proceed. I stand there feeling awkward for a few seconds before he asks, "You looking for the Agapovs?"

"I am. Cabin 4?"

"That's right. I believe they're in."

"Thank you."

Ryne opens when I knock, with Tails standing guard next to them. When he sees me, Tails wiggles his ass so hard he starts shifting himself across the worn wood floor. I laugh and pat my thigh, letting him know it's all right to jump up. I lean down, scratching his head and that sweet spot behind his ears. He goes perfectly still and squeezes his eyes shut, enjoying it.

Over my dog's head, I can see Dolly and Jeannie at the table having tea. There's a third mug still steaming, and Ryne promptly goes back to it after greeting me. Dolly pulls out the fourth chair and sets to making me a cup.

"Any luck finding the last three?" Jeannie asks.

"Not yet, but we knew that was going to be a challenge." I settle in so that Tails can rest his chin on my knees and continue to enjoy his under-the-table ear scratching.

Jeannie repeatedly smooths the plaid tablecloth. "Part of me wants them to be easy to find so they can come home, but part of me is also proud of them for doing exactly what I said they should do."

"Yeah, you certainly didn't make my job easy." I smile at her.

Dolly places a steaming mug of green tea down, and I let the bright, citrusy scent wash over me. "I hear you reached a deal with Mensel."

Jeannie lowers her head solemnly, but her face doesn't show worry or anger. She looks content. "Probation in exchange for my testimony implicating Mr. Drew and the pilots in the murders, as well as full details of the drug operation. The FBI seems more interested in how we were working than anything." She looks at me with a question in her eyes.

"The drugs are the start of the whole thing. There wouldn't have been murders without that operation."

She looks at her hands, examining the short fingernails. She's still feeling guilty, then. She should, of course. But I'm glad the deal is a good one for her.

"They're hoping to understand how it worked so that when operations spring up like that again, they can catch them sooner. Or hopefully prevent them in the first place."

"That makes sense." She's quiet for a long time, then she speaks tentatively. "They might be able to prevent it by making sure people aren't in such vulnerable positions."

"How do you mean?" I watch her closely as Tails nuzzles his wet nose into my knee.

"Well, he was intentionally recruiting from communities that he knew were isolated and didn't have a lot of money. He was intentionally going places with a lot of tribal members and people he thought the police wouldn't care all that much about. And he was kind of right, wasn't he?"

I allow myself a long moment to exhale. She's absolutely right, of course. I nod. "There definitely needs to be better connection with the communities. I think that's going to be a long road, and a lot of people will need to be involved. I'm guessing there will need to be a lot of conversations with Councils and local governments to figure out how that looks."

"Some towns aren't going to want the government and the police roaming around," Dolly says.

I'm sure Dolly wouldn't want that for her village, and I can't blame her. An outside force can be disruptive for the local culture, and a lot of people will feel like they're being spied on when they haven't done anything wrong. It's the perpetual conundrum of police work. You need to make people feel safe and protected, so they need to know you're there. You also have to let them know you're not out to get them while realizing that they may naturally resent your presence. In an ideal world, we wouldn't be needed. But this is far from an ideal world, no matter how beautiful the view outside Mr. Land's cabin.

"It's going to be long and delicate work, and I'm going to stay in Seward to do it. Mr. Drew may be gone and most of the scientists might be home, but there's still a lot of work to be done and I think it's worth doing."

"I can't say I'm jealous," Dolly says.

"When will you be back to work, Dolly?"

She laughs. "Tomorrow." I lean back in my chair in surprise. I figured she'd want as much time with Jeannie and Ryne as possible.

"Oh, don't look at me like that. I'm just leading a nature hike with the kids for a couple hours. I got permission to stay here in Seward overnight instead of at Exit Glacier. One of the newer guys is staying on grounds for emergencies instead."

"Ah, that makes sense."

"Jeannie, what's the plan for you?"

She laughs. "Whatever the FBI tells me for now. I can't leave Seward until they say, then they might have me go to Anchorage for more paperwork and interviews. After that, I don't know. They've just said I'll be checking in with a probation officer every week and I can't leave Alaska. I hope I'll be able to find a job and a place to live like normal."

Dolly shifts her focus to a wall, sighs, and gets up and goes to the little kitchenette again, turning her back to us. I can almost feel the worry radiating from her. Jeannie must feel it too. She scowls and stares into her mug. I'm sure Dolly was hoping Jeannie would go home to Nanwalek, but it sounds like that may not be the plan.

Instead of digging into the obvious sore spot, I turn to Ryne. "You, Ryne?"

"School starts up in a couple weeks. I'm a senior!" They grin, and the smile spreads clear across their face. At that, Dolly pats their shoulder and returns to the table.

"Congratulations!" Jeannie is grinning too.

"Yup, I'm taking some advanced studies classes and an independent study in chemistry." I raise an eyebrow. Ryne laughs. "I already had it planned and all. Mr. Wickey wrote the curriculum for me. It's not because of…well, I'm not sure science is going to be my field."

I tilt my head to the side. Tails settles under me, curling into a ball. "What are you thinking about post-graduation?"

"Well, college, of course."

Dolly squeezes her lips into a satisfied smile, and Jeannie grabs Ryne's hands.

"I'm not quite sure what I'll study yet. Maybe I've got kind of a knack for police work. Do you think so, Louisa?"

Dolly is giving me a look that could burn the flesh from my face, but I can't lie. I drop my eyes to Tails momentarily instead.

"It's true, I'm afraid." I look back up in time to see Ryne's grin and Dolly shaking her head, and then pursing her lips while glaring at me. I'll get an earful later. I attempt to hide my face in my teacup to stop Dolly's look from burning a hole through me. Sadly, the cup is too small. The fire coming from her eyes should keep my tea warm at least. "Ryne, you helped crack this whole case." I sneak a glance at Dolly to see what the odds are of her jumping over the table at me. She's leaned back, arms crossed. Clearly, she's planning to just kill me later. "And of course, there's always a need for good undercover work."

Dolly lets out a huff of air and Ryne laughs. I better tell Anna what I want on my tombstone. Dolly's still squinting at me as she speaks.

"You have a lot of time to decide, Ryne. And once you get to college you might find something else that catches your interest. Remember, you've wanted to be at least fifty different things so far. It was paleontologist first, wasn't it? Then you insisted I buy you that mail carrier costume. Then it was veterinarian, then…" We all laugh at Dolly's list.

"Okay, okay," Ryne says, leaning back in their chair. "I was, like, six when I had the post office costume."

"You get my point, though."

"Yes, Grams."

As soon as Dolly looks back at her refilled mug, Ryne gives me and Jeannie a wink. I cover my mouth to stifle a laugh.

CHAPTER FORTY

Mikey is sitting up when I knock on the open door to his hospital room. His eyes are looking much more focused and alert than last time I saw him. They're trained off to the left, toward the TV. I can hear what sounds like a documentary playing briefly before he flips it off.

"No Hallmark?"

Mikey doesn't smile. "I tried. Just couldn't do it." He watches me as I approach.

"Mind a visit?"

"No."

"I'm guessing you've got people in and out of here all day."

"And all night. The nurses check on me every couple hours, and my parents show up first thing in the morning. I'm pretty sure I'm permanently half asleep now."

I believe it. I remember when my mother was in the hospital, toward the end of her fight with cancer. There was a constant rush of so much activity that I never understood how the patients were supposed to rest. At least Mikey has a private room.

"They set you up with the executive suite, huh?"

Mikey looks around like he hadn't noticed the room he's been confined to for days.

"I guess so."

Usually in our relationship, Mikey is the talker. He's saying so little I'm not quite sure how to pick up the slack. I set my bag down and settle into the only visitor's chair. The stiff back is not entirely comfortable on my slowly fading bruises.

"Did you see the video I sent your mom?"

He finally cracks a smile. "Yeah. Kind of cool that it happened that way, with them all coming to the police station."

"A lot of the people we met during the Kyle Calderon investigation were there. I'm guessing they stayed in touch, and all started talking to each other the minute they got word. Stanley and Lena Gussido were there. Their son Marty is still missing, but they wanted to be supportive of the other families." I smile at the memory of that evening. I already know I'll come back to it over and over when I need a boost. It was one of the few truly rewarding moments in my career.

"I wish I could have been there," he mutters to the blanket pulled up over his stomach in the reclined bed.

"I wish you could have been too. But there will be a big celebration when you get back to Seward. Guaranteed."

"No, please." He holds his hands up as if to ward me off. "Please tell Valeria I don't want one. I don't even know when I'll come back to the station."

I tilt my head and look at him. It's unlike Mikey to turn down a party. I recall the one he threw for me what seems like years ago at the Bake. "Are you being serious?"

I know he is.

"Yeah. No parties. Please, Louisa?"

"Of course. Whatever you want." I'll tell Valeria, but I will have to impart how serious Mikey is. I wouldn't put it past everyone in Seward to want to throw him a surprise party regardless. Mikey's a popular guy both in spite of and because of his position.

"Will you hang around Seward?"

"Yes. I've already talked to Quint and Mensel. I'll be there when you get home."

I leave it at that.

Mikey doesn't.

"Louisa, what Mr. Drew said in the cave. About us reaching another agreement…"

I inhale sharply. "You remember." I was hoping he wouldn't, for so many reasons. No wonder he's glum.

"It's been coming back to me. Nothing to do but sit here and think, you know?"

I lean toward his bed, place my hand on the edge, careful not to disrupt the equipment.

"Mikey, we don't have to talk about that. You know how Mr. Drew was." I don't go so far as to say he was a liar, because I still don't think he was lying. But I've promised myself that Mikey isn't going to know I'm investigating until he's home and comfortable.

Mikey has other plans.

"You're going to look into it. I know you, Louisa." For the first time since I got here, he looks me square in the eyes, and there's a gravity in his stare that's new. It throws me off, and I stutter.

"I…not while you're—"

"But you will. And you *should*. It's your job." He finally breaks that uncomfortable eye contact and looks at the wall. "I'll make it easier for you. I *did* have an agreement with Mr. Drew."

"Mikey, if you want to tell me, you know I'm listening. But if you want to wait—"

"I don't. I'll just lie here and let it bother me like it's been doing."

I shift my weight and get comfortable. I carefully place my hands in my lap. There will be no record of this until he's ready for there to be.

"When I took over, it became clear that Chief Willington didn't just passively know about what Mr. Drew was doing. He was getting kickbacks from it."

"Like, Mr. Drew was sharing some of the money?"

"Indirectly, but yeah. Mr. Drew did things like set up a special scholarship program and then give the scholarship to Willington's son. He gave a lot of hefty donations to the force. Things like that."

"Gross."

"Yeah. But he was also giving a load of money to the city council, and to charities around town."

"He was buying off Seward."

Mikey nods very slowly. "Definitely. He was paying for people to turn a blind eye, and Willington was both encouraging and benefitting from it."

"Why? Because of their friendship?"

"Not entirely, I don't think. Willington has always maintained that he didn't really like Mr. Drew all that much, but he felt like he had to allow him to do what he was doing to keep Seward thriving. Remember his comment years ago about people like Mr. Drew not really having friends?"

"I do. But Seward wasn't in any danger before Mr. Drew, right? I mean, it was small like all the towns around here, but they were already starting to get tourists even before the cruise lines. There was fishing and some industry, right?"

"Yes, but Mr. Drew brought in not just a lot of money, but a lot of investors. And he invested a ton himself. You know most of the restaurants in town got money from him to start up. A lot of them still get his money. Most of them will probably survive without it, but it sure helps in the off season."

"So, Willington thought it was good for Seward, even though he knew what Mr. Drew was up to."

"Pretty much."

"And when you came in?" I cross my legs and lean my elbows on them, propping my chin in my hand. I don't even want to look like I'm interrogating Mikey while he lies in a hospital bed.

"Well, you know. I started out all gung-ho about getting Mr. Drew and taking down his operation and righting wrongs and all that. But then I started to see with my own eyes how tied up Seward's—and Kolit's— economy was with Mr. Drew. Kolit's doesn't have tourism, Louisa. Mr. Drew pretty much *is* their economy. *Was*." He takes a deep breath and blows it out forcefully. "Anyway, when I saw the connections firsthand, and I realized what it would mean to shut down Mr. Drew's illegal operations…I guess I started to second-guess myself."

"But you're the police chief, Mikey."

"I know. I know, and I take that seriously. I *took* that seriously. But the police work for Seward. And Seward seemed to want Mr. Drew and his drug money."

I shake my head adamantly.

"You can't say that. People wanted investment, of course, but they didn't know where it was coming from. You know Marli would never have chosen money over Branden. Do you really think someone *like* Marli would have chosen investment money over their loved one?"

Mikey's face has totally fallen—his jawline slack and his head hanging. From his expression, I fear I've pushed too hard.

That was me being gentle.

"I know that now. I should have known then. We saw how Mr. Drew's business affected Marli and the Stantons. It just…I just got pulled in, you know? The whole force knew about it. It was like— it was the status quo. They expected me to go along like Willington did. I thought—" He sighs and stares at the ceiling. "I thought the way to keep everyone happy was to not rock the boat. I was afraid that if I upended the operation right away, they wouldn't want me as chief anymore. They'd find a way to boot me out. And I wanted it so much."

I feel for Mikey. I really do. The anger at being lied to is already gone. When I look at his face, I see that young officer in Anchorage that I first met, so fresh and eager to impress. Naïve, in a way, but always wanting to do what was best for everyone else.

Mikey loves consensus, and this was his way of getting it, even if it was wrong.

"Is that why you were so reluctant to pull the Homer department in when we realized things were going on in Portlock?"

A look of annoyance briefly crosses Mikey's face. "Homer." He closes his eyes. "The chief there had been suspicious of Willington for years. That's why Mr. Drew always avoids Homer for trying to find workers. He still delivers drugs there, but that's it."

So, Mikey knew where Mr. Drew was and was not recruiting from and did nothing to stop it. *Ugh*. I need to get away from him suddenly so I can process this in peace.

"I understand." I lightly touch his hand. It's a lie and maybe he knows it because he pulls his hand away.

"So now the economy is going to be fucked *and* everyone will know I was going along with Mr. Drew and killing their children."

My head is swimming with complex feelings toward Mikey right now. I wonder if he can tell by my tone when I speak.

"You weren't killing anyone."

"But I was letting it happen."

I go silent. I can't argue with that because it's true.

A nurse pops her head in, reads the room, steals a glance at the monitor, and ducks back out. I'm sure she'll come back soon.

"Mikey, there will be plenty of time for you to explain once you've recovered. You made a mistake, absolutely. But the reasons you did it make some sense. Hell, Willington was in on it for decades and no one's putting him in front of a firing squad."

"They might still."

That's true. It's hard to say what exactly will happen to Willington since he's retired.

We sit for so long I assume that, when the conversation resumes, if it resumes, it will be with a different topic. The nurse returns to do her full complement of checks and leaves again.

"I'll need to formally resign my position."

"There's no need to—"

"No. I need to resign my position," he repeats sternly. "Will you dictate the letter for me?"

"Of course, if that's really what you want." I hesitate, and he doesn't take it back. So, I pull out my notepad.

"I won't be of much use to the force anyway."

"Now look." I set the laptop down hard on the flimsy overbed table next to me. "You can resign if you want, but you're not going to justify it that way. You do good police work, and you know it. How many cases have you solved in Seward?" He doesn't answer. He just stares at the opposite wall, refusing to make eye contact. "You can own up to this, and you should own up to this, but don't pull that bullshit. You can own your mistake and argue your case, and I bet you people will be pretty forgiving. Especially because you helped uncover the full operation. Hell, you got injured trying to stop him. You got injured protecting a teenager from a hardened criminal." I'm getting more heated the more I talk. Now I'm pointing my finger directly at his face, rising out of my chair. "So don't you throw some bullshit *I'm useless, nobody needs me* pity party. You're a police chief. The whole town needs you. The whole town is especially going to need you as they adjust, and as those men who came out of the caves try to get back to some semblance of a normal life. Okay?"

I'm loud enough that a couple staff appear in the doorway.

"Ma'am, we're going to need to ask you to settle down or leave," a male nurse says. "You can't be upsetting the patients."

"She's fine, Derrick," Mikey says.

"I mean all the patients, Chief. You can hear her clear down the hall."

I sit back down.

"I'm sorry. I didn't realize I was that loud. It won't happen again." Good for Derrick, putting me in my place. This is no setting for outbursts. Even if they're well deserved.

Mikey inhales with a slight wheezing noise, then coughs as he exhales. I'm still getting over my cough, too. We both catch our breath for a while.

"I think it's best not to make any serious decisions while you're on strong painkillers. Don't you?" I make sure my tone is even and smooth. He rolls his eyes toward the ceiling.

"I'm thinking rationally, Lou."

"Maybe, but didn't they specifically say you're not allowed to sign any legal documents after you've been under anesthesia?"

He huffs, and I can tell he wants to fight with me, but he lets it go.

"I don't want to make everyone cover me when I'm going to resign anyway."

"Valeria is doing an excellent job. You know she can handle it."

"Yes, but she doesn't *want* to do it. And Seward can get on with finding a new chief to help clean up this mess."

"I haven't heard her complain one time. And Seward, like you, needs to catch its breath for a minute."

His breathing is labored. He's agitated and I should leave him be. I slide my laptop into my backpack.

"Louisa, will you tell the FBI?"

"About your deal with Mr. Drew? You know I have to, but it doesn't have to be right now."

"No, I'm *asking* you to tell the FBI." He gives me a look of impatience that I've rarely seen on Mikey before. "If they know and the police departments know, they might tell me to resign and then I won't have to fight anyone about it."

"You want them to make the decision for you."

"Yes."

"And what if they agree to let you stay on? This might not go the way you're thinking it will."

He blinks at the ceiling a few times. "Just tell them, okay?"

"I will. Promise." I go to grab his hand but remember him recoiling and pat the edge of the bed instead. "You take it easy, okay? Get better soon and come back home. They won't allow Tails in, and he's anxious to see you. Everybody is." I suppose Mikey isn't very anxious to see them yet. Hopefully by the time he's ready to be discharged, he'll have worked through some of this and be ready to face the music.

"See ya." Mikey doesn't look at me when he speaks.

I need to drive back to FBI headquarters, but instead I just sit in the car for a long time, thinking. Investigating Mikey is going to be long and painful—especially because it seems cruel to do it while he's recovering. I don't want to be sent back to Anchorage to wait—I'll likely get dragged into another investigation and never sent back to Seward. I need a strategy that I can present to Mensel, and my brain is too cluttered to think through it right now.

Time to take my therapist's advice and consult someone I trust.

I dial Quint.

CHAPTER FORTY-ONE

I want to have this conversation with Mensel in person. Quint's advice was to not spin the situation at all—to just approach it straight on. Like Mikey said—there's procedure for what happens when a chief commits misconduct. Mensel will report it to the Department of Justice, and they'll investigate from there. I'll likely play little to no role, and neither will Mikey. It will be out of both our hands, and maybe it's better that way.

Mensel's office is a comfortable place to talk this through. The rectangular brick building certainly isn't meant to look friendly from the outside with its row of black-trimmed windows giving the impression of bared teeth from the sidewalk, but Mensel has countered the stark feel of the hallways and lobby by painting his office a deep blue and bringing in his own dark wood table and a comfortable leather chair, which is where I sit now, across from his heavy desk. Off to the side, positioned so he can see them while at his computer, are pictures of his family and his dogs. It's hard to picture Mensel at home. He's a bit like an elementary school teacher—you just imagine they live at work.

Mensel takes down the information carefully, asking a lot of questions. I recognize that he's more gentle with me for this talk than he normally is. He usually uses the same plain, straightforward speech with everyone. He doesn't tend to show a lot of emotion. Today, though, I swear I see a hint of concern around his eyes as I recount the details of how Mikey came to *ignore*—I intentionally don't use the phrase *cover up*—Mr. Drew's activities. When I've filled in all the details I can give, he carefully closes the notebook in which he's been writing, then slides it to the side. No one will accidentally glimpse his notes, which makes me feel better.

But make no mistake, Mensel will take this exactly where it needs to go without delay.

"Sir, what do you think will happen?"

He looks at me for several seconds. I don't get the impression that he's hesitating to tell me. Only that he's thinking it through himself.

"The Department of Justice won't take this lightly, especially given the number of men who have been killed since Mikey took over. Now granted, they weren't really from his jurisdiction, but his inaction is what caused Mr. Drew to recruit from further afield. I'm not sure if they'll place him on leave since he's hospitalized, but this won't be a short process. He may very well need to refrain from going into the station for several months when he gets home. Is the Seward department fit to oversee itself for a while?"

"Yes, sir. For as long as needed, I believe."

"All right. You'll be down there too, so you can provide any backup they need, I suppose. I know Quint has a good relationship with Seward. He will surely expect you to help out. If Harper is removed from his position, it will be up to you whether you'd like to continue toward working for us or try to get his old role."

The thought of taking over for Mikey never occurred to me, and I'm sure I look flustered. "Sir, I don't think I would want that. The FBI is my goal."

He actually lifts the corners of his mouth a tiny bit. "I was hoping you'd say that. Well then, make sure your training, full debrief, and evals go well. And for heaven's sake, Linebach, take a vacation. This Harper, Willington thing is out of your hands now. You still have to track down those missing men, and I'll want you looking into these missing women from Nanwalek and the villages around there, but Quint won't have anything for you in Anchorage right now. Seems like a good time to get away for a bit."

"I think I could arrange a few days at least."

"Well, that's something." He stands, indicating that our meeting is over. I'm sure he has plenty of other places to be. He shakes my hand firmly, holding it there for just a second.

"I know I've mentioned it before, but you're doing commendable work, Linebach. We're happy to have you working with us."

As I leave the building, almost everyone I pass gives a nod or a quick congratulations. I always think of the FBI as a sort of hive mind, imagining that as soon as something happens, a serious crime or a serious solve, they all know it simultaneously. It's easy to maintain that image as I leave the building. The movement of all these people, all walking fast, all headed in different directions and all working different cases, might look erratic to some. But for some reason, I can feel the order, and order speaks to me. Especially in a state that can feel so wild.

When I arrive back in Seward, even though it's late, I knock softly on Dolly's cabin door. Ryne is asleep and Jeannie is back at her own cabin, but we step out onto the porch with our hot mugs of honey and chamomile tea. The more I've talked about and written about and thought about the past couple months, the more I've been wondering about how Dolly was when we first met.

"Dolly, that first night when you dropped me at the cabin and told me about Jeannie, it was obvious you had a lot of disdain for Mikey." She breathes in deeply and stares off toward the water. "You thought Willington was the person behind the drugs. Did you think Mikey was in on it too?"

"Yes."

"Why didn't you say anything?"

"Because I already knew you were his friend, and that you'd been his partner."

I can't think of anything to say to that. She's right, of course. She barely knew me. She naturally wouldn't try to draw my attention to my friend as a suspect. And yet, she'd been at least partially right. Even if Mikey wasn't involved, he was allowing it to happen.

"Well, you had it figured out before most anyone else."

She turns slowly toward me, steadying her mug.

"Mr. Drew said, in the cave, that maybe he and Mikey could reach *another* agreement...I thought maybe he was just trying to mess with my head, but Mikey confessed it. He knew, just like Willington did, and he chose to cover it up for Mr. Drew."

Dolly's nostrils flare in the faint light of the lantern next to the door. "Why would he do such a thing?"

I breathe deeply, pushing away the natural instinct to protect Mikey.

"I don't entirely understand it myself, but I think he weighed his choices and decided it was in Seward's best interest."

"That damned fool."

"I know. He offered his resignation as chief of police."

"Good."

"Maybe."

It's hard to say what exactly Dolly is staring at off in the distance, or if she's looking at anything at all. "I don't feel good knowing I was right about that."

"No?"

"No. I can't feel angry at someone who shot a man to protect Ryne. Even if he did the right thing late."

I hadn't really thought about it that way. Mikey did come through in the end. I go to take a sip of tea and realize my mug is empty.

"Well, I should get back to Tails. But Dolly"—I turn toward her under the light hoping she can see how serious I am—"*Thank you*. You didn't need to do any of what you did. Even before Ryne went missing, you put yourself out there to help, and I will never forget it."

She turns her head to the side and waves her hand as if trying to bat the compliment away like she would a mosquito.

"No, I'm serious. You did amazing work. The Park Service is lucky to have you."

"Oh, they know it!"

I laugh. "I bet they do." She reaches for my mug, and I hand it over. "But if you ever decide on a career change..."

She gives me a stern look. "I get my pension in five years. Don't even start."

I just grin at her, already wondering if there will be a way to pull Dolly in on some FBI work again in the future. She seems to know what I'm thinking because she gives me much stank-eye as she opens the screen door.

"Good night, Louisa." It sounds like a reprimand.

CHAPTER FORTY-TWO

L ittle lower!" Cooper yells as two men try to match the sections of the ramp so a wheelchair can smoothly move up or down it. He's out of his sling, though he'll forever wear scars from the explosion in the cave. He knows Mikey has been placed on paid administrative leave. Valeria, working inside the house right now, knows she'll be running the department for the near future. She seems to have come to peace with it. One could even be fooled into thinking she was enjoying it. They're both still here, alongside me and Anna and a small team of construction workers from Seward, helping to rework Mikey's home.

AJ and Eliyah are working with Anna on lowering the kitchen counters and removing the upper cabinets. The new kitchen island with its built-in, easier to reach storage still sits on the back of Dolly's pickup. She's supervising some work in the bathroom. Mikey's tub had to be taken out, and a large no-threshold shower is going in. I think Dolly appreciates the distraction. Jeannie has been in Anchorage for a week. Now that she's finally finished giving all the information she could possibly give, Mensel had her take a look at a few operations around Anchorage that have been rankling us for ages. Who knows if she'll be able to help, but I know she'll try her best. Dolly is worried she'll like it in Anchorage and choose to stay, and with Ryne back in school, I think she's a little lonely. The prospect of being an empty nester looms.

The crew gets the ramp attached and starts fixing it in place. I step back toward the sidewalk. From here, little looks different. The only obvious change to Mikey's white house with its neat black shutters is the ramp that peeks out from its side entrance. The concrete stairs leading to the front porch can still serve for guests, and Mikey may still want to use the porch swing once he gets used to lifting himself in and out of his chair. Anna has taken down the ferns that hung from the porch roof and re-potted them in planters that now sit on either side of the door. It looks like a home anyone might be happy to return to.

When I step inside, it's a far less quaint scene. Dust is flying and there's the noise of circular saws and hand tools. The upper cabinets are down now, sitting tucked up against the pantry. Anna is using a power screwdriver to place a shallow shelf just above the stove, which sits pulled out from the wall, ready to be installed. It's a custom order, with a cooktop that will be safe for Mikey to reach across without burning himself. I'm sure he'll soon have had more than enough skin grafting. That's what he'll undergo next, and it should be the last procedure before he's released. We should be finished with the house just in time.

The bathtub is gone, donated to a nonprofit that furnishes low-income housing. The new shower is going in, its walls bright and fresh white against the hunter green of the rest of the room. I turn and place my hands on the sink, which has been lowered so that it should be just the right height. It took a bit of research getting all the right measurements, but Mr. Stanley Gussido was helpful. When he heard about Mikey's injury, he contacted Valeria to ask if his house was being redone. She connected him with Anna, and he's been invaluable in making suggestions, though so far, they've been communicating through pictures. He'll come out next week, making a special trip to test out the house. He and I have been collaborating on trying to track down his son, Marty, who we're pretty sure is in Maui going under the name Draper. The work has reenergized Stanley and he's eager to help however he can.

Everybody knows Mikey's being investigated and why, but it's a testament to the community that no one seems to give a damn. They're all intent on helping Mikey anyway. There's animosity toward Willington that's unmistakable, but Mikey and the other officers seem to have been automatically forgiven. I'm sure it helps that tales of Mikey's heroics in the cave have been circulating far and wide. I suspect Coop, who's been enjoying some special recognition himself. Dolly is the subject of much awed whispering, though she pretends she doesn't know it. She's jumpy and keeps referencing wanting to get home soon.

I step back out of the house to grab the mower from the shed. Anna and I will take turns doing our least favorite chore for the time being, though Anna insists she can design a garden for Mikey that won't require mowing. I've seen evidence of her success with plants in the form of dead cacti, but I'm keeping my mouth shut. If a few flowers have to die for the sake of keeping a wonderful woman happy, so be it.

As I pull the push mower out, she runs toward me, covered in sawdust and grinning. She pulls off her glasses and wipes them on the hem of her shirt, replaces them, and then leans in for a kiss. I drop the handle of the mower and wrap my arms around her waist. When our lips have parted ways, she leans her forehead against my hair. The wind blows, intermingling my loose brown strands of hair with her auburn ones.

"Good news, Officer."

"Oh?"

"I've found the perfect little getaway for us."

I give her nose a tap while pushing her hair behind an ear. "Do tell."

"There's a lodge right on the water in Lake Clark National Park. It's got a few cabins, a sauna, the whole deal. In the middle of absolute nowhere. You have to take a plane and then a boat to even get to it. And they cook for you!"

I close my eyes. "Mmm. That sounds wonderful."

"Tails is allowed too, so I hope he doesn't mind a boat ride."

"He's a seasoned sailor." By which I mean I have to hold him firmly in place so he doesn't stumble around the deck on rough waters. Balance isn't always his strong suit.

"So, how does Friday sound?"

"Think the house will be done by then?"

"Yup. I'm guessing we've got another day, then it's just cleanup and finishing touches."

"Then Friday sounds perfect."

"Oh, good. I won't have to cancel." She grins and bounces up and down in her work boots. I laugh. It's impossible to not share Anna's excitement. What she has planned sounds like exactly what I need. Suddenly, my smile fades. She notices too and rubs my shoulders with her hands. The breeze is turning cool.

"Everything okay?"

"Oh, yeah." I wrap my arms back around her. "Absolutely. It's just…"

I told myself we'd talk about this once we were at whatever destination she'd chosen for us, but once I start worrying about something, I can't get it off my mind. It just festers there and can ruin my mood if I let it. I find the best way to stop that cycle is to just say what needs to be said.

"I know a lot of people don't like labels and things, and I don't want to pressure you at all." I put a hand on my heart like I'm swearing to her. "It's just…Are we…What is…"

She puts her hand over mine. "Are we…a couple?" She turns her head to the side and winks at me dramatically.

I laugh at her expression.

"Exactly. Are we?"

"I'm in if you are."

"All in. One hundred percent."

"Well, then I'm glad we're on the same page."

I exhale, relieved.

The rules of dating have always been frustrating for me. I like things clearly defined at all times, but that's not how modern dating works. The line between friends and casual and serious is muddled. I like a nice signpost.

You are now entering Exclusive. Speed limit 65.

Anna grabs me up and kisses me again.

"Get a room!" It's Coop, walking up and down the ramp, looking for any weaknesses.

"If you insist! Better tell everybody to clear out of there!" Anna yells.

Coop laughs and hops up and down a little, testing the ramp's strength.

"I guess I should let you get to it." Anna nods at the abandoned push mower. "We still on for a shopping trip after work Monday?"

"You bet. You know I can't be trusted alone. I might end up with plaid everything."

Anna has promised to help me decorate my new rental house, a cute cabin a mile outside of town that Valeria was able to hook me up with. I'm very much looking forward to making it a home.

I watch Anna as she bounds up the ramp and back into the house, then I push the mower out onto the lawn, the golden sunlight slipping through the oak trees that separate Mikey's house from his neighbor. Between their leaves, which are losing their green and turning a reddish orange, I can see the mountains. Gray peaks are temporarily exposed in places, waiting for a fresh blanket of snow to cover them, and to cover Seward in quiet, soft winter.

About the Author

Bailey Bridgewater is a nomadic grant writer who travels the US and Canada hiking, writing, and checking out bookstores.

Books Available From Bold Strokes Books

And Then There Was One by Michele Castleman. Plagued by strange memories and drowning in the guilt she tried to leave behind, Lyla Smith escapes her small Ohio town to work as a nanny and becomes trapped with an unknown killer. (978-1-63679-688-8)

Digging for Destiny by Jenna Jarvis. The war between nations forces Litz to make a choice. Her country, career, and family, or the chance of making a better world with the woman she can't forget. (978-1-63679-575-1)

Hot Hires by Nan Campbell, Alaina Erdell, and Jesse J. Thoma. In these three romance novellas, when business turns to pleasure, romance ignites. (978-1-63679-651-2)

McCall by Patricia Evans. Sam and Sara found love on the water, but can they build a future amid the ghosts of the past that surround them on dry land? (978-1-63679-769-4)

Promises to Protect by Jo Hemmingwood. Park ranger Maxine Ward's commitment to protect Tree City is put to the test when social worker Skylar Austen takes a special interest in the commune and in Max. (978-1-63679-626-0)

Sacred Ground by Missouri Vaun. Jordan Price, a conflicted demon hunter, falls for Grace Jameson, who has no idea she's been bitten by a vampire. (978-1-63679-485-3)

The Land of Death and Devil's Club by Bailey Bridgewater. Special Liaison to the FBI Louisa Linebach may have defied all odds by identifying the bodies of three missing men in the Kenai Peninsula, but she won't be satisfied until the man she's sure is responsible for their murders is behind bars. (978-1-63679-659-8)

When You Smile by Melissa Brayden. Taryn Ross never thought the babysitter she once crushed on would show up as a grad student at the same university she attends. (978-1-63679-671-0)

A Heart Divided by Angie Williams. Emmaline is the most beautiful woman Jack has ever seen, but being a veteran of the Confederate army that killed her husband isn't the only thing keeping them apart. (978-1-63679-537-9)

Adrift by Sam Ledel. Two women whose lives are anchored by guilt and obligation find romance amidst the tumultuous Prohibition movement in 1920s California. (978-1-63679-577-5)

Cabin Fever by Tagan Shepard. The longer Morgan and Shelby are stranded together, the more their feelings grow, but is it real, or just cabin fever? (978-1-63679-632-1)

Clean Kill by Anne Laughlin. When someone starts killing people she knows in the recovery world, former detective Nicky Sullivan must race to stop the killer and keep herself from being arrested for the crimes. (978-1-63679-634-5)

Only a Bridesmaid by Haley Donnell. A fake bridesmaid, a socially anxious bride, and an unexpected love—what could go wrong? (978-1-63679-642-0)

Primal Hunt by L.L. Raand. Anya, a young wolf warrior, finds herself paired with Rafe, one of the most powerful Vampires in the Americas, in an erotic union of blood and sex.(978-1-63679-561-4)

Snake Charming by Genevieve McCluer. Playgirl vampire Freddie is on the run and a chance encounter with lamia Phoebe makes them both realize that they may have found the love they'd given up on. (978-1-63679-628-4)

Spirits and Sirens by Kelly and Tana Fireside. When rumored ghost whisperer Elena Murphy and very skeptical assistant fire chief Allison Jones have to work together to solve a 70-year old mystery, sparks fly—will it be enough to melt the ice between them and let love ignite? (978-1-63679-607-9)

Aubrey McFadden Is Never Getting Married by Georgia Beers. Aubrey McFadden is never getting married, but she does have five weddings to attend, and she'll be avoiding Monica Wallace, the woman who ruined her happily ever after, at every single one. (978-1-63679-613-0)